Homecoming

Homecoming

The Southern Family in Short Fiction

edited by Liz Parkhurst & Rod Lorenzen

August House Publishers, Inc.

LITTLE ROCK

Published by August House, Inc.,
P.O. Box 3223, Little Rock, Arkansas, 72203,
501–372–5450.

Printed in the United States of America

10 9 8 7 6 5 4 3 2 1

LIBRARY OF CONGRESS CATALOGING-IN-PUBLICATION DATA

Homecoming: the southern family in short fiction /
edited by Liz Parkhurst & Rod Lorenzen.
—1st ed. p. cm.
ISBN 0-87483-112-1 (alk. paper): $17.95
1. Short stories, American—Southern States.
2. Family—Southern States—Fiction. 3. Southern States—Fiction.
I. Parkhurst, Liz Smith. II. Lorenzen, Rod.
PS551.H64 1990
813'.01083275—dc20   90-33449
CIP

First Edition, 1990

Cover illustration by Traci Haymans
Jacket design by Communication Graphics
Typography by Lettergraphics
Editorial assistance by Ed Gray

AUGUST HOUSE, INC.   PUBLISHERS   LITTLE ROCK

Acknowledgments

"A Man Among Men" by Mary Hood, copyright ©1984 by Mary Hood, is reprinted by permission of the University of Georgia Press.

"Earl Goes to the Site and Stares Until He Sees" by Dennis Johnson, copyright © 1987 by Dennis Johnson, is reprinted by permission of the author.

"I Just Love Carrie Lee" by Ellen Douglas, copyright ©1989 by Ellen Douglas, from *Black Cloud, White Cloud,* is reprinted by permission of the University Press of Mississippi.

"Artists" by Lee Smith, copyright © by Lee Smith, is reprinted by permission of the Liz Darhansoff Agency.

"Old Frank and Jesus" by Larry Brown, first published in *Facing the Music,* copyright ©1984, 1985, 1986, 1988 by Larry Brown, is reprinted by permission of Algonquin Books of Chapel Hill, a division of Workman Publishing Co.

"Happy Birthday, Billy Boy" by Ruth Moose, from *Dreaming in Color,* copyright ©1989 by Ruth Moose, is reprinted by permission of the author.

"Love Life" by Bobbie Ann Mason, from *Love Life,* copyright ©1988 by Bobbie Ann Mason, is reprinted by permission of Harper & Row, Publishers, Inc.

"Leaving" by Shirley Cochrane, copyright © by Shirley Cochrane, first published in *Mississippi Review,* is reprinted by permission of the author.

"Everyday Use" by Alice Walker, from *In Love & Trouble,* copyright ©1973 by Alice Walker, is reprinted by permission of Harcourt Brace Jovanovich, Inc.

"A Christmas Memory" by Truman Capote, copyright © by Truman Capote, is reprinted by permission of Random House, Inc.

"Spittin' Image of a Baptist Boy" by Nanci Kincaid, copyright ©1989 by Nanci Kincaid, first published in *Carolina Quarterly,* is reprinted by permission of the author.

"Kin" by Eudora Welty, copyright ©1952 and renewed 1980 by Eudora Welty from her volume, *The Collected Stories of Eudora Welty,* is reprinted by permission of Harcourt Brace Jovanovich, Inc.

Contents

A Man Among Men

MARY HOOD

HIS OLD MAN LAY in Grady Miller's best steel casket with the same determined-to-die look on his face that he had worn throughout his final two months of decline, from the night Olene had run red-eyed back through the Labor Day rain with his uneaten supper on its wilting picnic plate to report, "He's gone in that camper and put on his nightshirt and gone to bed. For keeps." She had shaken the rain from her jacket and scarf, using one of the green-checked napkins to dry her face. "He's talking funny. I don't like the way he's talking. Made me lay out his dark suit where he could see it and told me, 'No shoes, no use burying good leather, just see my socks are clean,' all because of a dog. A dog!"

"Daddy thought the world of Smokey Dawn," Thomas pointed out.

He and the old man had spent their entire holiday looking for the hound, as far south as Buck's Creek, all around the public hunting lands, calling, calling from the windows of the truck. She had never stayed out so long. She had never trashed in her life. From time to time the old man raised his arm and hissed, "Listen!," his bladey hand like an ax. Once it was the waul of a blue-tailed rooster, strutting in a dried cornfield; it almost sounded like the dog. The cock stepped toward them, icy eye taking it all in. "Shoot!" The old man fell back against the seat, disappointed. They drove on.

There was a strange feel to the weather; the sky was so overcast the morning glories in the corn were still wide open. "Weatherbreeder," the old man said, staring at the clouds, but he wasn't looking for rain. In a

9

few miles he spotted them—three buzzards—freckles on the flannel belly of the afternoon. The old man tensed up and leaned forward, still hoping, and peered down the dirt lane to where she lay in the goldenrod. Before Thomas got the truck full-stopped, his daddy was scrabbling out. He thrashed his hat all around to keep the birds aloft. He still had that sense he was rescuing her. His tough old shoes barely cleared the dust as he hastened toward the corpse, stumbling over pebbles and lurching on, stiff-footed.

Thomas lagged back, letting him handle it. He lit his cheroot on the third match; there was an east wind, mean and cold, shaking the young pines. Handfuls of sparrows sifted themselves out of the blow, deeper and deeper into the thickets.

His daddy was shivering.

Thomas shed his jacket and offered it to the old man, who wasn't dressed for the knifing wind. He took it, knelt, and wrapped the dog in it. "I reckon it was her heart," he said, beating his parchment fist against his chest. "No bigger than a fiddle when I got me my first redbone pup, Billy Boy it was." He looked away as Thomas lifted the dog and carried her back to the truck. The old man walked alone, counting up his losses: "After Billy it was Babe...and Ginger Tom out of Babe and French Lou—she had the straightest legs of them all—and Red Pearl and Rabbit Joe, one-eyed but it never cost him a coon, heart like a tiger...did I say Racing Joe? And Joe's Honey and Honey's Nan..." He flinched when Thomas slammed the tailgate: a solemn closing, the end of an era. They headed home. "And Jolly, and Honey's Nan, I mention her yet? And Prince Ego and Skiff. And Smokey," he said, "Smokey Dawn." He stared toward the darkening west, his eyes cold and gray as a dead-man's nickels. "Well, that's about it." They rode in silence then.

By the time Thomas parked, at home, the old man's interest had waned to a single, final point. "Dig it deep" was how he put it. "I don't want a plow turning her up some day." He headed for his mobile home and went in and closed the door.

When Olene saw the windbreaker over the dog's body, she said, "I'm not washing that in the machine."

"Dean's not home yet?"

"I'm not worried." She laughed. "When you're seventeen you run on nerve and Dr. Pepper, not Daylight Saving. You'll have to bury her yourself."

It was already raining—the first huge cold drops—when he went to get the mattock.

Olene had never had much patience with the old man's sulks. "Do something," she said, after supper, just as the phone rang. She went on scraping the old man's untouched food into the garbage. "Turned his head to the wall, not one bite would he taste, and me on my feet chopping and cooking since noon." All the time Thomas was on the phone she kept reciting her welling grievances at his back. She broke off when he reached for his uniform jacket on its hook.

"Now what?"

He zipped the jacket to his chin, then unzipped it halfway; he dug out his truck keys and clipped his beeper to his belt. "A car hit a deer on the quarry road."

"Couldn't someone else?"

He unlocked the cabinet and took down his service revolver. "I had last weekend off, remember?"

"We didn't do anything."

He loaded the gun and clicked it shut. "I'll just step on across and check on Daddy before I go." Lightning showed the walk to be running like a brook. "And it's not a camper," he said as he plunged out into the deluge.

He splashed across the flagstones to the mobile home. The windows were open; it was cave-damp and dark inside. The wet curtains dragged at his hands as he cranked the jalousies shut. He turned on the lights and ran the thermostat up. At the bedroom door he hesitated. "It's Thomas," he announced softly.

"Come on."

Thomas took the old man's hand and clasped it; it was cold. His daddy puzzled him out a feature at a time from his pillows. He shook his head; they were strangers. "I recollect you now," he bluffed. "We were running Blue Jolly and Nan..." He trailed off, uncertain. "That old coon—tail shot off four years back—no fight left in her, no fight. So fat she dropped into the dogs and just let 'em rip. No play in the pack for that. Funny..." He yawned for breath. "Funny..." He opened his eyes and stared all the way through Thomas, clear out the other side into the young century when someone, someone...

"*Who?*" he asked irascibly. He focused again, present tense. "My memory's shot to chow," he confessed. He glanced indifferently around the room, recognizing nothing but his suit on the chair. "I'm checking out of here," he announced abruptly, flailing himself upright, then falling back, exhausted. "You help me, mister?"

Thomas nodded.

"You notify my son. Little Earl—Earl Teague, Jr.—on the Star Route..." He gestured with his thumb, south.

Thomas watched the pulse wriggle in the old man's temple. Was he just sulking, like Olene said? Or was it another of the little strokes that left him more and more a stranger?

"Daddy?" Thomas said, sharp, calling the cloudy eyes back into focus.

Frowning, he examined Thomas' face and resumed, "Highly thought of...in the book...look him up...Earl Teague, Jr. He'll come take care of me."

"But what about Thomas?" Thomas asked, for the record.

The old man seemed to have dozed off.

"Daddy?"

He blinked awake. "Who is it?"

"Thomas."

"Not him," he said, irritated. He had never suffered fools gladly. "He's dead." He looked at Thomas and yawned.

You son of a bitch, Thomas thought. He wanted to shake the old man, wake him, make claims. But what was the use of that now? Or ever? When Little Earl was killed by the train, hadn't his daddy stared at Thomas standing by the closed coffin and asked, "Why couldn't it have been you?"

That was when Thomas knew.

2

His old man lay in Grady Miller's front parlor between the adjustable lamps casting their discreet 40-watt pink-of-health upon him head and foot. He was dressed in his Sunday best. Olene had tucked a rose into his lapel. She came up to Thomas standing there and ran her arm through his. "Isn't he sweet?" she said, giving the little bouquet of buds and baby's breath a pat, smoothing the streamers across the old man's chest. GRANDDADDY was spelled out in press-on gold letters on the satin ribbon. She had ordered that, in Dean's name. The boy hadn't seen the old man since the last week of the hospital stay, when life-support was all that tethered him to the world. He hadn't seen him dying, and he hadn't seen him dead. Thomas' simmering resentment of that finally boiled over on Saturday night when Dean came in late for supper, said he wasn't hungry, and announced that the clutch had torn out of his Chevy again.

"Ten days!" Thomas said. "This time it lasted ten days!"

"Three weeks," Olene corrected. She looked it up in the checkbook. "He can drive mine."

"He won't need it; he's coming with us," Thomas said.

"I can fix it myself in three hours if I get the parts."

"Not tonight." Thomas finished his coffee, standing. He set the cup in the sink.

"I'm not going down there."

"Your granddaddy—"

"Is dead and I'm not. I'm sure as hell not," Dean said. He laughed. He drank what was left of the quart of milk right from the carton. When Thomas back-handed him, it knocked his sunglasses and the empty milk carton across the kitchen. One of the lenses rolled over by the trash.

"No!" Olene stepped between.

"I'd beat his ass till it turned green if I thought it would do any good," Thomas said, over her head. Still he couldn't see into the boy's eyes. How long had it been since they *saw* each other? He turned away, shrugged off Olene's restraining hand. In the silence, which prolonged, the boy wiped the milk mustache off with his fist.

When Olene saw the look on his face, she said, "He's just trying to raise you."

"All he raises is objections," Dean said.

Thomas headed up the stairs, two at a time, to shave and dress for the wake. "Don't wait up," Dean bragged as he left. He took Olene's car.

It was the first time he had stayed out all night that they didn't know where to find him.

On Sunday morning (the old man's funeral would be that afternoon) the beeper summoned Thomas on a dead-body call. He left Olene and the men's Bible class on honor guard at Miller's and headed across town to Doc Daniels' pharmacy. Doc was the one who had spotted the body in the weeds, followed the footprints from his broken-in back door out through the frost and down the gullied fill-dirt specked with soda cans and gum wrappers. Doc had called, "Hey! *Hey!,*" a wake-up call, in case it was sleep and not death he had been stalking, but when he got close enough to be fairly sure he hurried back to the phone to spread the news. The EMS driver got there first and made a tentative diagnosis—overdose—but now they were waiting on the coroner and Thomas to arrive.

When Thomas got there, Doc led the way again, down the clay bank, his white bucks getting pinker with every dusty step. Thomas was in a hurry; Doc caught at his sleeve to stay apace. He was panting to keep up. Together they leaped the last gully. All the way Doc was telling, telling, fixing his magnified gaze on Thomas' profile.

"Look at him," Doc accused, as they came to the corpse.

A boy, curling a bit toward the fetal pose, lay on his left side. For a moment Thomas thought he knew him—a trick of the mind after a sleepless night—dirty sneakers, faded jeans, blue windbreaker, watch cap. He swayed, rubbed his eyes, then knelt for a closer look, resting his hand on the boy's stiff, angled knees.

Behind him Doc was saying, "This makes the sixth time I've been robbed. I've got payments to make like anyone else—"

Thomas searched the boy's pockets for ID. He flipped through the haggard wallet. Doc leaned forward, squinting. "So who gets the bad news?" he wondered.

Thomas stood up. "I'll tell them," he said, and started up the bank to his truck. He took the time to smoke one of his little cigars. He answered no questions. The crowd moved back to let his truck pass. He drove fast though there was no hurry.

He crossed the tracks at midtown and turned right onto a forgotten road hardly more than an alley paralleling the rails. He headed south till the paving turned to gravel; it peppered the underside of his truck as he negotiated the lane's washboard heaves and hollows. He rolled his window up against the dust rather than slow down.

The road dead-ended in a grove of blighted elms beyond a bare yard, clean-swept with a broom in that country way of deterring snakes. Mazes of rabbit fence held back the frost-nipped remains of faded petunias. On the staggering mailbox, in decrescendo, red paint not a season old announced ELSIE BLAND beneath the former tenant's name, shoeblacked out. A dingy cat leaped up onto the truck hood, settled on the cab roof, and held aloof from Thomas' hand. From the grayed house came the sound of fast sad blues, decades old, scratchy—an ancient, sturdy record salvaged from attic or rummage sale. Before Thomas crossed the porch the music sped up to 78 rpm; people were laughing. They didn't hear him.

He knocked again. Louder.

A laughing woman materialized behind the rusty rump-sprung screen door, wiping her eyes with her fingers and shaking the tears away. "Sounds like mice in them cartoons," she explained. She leaned into the dark to call, "Jude? Jude! You shut that down now, *shut* it." To Thomas she said, "It's Sunday, I know, but I didn't reckon it'd hurt anything for him to listen. We been to church this morning, early." She guessed he was a preacher.

Because they did not know each other, because he had come in his pickup truck instead of the cruiser, because she did not notice the blue light on the dashboard behind the windshield reflecting October, because he was dressed for his daddy's funeral and wasn't in uniform, he could see she had no idea at all who or what he was. He held up his badge and said, "It's the Law, ma'am. I'm Tom Teague. Are you Mrs. Bland?" And because he had come on official business and there was more than courtesy conveyed in his manners—some additional intimation of apology for bad news, perhaps the worst news—the solemnity communicated itself through the rusty screen and into her heart instantly and flamed up into remorse, as though the fires of regret and grief had long been laid and awaited but the glint off Thomas' badge to kindle them.

"My boy Ben! Killed oversea in the service!" she screamed, voicing her oldest premonition, her dreams that woke her, brought her to her knees in the nightwatch. She had a map of the world with Lebanon marked on it in ballpoint, circled and circled, to help her focus her prayers.

"No," Thomas said. He tried the door. It was latched. "Mrs. Bland..." he appealed. Something in his tone arrested her wild attention. The needle scratched loudly across the old record and resumed playing again, at proper speed, the fast sad blues. She settled her eyes on Thomas'.

Quieter, she said, "Then it's about Ray." She unhooked the screen and admitted trouble into her scrub-worn rooms. Every windowsill had its beard of green plants in foil-covered pots. Above the mantel with its clutter of photographs hung a lithograph of radiant Christ.

"Jude, honey," his mama suggested, "about time for your train."

Jude came in from the kitchen, a man who would be a boy all his life. "We got to discuss," she told him. "You go on out." No introductions.

Passing by, the boy stuck out his hand to Thomas. "Pleased to," he said. The old ladies that Elsie cleaned for praised his manners and willingness to climb ladders; they let him unclog their gutters for cookies and dimes.

The train at the town limits sounded its whistle. The boy hurried out to admire the pink Albert City Farmers grain cars rolling past on tracks not a city block away.

"Just a little something went wrong when he was borned, a good boy, no trouble, not like Ray." Elsie breathed faster. She aimed her sharp nose at Thomas and angrily asked, "What about him? Tell me what he done."

"I'm afraid it's bad news, Mrs. Bland."

She thought it over. "Bound to be." She pushed herself up out of the chair and fetched one of the photographs from the mantel. She handed it to Thomas. Its cheap metal frame was cold and sharp as a knife. There was the face of the boy Doc had found in the weeds. Thomas cleared his throat. He handed the picture back; for a moment they both held it, then he let it go.

"He's dead," he told her. There was nothing to tell but the truth, and it only took two words. Thomas thought that was how he would want to hear it, if he ever had to. Elsie heard it, Thomas thought, without surprise. She seemed stupefied, though, and it was a minute before she repeated, "Dead." She sat staring at the photograph in her lap.

"He's the one like his pappy," she specified. She just sat there. Silent.

"You'll want to ask me some questions," Thomas suggested.

Elsie looked out the window at Jude. "He purely loves them trains. Don't miss a one. Always try to locate near the tracks for him."

Georgia, Clinchfield, and West Point stock rolled past, slowing, and the British Columbia car with its magnolia logo stopped directly in view as the L&N engines switched back and forth uptown, shunting a feed car aside.

"He's the good one," Elsie said. Canny, she studied Thomas' face, reading there her familiar, bitter lesson. "Ray done bad?" she guessed. She set the photograph back in its place on the mantel. "You don't love them for it, but you love them. There's good in between the bad times." She smoothed a wrinkle in the mantel runner, chased the fold ahead of her fingers to the fringed end, then chased it again.

The train, readying itself for the run north through the deep cuts and poplar hills, revved its engines until the whole house rumbled, making itself felt in every bone.

"The Lloyd Jesus knows I love all my boys!" she cried, her face lifted to the calendar Christ as she wept. When she was calmer she wiped her face on her apron and took her seat again, her tear-shining hands inert on the arms of her chair, her swollen feet in their strutted oxfords braced heel by heel for the truth. "All right," she consented. She sniffed deeply, inhaling the last of her tears. "You tell me what it is. What'll be in them newspapers. Tell me in so many words. I don't want to read about it." Her voice was worn down with speaking up for herself and her sons, husky from making itself heard over mill racket, muffled by sorrows. "I hate to read about it," she explained, then cleared her throat with a sigh and waited.

That was when Thomas, though it wasn't his intention, admitted, "It could have been my own son. I thought it was."

3

His old man lay in Grady Miller's lifetime-guaranteed burial vault, and the mourners—those windblown few who waited for the closing and the anchoring of their wreaths in the raw clay—drifted like dark leaves against the whited wall of Soul's Harbor Church. Olene's sinuses were acting up; she couldn't wear a hat over that hairdo and she had left her scarf in her other coat. She withdrew to the sanctuary of the darkened church itself. Miller's assistants were already folding the chairs, rolling up the fake grass, loading the pulleys and frame and plush seat covers into their van. The pastor gave Thomas a little tap with his Bible as he went by, saying, "We'll keep in touch," and headed briskly for his car. His wife was already buckled in, ready.

There came that general, genteel exodus, with no backward glances, as life went on. The road and margins cleared of traffic and then it was so quiet; there was only the flutter of the canopy's scalloped canvas as the wind rocked it on its moorings. The grave-diggers' words were blown far afield, toward the kneeling cattle, fawn-colored jerseys, on the distant hill. They looked legless; they reminded Thomas of that deer on the quarry road Labor Day night, her front legs sheared in the accident, yet somehow she was still alive.

He had knelt beside her. Her doe eye, widely dilated, stared vacantly up at the sky, her nostrils flaring with each quick breath. She was dying, and it was taking too long.

"Where the hell is the Ranger?"

The inevitable crowd had begun to gather. G.W. Laney, first responder, stamped and snorted like a dray beast. He was a volunteer, whose wife had given him an emergency light for his birthday. Its intermittent red sweep refreshed his sunburn and turned the rain to blood. His scanner spat static. Thomas had a headache. He and G.W. laid a tarp over the deer.

"Back 'em up," Thomas told him, and G.W. herded the bystanders deeper into the dark. "Appreciate y'all coming, folks, but how about clearing on off for home now?" They mostly went. Thomas couldn't see how the deer was still alive. He checked her again, ran his hand down her neck.

"I'm not waiting," he decided.

At the gunshot, the door of the ditched car ratcheted open and a young man climbed uphill out into the downpour. Thomas stared. They hadn't told him it was Dean! The boy had a bloody handkerchief tied around his left palm. They stood in the rainy circle of flashlight and Thomas asked, first off, "Whose car have you wrecked this time?"

"Ginnie let me drive. You know Ginnie—Doc Daniels' daughter."

The kind you find dead in a ditch some day, Thomas thought, watching her get out now, her jacket held over her head to keep the rain off her bright hair. Her T-shirt advertised Squeeze Me, I'm Fresh. She sided with Dean, facing Thomas down, two against one.

"It's totaled," Thomas said, surveying the wrecked sedan.

"I'm insured," Ginnie said. "But still I bet Daddy'll shit a brick." She laughed. Dean started to laugh, then didn't. Then did. Ginnie flicked a few tiny cubes of safety glass off his shoulder.

"You been drinking?" Thomas asked, officially. And unofficially.

"Naw, uh, just beer. Just one." Dean shut his eyes, stood on tiptoe, and begun touching first one index finger, then the other, to his nose. "See?"

"You need a doctor?" Thomas kept his voice casual as he eyed that blood-blackened bandage.

"It's just a cut." Dean was exhilarated by the adrenalin. "Damn deer bust right out on me! Like a bomb. Clean through the windshield." He avoided looking at that mound under the rain-glittering tarp.

"How fast were you going?" Thomas shone the flashlight along the pavement. "Where'd you brake?"

"You saying it's my fault?" The boy's raw fist in its bandage tightened.

"I'm saying what I'd say to anyone."

Dean crossed his arms over his chest when he heard that and bent a hot, hurt look on his father—part anger, part disappointment—as though he had been handed a stone instead of bread.

Thomas knew that look well enough. "Sue me," he told the boy. The wrecker was backing up to Ginnie's car and the Ranger had arrived, with a notebook to fill with facts. He began asking Dean and Ginnie the hard questions. When he finished and had no charges to file, Thomas offered, "Y'all need a lift?"

Ginnie said, that quick, "We're going with G.W.," and G.W. grinned, because he hadn't asked them and because Ginnie was like that, fixing things to suit her. (She had a way of daring him that sent Dean diving off the rocky cliff over the reservoir at least once a summer, risking his neck for one moment of her laughter, and before the peony of spray had settled around him, before he had surfaced, she was bored, thinking up something else. Thomas had warned them off those rocks, but Ginnie was worth the risk, worth the slow climb back up the cliff to her lacquered toes.) She swung herself up into G.W.'s front seat and Dean got in back.

"Keep it between the ditches," Thomas had called as they rolled off, white water fluming up from beneath the wide tires of the Jeep.

"How much longer?" Thomas wondered. He had objected to the machine, backfilling, so the men were shoveling by hand.

One of the mourners, with an estimating glance over toward the undertaker's canopy, said, "Now, I think. They're about done." The grave was covered and the wreaths were being laid. The ribbons rattled in the wind.

Thomas led the way, alone. Friends who had stayed set out in a broken rank behind him, by twos and threes, across the intervening graves, picking their way around the minimal obstacles of granite and marble, not talking. The throaty mufflers of Dean's orange Chevy caught their attention from the moment he rounded the curve by Foster's store. He burned a week's worth of rubber off his tires and stopped in a scour of gravel at the foot of the hill. Thomas turned to watch. They all did.

Dean had a bucket of bronze mums. He came on fast, loping across the field, hurdling the cemetery wall, catching up. They made way for him, but still he hung back, only stepping up to set the flowers at the headstone, between his grandparents' graves. Then he rested on Little Earl's footstone, catching his breath. He had nothing to say when they greeted him. Sullen, he raised the hood of his jogging suit and tied it snug, but they could still see his black eye. He stood suddenly and stamped his foot. "Cramp," he explained, doing some exercises to stretch the kink from his calf. "Gotta work it out." He jogged off east across the field, over unclaimed ground, then down toward the gravel pit, and around again.

As they watched him go, one of the men said, "Give him time, Tom, he's just a kid." That was what Olene was always saying. But wasn't that what everyone had said about Little Earl? Wild as sunspots and dead at twenty-four after losing a race with a locomotive, and not a day in that whole wasted life had he ever thought of anyone but himself.

The others paid their last respects to the old man, calling him a man among men, shaking Thomas' hand, and heading on down the hill to their cars. The diggers, behind the church, loaded their backhoe onto its trailer, threw in their handtools, and drove off.

When they had gone, Dean trotted back. "I wasn't going to come," he said. He pulled up his left sock, then stood not quite facing his daddy. They were alone now.

"You just about missed it," Thomas agreed. Why had he bothered to come? Thomas couldn't look at him, at that bruised eye. Had he hit him *that* hard? Where the hell had he been all night?

"Your mother was worried sick," Thomas said. He fumbled with his matches. Dean didn't say anything, as usual, just looked around. "She's in the church," Thomas told him. The boy shrugged.

"You're the ones who let the air out of the cruiser's tires, aren't you? You and Ginnie." He'd figured that out in fifteen seconds. Did they think he was a fool?

"Sue me," Dean said. Thomas blinked when he heard himself quoted. The boy stepped up to the curb of the plot and balanced on his toes, taller than his daddy, then stepped back down. "I was pissed," he said.

Before Thomas could decide if that was an apology, the door of the church skreeked open, then slammed. Olene stood on the steps, her eyes shaded by her upheld hands as she stared their way. She waved and shouted something, but the wind scattered her words. She gave up, but stayed out, as though she wanted to keep an eye on them. She sat on the top step in what was left of the sun, hugging her cold knees.

"And leave Ginnie out of it," Dean added.

"I figured it was you." Thomas unpocketed his fists to stoop and right a spray of carnations the wind had tipped over. The shoulders of his suit were white from leaning against the chalky shingles of the church. The scent of dying flowers choked him. Just that mere whiff made him remember all the other times, but he didn't want to remember. A phoebe settled hard, rocking a little on the rusty gate, feebly singing. Thomas concentrated on the bird.

When he caught Dean looking at him, he nodded toward the boy's car and said. "You fixed the clutch." He was getting hoarse.

"Yeah." Dean almost smiled.

The wind was strong enough to lean on, like it would never die. Dean glanced at his watch and sighed. He held out his hand, signaling *five minutes more* to Olene, waiting.

Thomas crossed his arms. "Don't let me keep you."

One by one, Dean popped the knuckles of both hands, taking his time. Thomas hated that. "You going to stay out here all night?" Dean asked.

"Look who's talking."

"At least I was warm," Dean said.

Thomas checked the sky. "This time it didn't rain. It always rains." He watched the blue pickup truck bump across Langford's far pasture, and the cows begin walking toward the hay in back. One of the calves bawled and ran to catch up with its mother.

Olene came across the cemetery, making careful steps in her high heels, holding her coat shut. "Thomas?" she called. She lurched, stopped, and removed her shoes, then came on, faster, over the grass. "I'd rather have pneumonia than broken bones," she said. She looked from Thomas to Dean and back again. Thomas took her shoes and put them in the pockets of his suitcoat. She reached up to touch Dean's bruised eye, but he pulled away.

Olene knelt to gather up the remains of the everlasting and lilies she had planted. "Look what they did," she said. The careless mower in his zeal had laid them low. The diggers had chipped the granite corner monogram and snubbed the rose, the only volunteer. Thomas toed a stray clod from his daddy's footstone, which was already in place, part of the package deal when they buried his mother.

"All they've got to do is cut the date of death," Olene said, bending to tap the cold stone. "It's been a while, but they can match Mama Teague's numbers exactly." Olene dusted her hands and hugged her coat tighter to her. "I'm freezing to death," she said. "I'll be next."

"We'll go," Thomas said. Olene ran on and got into Thomas' truck and shut the door, but Dean stayed. Thomas was shivering. He made a giveaway gesture at the ground: farewell. "Maybe Mama can do something with him," he said. "I sure as hell never could."

The phoebe on the iron gate flew out and back, out and back, preying and preening. The wind had finally let up, and for a moment there was no other motion in the world but the lone bird, weakly singing. Then Dean stepped across Little Earl's grave and brushed the chalk dust off Thomas' shoulders, brushed and brushed.

That was when Thomas began to cry.

MARY HOOD lives and works in the foothills of north Georgia. She has published two collections of short fiction and recently completed a novel.

Earl Goes to the Site
and Stares Until He Sees

DENNIS JOHNSON

I DECIDE IT'S TIME to go to Washington, D.C., to look for the father of my children. Of course, I have to take the kids along.

We've gone to fetch my husband, Earl, three or four times now. It's become sort of a routine. As soon as the kids get home from school, we leave. The two little ones get excited and anxious. They love the three-hour car trip down to the big city. They love sleeping in a hotel and eating bought food. They don't find it strange that their father wanders off. Maybe they think he is a spy on a secret mission; that is all they need to know.

I try not to think about it. I only know I couldn't make the trip without my children. Marlon, my big boy who's eighteen, not only does the driving, but is a pretty smart mechanic and good at coaxing the car all the way to the city. He is unhappy about missing a day of basketball practice, but he wouldn't let us go without him. He sits next to me, erect, all six foot five inches of him: a soldier doing his duty.

I close my eyes for a bit and remind myself that Earl is tall, too, and not hard to find. We've always been able to locate him in a day.

In the back seat, Dustin, age nine, and Jimmy D., seven, are having a punch contest. This is where you punch your brother on the arm as hard as you can. The idea is to start out laughing, but then to get progressively meaner. Jimmy D.'s wail comes up like a police siren.

I open my eyes and pull around in my seat. "Dustin!" I say.

"He asked for it, Mom."

"Nobody asks to cry, knucklehead," I say.

"We're almost there, Ma," says Marlon, and I look ahead and see the city. The buildings give off a clean, golden light as the sun sets behind us. As always, the sight of our nation's capital fills me with dread.

We're on the road overlooking the memorials. Pointing to a dome, Dustin starts in again with his history stories. "Thomas Jefferson," he says, "had slaves." "No," says Jimmy, glaring at the monument as if the truth were visible. "Yes," says Dustin, folding his arms.

By now, Marlon knows which exit to take, and he steers with one hand toward the Harrington, the downtown hotel where I will sleep tonight in a single bed, my children on the floor around me in their sleeping bags.

We pass the Treasury Building, and I think about money. The longer it takes to locate Earl, the more we spend. The car makes a rattling sound as Marlon accelerates. We will look for Earl on foot, in order to rest the car and save gas. The first time Earl went to Washington, it was a family trip. That was when Marlon was a baby, crying all the way.

Every time we've been to Washington there has been a demonstration of some sort going on, and this time is no exception. As we approach the Capitol Building in the morning, there is a podium visible on the steps, and a plump black man is giving a speech in a bullhorn voice we can't understand. On the quarter-moon lawn, among the statues, the audience is spread out in bunches: mostly city-looking people, mostly blacks, a few shaggy, bearded whites wearing big slogan buttons. A few more white men, wearing suits and sunglasses, are standing under the trees around the lawn, watching the crowd.

"What's this one about, Mom?" asks Dustin.

"Civil rights," says Marlon. "But it can't be too important, ain't no TV cameras."

"Let's try the side entrance," I say. "Too many people here." We go off Pennsylvania Avenue to the south wing.

"Lotta people," I say to the guard there.

"Zoo," he says. "Demonstrations." He shakes his head.

"How long'll it last?" I ask. "I'm looking for somebody, but we won't find him in this crowd."

"Well, this one's supposed to finish up by eleven, but then there's another scheduled for just after that. Try late afternoon."

We huddle on the sidewalk to think this one out. Usually, Earl can be found in the Capitol. It's easy to find him in there. There are only so many places regular people are allowed: either sitting in the gallery for the twenty minutes they let you, watching the Senate in session; or on a bench in the enormous marble hall that the tour guides call the Rotunda. That's the most likely spot. I have twice found Earl on those benches, watching people hurry through the echoes, hoping he can catch a senator alone. He wants to talk to a senator.

"What now?" says Marlon.

"Let me think," I say. I'm trying to figure how much walking the kids can take. I look over at them and Jimmy D. suddenly thrusts a finger into Dustin's chest.

"What's this?" he says.

Dustin looks down to see. Jimmy D. dribbles his finger up Dustin's face, boinking his nose. Jimmy lets go a big laugh. Dustin belts him one on the shoulder.

They're about to go at each other when Marlon steps in. He grabs them each by the back of the neck and squeezes until their faces scrunch up. "Ma's tryin' to think," he says.

I rub my temples, trying to press out the worry about my husband. He's been making more and more of these trips. When he gets home I try to pretend nothing's wrong, but it's hard. I've been thinking I should ask to go with him one time, except there's the kids to worry about and I don't think he wants me along anyway.

"That's enough thinkin' for now, Ma," Marlon says. He hoists Jimmy D. up over his shoulder like a sack of beans and says, "What say, let's try the White House." My sons head off down Pennsylvania Avenue, and I follow.

It's a long walk, but we have to go there. Earl always takes a tour of the White House when he is in Washington. This is because he heard on the news once that the President made a surprise appearance to chitchat with a tour group. As far as Earl can find out, this has only happened that one time. Still, he figures it is worth a try. After all, Earl says he comes to Washington to talk to a senator, to find out if they're normal people; but seeing the President—seeing him walk and talk—that would really tell Earl what he wants to know. You would think there's a better chance of meeting the Queen of Sheba, but once, while taking a tour, Earl's group came upon the Presidential spokesperson in the hall outside the Blue Room. This excited Earl to no end. The Presidential spokesperson told the tour group, "The President says 'Hello.' "

But as we walk along between the big stones of the Justice Department and the Federal Bureau of Investigation, I remember something I saw on the morning news program back at the hotel.

"Oh, shoot," I say. "Wait. The President isn't here. He's vacationing at the California White House." The television had shown pictures of him riding horses with the First Lady and one of the First Sons. "Your father would know that," I tell the boys. It's true. Earl follows the news very carefully.

"Now what, Mom?" says Dustin.

"We could eat," suggests Marlon.

"One hour ago," I say, "you had pancakes, a cheese omelet, biscuits and gravy, toast, grits, and a bowl of cling peaches."

"Big game against Culpepper tomorrow," he says.

"Did you know that William Howard Taft got stuck in the White House bathtub once?" says Dustin.

"Wait," I say. "Let's try one more place before lunch."

"Can we go to the history museum?" asks Dustin.

"No," I say. "We don't have the time." I got another place in mind, but it's a long walk. "We got to find your daddy," I say.

We found Earl at the black wall once, searching for his cousin Deke's name among the tens of thousands written there. Deke the Geek. Earl had not been friendly with his cousin, and as my father used to say, "You got to be some kinda jackass to get on Earl's bad side." This was true. Deke was tall and skinny and had an awful complexion and a nasty temper. He had the biggest Adam's apple I ever saw, and he didn't shave around it very well. He got drunk and sick at our wedding and knocked over some folding chairs. He was a jerk, but he didn't deserve what he got, which was killed in a war.

It was after that when Earl began to seem distracted, and I used to think that it was because of ruminating about old Deke. I don't think that anymore. Now I think Earl just read the paper too much. He'd sit down after dinner and really eyeball every page. I noticed once that the longer he read, the more scrunched up his eyebrows got. Then one day he started a subscription to *Newsweek* magazine. Soon after, he took to watching the six o'clock news, and then the eleven o'clock news, and sometimes on winter days when it was too cold for him to go out and work, he would watch the morning news, too. He took in information like he was preparing for something. And then finally, after years and years, he started making the drive down from our West Virginia hills into Washington.

Earl, you see, is a hard-working man who is used to making things. He is a mason, a bricklayer. He makes simple back porches, he makes complicated houses. Fireplaces, foundations, chimneys, sidewalks, even part of a road in the pedestrian mall in downtown Charleston. You tell Earl what you want, he goes to the site and stares at things until he sees how to do it. When he tries to operate from blueprints, he loses sight of what he's making. So when he goes to Washington, D.C., to figure out how something's done, I don't stop him. It doesn't seem as weird to me as it does to, say, his mama. "My boy," she says to me, "has gone nuts." No, I want to tell her, although the words don't come out. It's just that Earl don't know how to take care of himself, and he loses his place and forgets we're waiting on him. So I go get him. It's as simple as that.

The frozen grass crunches beneath our feet as we tramp across the Mall. Jimmy D. walks up behind Dustin and sticks his foot between Dustin's legs. Dustin falls down on his face but pops back up and takes off after Jimmy. They run off, both of them hollering, Dustin with one fist raised over his head, hoping to clobber his brother. I call out to them, but they're gone. Marlon clucks his tongue. "I'll take care of this, Ma," he says, and returns dragging a squirming little brother in each hand.

I am surprised by my own anger. "Once more," I say to them, "just once more with this dum-dum stuff and I'm gonna paint your back porch red, you hear me? You're brothers! Act like it! We're here to find your daddy. Don't you understand?" But this is a dumb thing to say. How can they understand? They don't even think about it cause they figure there's nothing to be done. At the dinner table one time they tried, they asked their daddy about it, and he told them he just wanted to talk to someone in charge, like talking to a foreman on a job. "I want to talk to a senator," he said. "Oh," I said. "And what you got to say?" "It'll come to me," he said. Then he just put down his fork and stared off. Dinner ended with the rest of us looking down into our plates.

I finish my hollering and we stand there in awkward silence. Then Marlon lets loose one of his famous belches.

Dustin and Jimmy D. giggle, and I wish Earl could hear it. I look around and notice the buildings across the grass. "Let's get a snack and look around the history museum," I say.

I sit on a bench outside the Smithsonian Institution holding two half-finished cups of cherry cola, while Marlon leads Dustin and Jimmy D. off to their favorite exhibit: a stuffed horse that used to belong to some general. There are also guns and swords in that room, weapons that used to belong to famous soldiers.

I don't care for that room and my calves have begun to cramp from all the walking, so I sit. It's pushing into afternoon and the air has warmed up some. The sky is getting all blue-gray; it looks like snow. We should be moving on, but I don't want to rush the kids. I imagine Dustin chattering on and on about the Battle of Bull Run, or reciting Patrick Henry's "Give Me Liberty or Give Me Death" speech, or telling how Francis Scott Key wrote the national anthem on the back of an envelope, just like Lincoln did the Gettysburg Address. Jimmy D., and even Marlon, listen with their mouths open as Dustin tells the things he's learned in school, and then some.

He gets this from his father. Not the history so much as the jabbering. It is something I wish Earl would learn back from his son. For years now, he's been getting quieter and quieter. But at one time he was a real talker. Not that his words had ever been quite to the point. They were spacy, wandering, dreamy, like him, like some guy in the pictures. I remember when we were courting, Earl would pick me up after I was done ripping tickets in the movie theater and he would hold me in his arms, but instead of soulful words of love, he would prattle on and on, in a voice of deep satisfaction, about leaves, or water, or stars, or cement. One time, something welled up in me and I interrupted him. Words of love gushed out of me, streamed out, tumbling over each other, an offering that left me so weak I would have fallen if we hadn't been hugging at the time. I looked up and he was staring at me, eyes wide, hair tousled. "And just what am I to you, Earl E. Swanson?" I asked. His eyes opened as he said—as if it made all the sense in the world—"Why, you're the girl in my arms." I laughed and held him to me for all I was worth. I closed my eyes and pressed my face into his chest, and I had the feeling that if I ever opened my eyes again, a home would have suddenly been built around us. And that is exactly what happened.

"*Yo, Mom!*" says a voice. "Earth to Mom. Come in Mom."

I open my eyes and there are my boys. Marlon is grinning, but the two little ones look worried.

"Mama," says Jimmy D., pressing up against my leg.

"Don't worry, Ma," says Marlon. "You know he's okay. We'll find him." Then, as I get up, he puts an arm around my shoulders—he has to stoop a little to do this—and says, "You shouldn't space out like that, Ma. Your children find it frightening."

"Mom," Dustin says, "did you know Stonewall Jackson liked to suck lemons before a battle?"

Across town now, exhausted from our march, we are at the wall. Around us, monuments and memorials and government buildings are all competing with each other for the horizon. But right here, we are surrounded by grass, a few trees, and a monument that is barely higher that my head: the black, shiny stone wall, stretching off a long way, holding back a grassy mound. Thousands upon thousands of names are carved into it, and it's spotted with small flags, flowers, medals, and photos. There are letters taped to it here and there, like people expect them to be picked up by some angel mailman.

It takes a minute to get Jimmy D. to move. He holds his body still, and I have to squat down and rub his back. "We won't stay long, baby," I tell him. "Stay close to Mama and it'll be all right."

Like me, he finds this stitch in the earth a frightening thing. Dustin, on the other hand, likes it for what it is: a memorial to dead soldiers. It excites him, because he has seen movies and television shows about these men, and he knows for a fact that they all died like heroes.

We are silent as we walk along. Jimmy D. clings to my leg. Dustin walks with his mouth open. Marlon keeps his head lowered, eyes squinting glances as if into the sun.

There are not many others here. We pass an old couple in corduroy coats and wool hats, leaning on each other, hands in pockets. Farther on, a bearded man in a wheelchair sits at an angle to the wall. He is wearing an olive army jacket and a beat-up cowboy hat, and he's chatting happily over his shoulder to the wall, laughing and talking all by himself.

"Holy cow," Marlon whispers to me. "Do you see that?" He sucks in a whistle as we pass by.

"Yes," I say. "Get Dustin."

Dustin has stopped behind us and is standing stock still, staring back at the happy man in the wheelchair. Marlon cuffs him on the back of the head. "Ain't no TV you're starin' at there, nosy," Marlon says, and pulls him back, and the four of us move off again along the path.

We come to the place where the wall folds back into itself, into a V-shaped opening, and we turn the corner slowly, as if afraid, almost, of seeing Earl.

But Earl isn't there. Peering into the heart of the memorial, the names of all those human beings converge into a black, glistening nothing.

Back in the middle of the city, the snow finally starts to fall in big, quiet flakes as we trudge up Maryland Avenue, past a giant, gray-stone government building that claims to be the minister of our Health, Education, and Welfare.

All that's left for us is one more trip to the Capitol, in the hope that the protesters have packed it in and left democracy open to tourism. The kids are grouchy. I could leave them off at the hotel, but I want them with me; somehow, I'm grateful they are crabby and want only food and sleep.

It is late in the day and the air seems to be exactly caught between light and dark. We pass by some raw-looking public gardens and an icy reflecting pool, and there—with a statue in the foreground of some bearded leader holding a sword—is the Capitol. Men in suits and women in high heels and people in uniforms stream up and down the wide steps. It looks like business as usual. We hesitate—like rabbits about to cross the interstate—then move on up the long steps.

Walking past a bunch of scowling guards, we come in by a busy tourist desk staffed by young men and women with short blond hair. There is a thick velvet rope leading off to one side and a sign says "ALL TOURS." In the bustle I slip the children past it and around a massive marble column out into the opening beneath the dome. We stand there looking around. "Is this where the President works?" asks Jimmy D. "Not really," says Marlon.

We begin to skirt the circle. People hurrying all around, scurrying every which way; we move slowly. It is as if there is an undertow, as if we were wading at Myrtle Beach.

Directly across the rotunda is a wide bank of elevators with a bunch of bureaucrats pacing in front of them; people looking at watches, carrying briefcases. The space around us echoes with shuffled voices and footsteps.

The children and I huddle together by one of the smooth columns, a column wider and taller than the most mighty tree in West Virginia. Dustin and Jimmy D. stand close against my legs, and then Marlon puts his hand on my shoulder. I look across the huge stretch of marble and see my husband. He is standing in his plaid flannel coat, looking up at a small statue on a pedestal. The statue is of a man wearing a wig and a long coat and knee breeches, standing with chin held high and one arm outstretched. The arm reaches over Earl's head, as if patting him down.

I can't move. I want to call out to Earl, to call him to us, to take him back home. Once there I can make him see that the girl in his arms will have to be enough. But I know that here, in this hollow space, if I dared to call out the truth to him, my voice would carry up into the dome above us, and not be heard at all.

DENNIS JOHNSON holds an M.F.A. degree from the University of Iowa and teaches English at Allegheny College in Meadville, Pennsylvania. He is currently working on a collection of his stories and editing an anthology of novellas.

I Just Love Carrie Lee

E L L E N   D O U G L A S

ALL THE TIME WE WERE away from here, living in Atlanta, I paid Carrie
Lee's wages—seven dollars a week for eight years. Of course, part of the
time, after Billy married and came back to Homochitto, she was working
for him in the country. She rides the bus to Wildwood, seven miles over
the river, every day. I don't know why she doesn't move back over there,
but she likes to live in town. She owns her own house and she likes to
visit around. The truth of the matter is, she thinks she might miss
something if she moved over the river; and besides, she never has had
any use for "field niggers." (That's Carrie Lee talking, not me.) Anyway,
as I was saying, I did pay her wages all those years we were away from
here. I knew Mama would have wanted me to, and besides, I feel the
same responsibility towards her that Mama did. You understand that,
don't you? She was our responsibility. So few people think that way
nowadays. Nobody has the feeling for Negroes they used to have. People
look at me as if they think I'm crazy when I say I paid Carrie Lee all that
time.

I remember when I first had an inkling how things were changing. It
was during the Depression when the Edwardses moved next door to us.
They were Chicago people, and they'd never had any dealings with
Negroes. Old Mrs. Edwards expected the baseboards to be scrubbed every
week. I suppose she scrubbed them herself in Chicago. Oh, I don't mean
there was anything wrong with her. She was a good hard-working
Christian soul; and *he* was a cut above *her*. I've heard he came from an old

St. Louis family. But a woman sets the tone of a household, and her tone was middle-western to the marrow. All her children said "come" for "came" and "I want in," and I had a time keeping mine from picking it up.

To make a long story short, she came to me one day in the late fall and asked me what the yardmen in Homochitto did in the winter.

"What do you mean?" I said.

"I mean where do they work?"

"Well," I said, "mine sits around the kitchen and shells pecans and polishes silver all winter."

"You mean you keep him on when there's actually nothing for him to do?" she said.

"He *works* for us," I said. "He's been working for us for years."

"I haven't got that kind of money," she said. "I had to let mine go yesterday, and I was wondering where he would get a job."

I tried to explain to her how things were down here, how you couldn't let a man go in the winter, but she didn't understand. She got huffy as could be.

"I suppose that's what you call *noblesse oblige,*" she said.

"You could, if you wanted to be fancy," I said.

And do you know what she said to me? She said, "They're not going to catch me in that trap, the *Nee-*grows. I can do all my own work and like it, if it comes to that. I'm going to stand on my rights."

They didn't stay in Homochitto long.

Wasn't that odd? Everyone is like that nowadays. Maybe not for such a queer reason, but no one feels any responsibility any more. No one cares, white or black.

That's the reason Carrie Lee is so precious to us. She cares about us. She knows from experience what kind of people we are. It's a boon in this day and age just to be recognized.

The truth of the matter is I couldn't tell you what Carrie Lee has meant to us. She's been like a member of the family for almost fifty years. She raised me and she's raised my children. Ask Sarah and Billy, Carrie Lee was more of a mother to them than I was. I was too young when I first married to be saddled with children, and too full of life to stay at home with them. Bill was always on the go, and I wouldn't have let him go without me for anything. It was fortunate I could leave the children with Carrie Lee and never have a moment's worry. She loved them like they were her own, and she could control them without ever laying a hand on them. She has her own philosophy, and while *I* don't always understand it, children do.

Carrie Lee is a bright Negro—both ways, I mean, and both for the same reason, I reckon. I don't know exactly where the white blood came from (it's not the kind of thing they told young ladies in my day), but I can guess. Probably an overseer. Her mama was lighter than she, and married a dark man. The old mammy, Carrie Lee's grandmother, was black as the ace of spades, so Mama said. I judge some overseer on Grandfather's place must have been Carrie Lee's grandfather. She has always said she has Indian blood, too, said her mama told her so. But how much truth there is in that I don't know. The hawk nose and high cheekbones look Indian, all right, and there is something about her—maybe that she won't make a fool of herself to entertain you. You know she's different. And she could put the fear of God into the children, like a Cherokee chief out after their scalps.

Billy says Carrie Lee taught him his first lesson in getting along with people. He was the youngest boy in the neighborhood, and of course the other children made him run all their errands; they teased and bullied him unmercifully until he was big enough to stand up for himself. This is the kind of thing they'd do. One day in the middle of my mah-jongg club meeting, he came running in the house crying. Some of the children had mixed up a mess of coffee grounds and blackberry jam and tried to make him eat it. It was an initiation. They formed a new club every week or two and Billy was the one they always initiated.

"Mama's busy, honey," I said. "Tell it to Carrie Lee. She'll tend to 'em for you."

Carrie Lee took him on her lap like a baby and rocked him and loved him until he stopped crying, and then he sat up and said, "But Carrie Lee, who am I going to play with? Everybody's in the club but me."

And she said, "Honey, they bigger than you. If you wants to play, you gits on out there and eats they pudding. If you don't like it, you holds it in your mouth and spits it out when they ain't looking."

"But s'pose they feed me more than I can hold in my mouth?" he said.

"Honey, if they does, you got to make your mouth stretch," she said.

Billy has never forgotten that.

Carrie Lee came to work for Mama when she was fourteen years old.

She was only a child, it's true, but even then she had more sense than most grown Negroes. Mama had seen her on their place outside Atlanta and taken a fancy to her. *Her* mother (Carrie Lee's, I mean) cooked for the manager's family there, and Carrie Lee was already taking care of five or six younger brothers and sisters while the mother was at work. You can imagine what it meant to her to come to town. Mama clothed her and fed her and made a finished servant of her. Why, she even saw to it that Carrie Lee went to school through the fifth grade; she'd never been able to go more than a couple of terms in the country. Fifty years ago, practically none of the Negroes went more than a year or two, if that long. When they were seven or eight, they either went to the field or stayed at home to nurse the younger ones.

By the time we moved to Homochitto, Mama couldn't have gotten along without Carrie Lee, and so she came with us. At first Mama was miserable here—homesick for Georgia and her own family and the social life of Atlanta. Compared to Atlanta, Homochitto then was nothing but a village. And the weather! We had never been through a Mississippi summer before, or, for that matter, a Georgia summer; we'd always gone to the mountains—Monteagle, or White Sulphur Springs, or some place like that. But that first year in Homochitto Papa couldn't leave, and Mama got in one of her stubborn spells and wouldn't go without him. To tell you the truth, I think she wanted him to see her suffer, so he'd take her back to Atlanta. She used to say then that no one understood how she felt except Carrie Lee. And I suppose it's true that Carrie Lee missed her family too, in spite of the hard life she'd had with them. In the mornings she and Mama would sit in the kitchen peeling figs or pears or peaches, or washing berries, preserving together, and Carrie Lee would tell stories to entertain Mama. I'd hang around and listen. I remember one day Carrie Lee had said something 'specially outrageous, and Mama said, "Carrie Lee, I don't believe half you say. Why do you make up those awful tales?"

Carrie Lee stopped peeling pears and began to eat the peelings. She always did eat the peelings when they were preserving, everything except figs—a hangover from hungry days, I reckon. She hushed talking a minute, eating and thinking, and then she looked at Mama and said:

"To keep us from the lonely hours,
    And being sad so far from home."

It was just like a poem. I had to get up and run out of the house to keep them from seeing me cry. Do you suppose she understood what she'd said and how beautifully she'd said it? Or is it something about language that comes to them as naturally as sleeping—and music?

When Mama died, I felt as if she had more or less left Carrie Lee to me, and I've been taking care of her ever since. Oh, she's no burden. There's no telling *how* much money she has in the bank. There she is, drawing wages from Billy and from me, owns her own house and rents out a room, nobody to spend it on but herself and one step-daughter, and she never has to spend a dime on herself. Between us, Sarah and I give her everything she wears; and as for her house, every stick she has came out of our old house.

When we sold the house, after Mama died, Carrie Lee took her pick of what was left. Of course, I had gotten all the good pieces—the things that were bought before the war—but she wouldn't have wanted them anyway; nothing I chose would have suited her taste. She has a genius for the hideous. She took the wicker porch chairs—you know, the kind with fan backs and magazine racks in the arms and trays hooked onto the sides for glasses—and painted them blue and put them in her living room; and she took a set or crocheted table mats that Mama made years ago. (They were beautiful things, but if you've ever had a set you know what a nuisance they are. Not a washwoman in Homochitto does fine laundering any more, and *I* certainly wouldn't wash and starch and stretch them *myself*. And besides, where would anyone in a small apartment like this keep those devilish boards with nails in them, that you have to stretch them on?) Anyway, Carrie Lee took those place mats and put them on the wicker chairs like antimacassars, if you can believe it. But that's just the beginning. All the junk collected by a houseful of pack rats like Bill's family—the monstrosities they acquired between 1890 and 1930 would be something to read about. And Bill and Mama had stored everything in Mama's attic when Bill sold his father's house in 1933. Why, I couldn't say, except that Bill always hated to throw anything away. That's a trait that runs in his family: they hang on to what they have. And if his father hadn't hung on to Wildwood during hard times and good, where would we be now?

Fortunately, he did hang on to it, and to everything else *his* father left him. You know, Bill's family didn't have the hard time most people had after the Civil War. His grandfather started the little railroad line from Homochitto to Jackson that was eventually bought by the Southern. He was a practical businessman and he didn't sit back like so many people, after we were defeated, and let his property get away from him out of sheer outrage. And so, the family was able to travel and to buy whatever was stylish at the time. Carrie Lee loved everything they bought, and she has as much of it as she can squeeze into her house: heavy golden oak sideboard and table, a fine brass bed polished up fit to blind you, a player piano that doesn't work, with a Spanish shawl draped over it, and on the walls souvenir plates from Niagara Falls and the St. Louis Exposition, and pictures of Mama and me and the children, sandwiched in between pictures of all her sisters and brothers and their families. It's too fine.

Actually, there are some people around here who disapprove of Carrie Lee and me; but as far as I'm concerned they can say what they like. I just love Carrie Lee and that's all there is to it. When she comes to call, she sits in the parlor with the white folks. She has good sense about it. If she's in the house on Sunday afternoon visiting with me, and guests come, she goes to the door and lets them in as if she were working that day, and then she goes back to the kitchen and fixes coffee and finds an apron and serves us. Everything goes smoothly. She knows how to make things comfortable for everybody. But half the time, whoever it is, I wish they hadn't come. I'd rather visit with Carrie Lee.

And people who talk about it don't know what they're saying. They don't know how I feel. When Bill died (that was only a year after Mama died, and there I was, left alone with a houseful of *babies* to raise and all that property to manage), who do you think walked down the aisle with me and sat with me at the funeral? Carrie Lee. If I hadn't been half crazy with grief, I suppose I might have thought twice before I did a thing like that. But I did it, and I wouldn't have let anyone prevent me.

Weddings are a different matter, of course. If you have them at home, it's no problem; the colored folks are all in the kitchen anyhow, and it's easy enough for them to slip in and see the ceremony. I know Winston and Jimmy and the ones we've known for years who turn up at weddings and big parties would *rather* stay in the kitchen. Jimmy takes charge of the punch bowl and sees that all the help stay sober enough to serve, at least until the rector goes home.

But it's not customary in Homochitto to include the servants at a church wedding. There's no balcony in the Episcopal church like the slave gallery in the Presbyterian church, and so there's no place to seat them. I couldn't do anything about that at Sarah's wedding; I just had to leave the rest of the servants out, but we did take Carrie Lee to the church.

I'll never forget how she behaved; if she'd been the mama, she couldn't have been more upset.

Sarah was only nineteen, too young, way too young to marry. To tell you the truth I was crushed at the time. I never, *never* thought any good would come of it. Oh, I realize I was even younger when I married. But in my day young ladies were brought up for marriage, and marriages were made on other terms, terms I understood. Bill was nearly thirty when we married, and he had exactly the same ideas Papa had. He simply finished my education. Which proves my contention—that a woman is old enough to marry when she has sense enough to pick the right man. If she doesn't, she isn't ready. That's the way it was with Sarah.

Wesley was just a boy—a selfish, unpredictable boy. He never understood how sheltered Sarah had been, how little she knew of the world, how indulgent we had been with her as a child, how totally unprepared she was for—for him. And afterwards she said it was all my fault. That's children for you. But I hadn't meant to prepare her for *Wesley*. I wouldn't have had him!

To go back to the wedding, Carrie Lee rode to the church with Sarah, and put the finishing touches on her hair and arranged her train. I didn't see this because of course I was sitting in the front of the church, but the people in the back said when Sarah and Brother George started down the aisle, Carrie Lee ran after them, straightening Sarah's train, the tears streaming down her face. I believe she would have followed them to the altar, but Edwin Ware slipped out of his pew and got her to go back. She was crying like a child, saying, "My baby. She's *my baby.*"

You'd never have known she had children of her own the way she worshipped mine—still does.

But she had a married interlude. She was too old to carry a child; she had two miscarriages and lost one shortly after it was born. But she raised two or three of her husband's children. Negroes are so funny. Even Carrie Lee, as well as I know her, surprises me sometimes. She turned up at work one morning just as usual. (She never came until ten-thirty, and then stayed to serve supper and wash the dishes at night.) Bertie, who was cooking for me then, had been muttering and snickering to herself in the kitchen all morning, and, when I came in to plan dinner, she acted like she had a cricket down her bosom.

"What in the world are you giggling and wiggling about, Bertie?" I said.

Bertie *fell* out.

Carrie Lee, forty if she was a day, stood there glowering. "You know Bertie, Miss Emma," she said. "Bertie's crazy as a road lizard."

Bertie pointed her finger at Carrie Lee and then she sort of hollered out. "She *ma'ied*, Miss Emma! She ma'ied."

You could have knocked me over with a feather. I didn't even know she was thinking about it. "Are you really, Carrie Lee?" I said.

"Yes'm."

"Well, Carrie Lee!" I said. "My feelings are hurt. Why didn't you tell us ahead of time. We could have had a fine wedding—something special."

I *was* disappointed, too. I've always wanted to put on a colored wedding, and *there,* I'd missed my chance.

Carrie Lee didn't say a word. I never *have* been able to figure out why she didn't tell us beforehand.

And then that nitwit, Bertie, began to laugh and holler again. "She don't need no special wedding, Miss Emma," Bertie said. "Ain't nothing special about getting ma'ied to Carrie Lee."

I was tickled at that, but I was surprised, too. Oh, I'm not so stupid that I don't understand how different Negro morals are from ours. Most of them simply don't have any. And I understand that it all comes from the way things were in slavery times. But our family was different. Grandmother told me many a time that they always went to a lot of trouble with the slave weddings and, after the war, with the tenants'. She kept a wedding dress and veil for the girls to wear, and she made sure everything was done right—license, preacher, reception, and all the trimmings. There was no jumping the broomstick in our family. And Carrie Lee's people had been on our place for generations. I never would have thought she'd carry on with a man.

She seemed devoted to her husband. If she had carried on with one, she must have carried on with others, but I reckon she'd had her fling and was ready to retire. The husband, Henry, was a "settled man," as they say, fifteen years older than Carrie Lee, and had a half-grown son and daughter and two or three younger children. He farmed about thirty acres of Wildwood. I had known the family ever since we moved to Homochitto. (Can you imagine that—my own place, and I didn't know about him and Carrie Lee!)

Later on, shortly before he died, he managed with Carrie Lee's help to buy a little place of his own.

I always let Carrie Lee off at noon on Saturday and gave her all day Sunday, although I hated running after the children. When they got old enough to amuse themselves, it wasn't so bad, but when they were little...! Usually I got Bertie to take over for me. But I never believed in working a servant seven days a week, even when everybody did it, when they were lucky to get Emancipation Day and the Fourth of July. I never treated a servant like that. Bertie had her day off, too.

Henry would be waiting for Carrie Lee in his buggy when she got off on Saturday, and they'd catch the ferry across the river and drive out to Wildwood; and early Monday morning he'd send his son to drive her in to town—it was a couple of hours ride in the buggy. She didn't want to sell her house and move to the country (thank God!) and Henry wouldn't move to town. As Carrie Lee said, he didn't know nothing but farming, and he wasn't fixing to change his ways.

Once in a while she'd take the children to the country with her on Saturday afternoon, and I'd drive over after supper to get them. Every Saturday they begged me to go; it was the greatest treat in the world to them to ride to Wildwood in the buggy, and they were crazy about the old man. For a while I kept their horses there, and when Billy was older he used to go over there to hunt. Henry taught him everything he knows about hunting. That was before cottondusting killed all the quail in this part of the country.

Well, Carrie Lee lived like that until we moved back to Atlanta, riding to the country every Saturday afternoon and coming in at daybreak on Monday morning. It's hard to understand how anyone could be satisfied with such a life, but Carrie Lee has a happy nature, and of course the fact that she was so much better off financially than most Negroes made a difference. Besides, I wouldn't be surprised if she wasn't glad to have the peace and quiet of a single life during the week. You might say she had her cake and ate it too.

Then I left Homochitto for several years. It's the only time Carrie Lee and I have ever been separated for more than a month or two.

I'd always heard Mama talk about Atlanta; she kept after Papa to go back, right up to his dying day. I'd been too young when we moved to care, but later, after Mama and Bill died, I got the notion that someday I'd go back. So finally, I went. The children were away at school, Billy at Episcopal High and Sarah at Ardsley Hall, and there was no reason for me to stay in Homochitto.

I thought of course Carrie Lee would go with me, but she didn't. For all her talk in Mama's day about how she missed Georgia, she didn't go back. She stayed with Henry. And, as I told you, I paid her wages all the time I was gone. We wrote to each other, and we saw each other when I brought the children to Homochitto for a visit. They never got used to Atlanta and never wanted to stay there in the summer. Then Billy settled in Homochitto and began to farm Wildwood himself, and I came home.

I wish I had kept some of Carrie Lee's letters. She has a beautiful hand. She used to practice copying Mama's script, and finally got so you could hardly tell them apart. It always gives me a turn to get a letter from her, addressed in Mama's hand, and then, inside, what a difference! When she writes something she thinks will amuse me, she puts "smile" after it in parentheses. Did you know that practically all Negroes do that, even the educated ones? I sometimes see pictures of all the ones that are so much in the news nowadays—diplomats and martyrs and so forth, and I wonder if they put (smile) in their letters.

Carrie Lee used to advise me in her letters, where she would never do such a thing face to face. Like one time, I remember, she wrote me, "All the babies is gone, yours and mine. I writes Miss Sarah and Mr. Billy and they don't answer me. True, I got the old man's kids, but you haven't got none. When will you get married again, Miss Emma? Find you a good man to warm your bed." And then she wrote (smile)—to make sure I understood she wasn't being impudent, I reckon.

It was while I was living in Atlanta that Carrie Lee got her picture in the magazine. I never quite understood how it happened, unless through ignorance on all sides—ignorance on the part of the photographer about Carrie Lee's real circumstances, and ignorance on her part about what the photographer wanted. We all laughed about it afterwards, although, of course, I never mentioned it to Carrie Lee.

When we left Homochitto, she had moved over to Wildwood and rented her house in town. That's how they saved enough money for the old man to buy a place of his own. I think she gave him every cent she made. But they had their pictures taken the winter before they bought the place, the last winter they were on Wildwood.

I'll never forget how shocked I was. I had gone out for dinner and bridge one night, and was quietly enjoying a drink when one of the men at the party picked up a copy of *Life* or *Fortune* or one of those magazines.

"By the way," he said to me, "I was reading about your old stamping ground today."

I might have known he was teasing me. None of those magazines ever has anything good to say about Mississippi. But I was interested in news of Homochitto, and never thought of that; and of course *he* didn't know it was Carrie Lee. I sat there while he found the article, and there she was—there they all were, Carrie Lee, Henry, and all the children, staring at me practically life-sized from a full-page picture.

The article was on sharecropping, and *they* were the examples of the downtrodden sharecropper. I must admit they looked seedy. I recognized my dress on Carrie Lee and one of Sarah's on the little girl. They were standing in a row outside the old man's house, grinning as if they knew what it was all about. At least, all of them except Carrie Lee were grinning. She's not much of a grinner.

A November day in the South—the trees bare and black, the stubble still standing in the cotton fields, an unpainted Negro cabin with the porch roof sagging, half a dozen dirty, ragged Negro children, and a bedraggled hound. What more could a Northern editor have asked?

What will these children get for Christmas?

I could have told him what they'd get for Christmas, and who had bought the presents and sent them off just the day before. And I could have told him whose money was accumulating in the teapot on the mantel piece.

To do them justice, I'll say I don't believe Carrie Lee or Henry had the faintest idea why he'd taken their pictures. They just liked to have their pictures taken. But the very idea of them as poverty-stricken, downtrodden tenants! I couln't have run them off Wildwood with a posse and a pack of bloodhounds.

We got a big kick out of it. I cut the picture out and sent it to Sarah.

The old man died the year after they began to buy their farm, and then Carrie Lee moved to town, and shortly after that I came back to

Homochitto for good. Henry, Jr., took over the payments on the farm and lives on it. He's a sullen Negro—not like his father—but he's good to Carrie Lee. In the summer he keeps her supplied with fresh vegetables; he comes in and makes repairs on her house to save her the price of a carpenter; things like that. But he's sullen. I never have liked these Negroes who're always kowtowing and grinning like idiots—"white folks' niggers," some people down here call them—but it wouldn't hurt that boy to learn some manners. I told Carrie Lee as much one time.

I had gone into the kitchen to see about dinner, and he was sitting at the table with his hat on—this was after we moved back here, and old Henry was dead—eating his breakfast—*my* food, need I add. He didn't even look at me, much less get up.

"Good morning, Henry," I said.

He mumbled something and still didn't get up.

"Good morning, Henry," I said again.

"Morning," he said, just as sullen as he could be.

I went to Carrie Lee later and told her that any man, black, white, blue, or green, could get up and take off his hat when a lady came into the room. That's not prejudice. That's good manners.

"He ain't *bad,* Miss Emma," she said. "Just seems like he always got one misery or another. Born to trouble, as the sparks fly upward, like the Good Book says."

"Well, he'd feel a lot better, if he'd get a smile on that sullen face of his," I said. "Sometimes people bring trouble on themselves just by their dispositions."

"Ah, Miss Emma," she said, "ever since he married, it's been *root, hog, or die* for Henry, Jr. He ain't settled into it yet."

Of course, I didn't know then about the boy's sister, Carrie Lee's stepdaughter. Didn't know she had left Homochitto, much less that she had come back. She apparently married and moved to *"Dee*-troit" while we were living in Atlanta. I didn't see her until some time after she came to live in town with Carrie Lee, just a few years ago. Henry, Jr. finally had to turn her over to Carrie Lee. I can't blame him for *that,* I don't suppose. By then he had five children of his own, and there was scarcely room for them in the house, much less the sister.

I found out about the sister because Sarah left Wesley. That was a hard year. Sarah packed up the children and everything she owned and came home from Cleveland, inconsolable. I suppose I could have said, "I told you so," but I didn't have the heart. She'd married too young, there's no getting around it, and by the time she was old enough to know her own mind, there she was with two children. I tell you, people say to me: "You don't know how lucky you are that Bill left you so well-fixed. Never any money problems." They don't know how wrong they are. Money's a preoccupying worry. It keeps your mind off worse things. If you don't have to work or to worry about money, you're free to worry more about yourself and your children. Believe me, *nobody's* exempt from disappointment. I'm *proud* of the way I've raised my children. I've taught them everything I know about good manners and responsibility and honor, and I've kept their property safe for them. I've tried to give them everything that my family and Bill gave me. But when love fails you, none of it is any use. Your bed is soft and warm, but one dark night you find that sleep won't come.

I was half crazy over Sarah. She slept until noon every day and moped around the house all afternoon. Then she'd start drinking and keep me up till all hours crying and carrying on. "What am I going to do? What am I going to do?"

She still loved that good-for-nothing man.

I borrowed Carrie Lee from Billy to take care of Sarah's babies while she was here. I'm too old to chase a two-year-old child, and Sarah hardly looked at the children. She was too busy grieving over Wesley. So Carrie Lee was a boon; she took over, and we never had a minute's concern for them. Like all children, they adored her.

Billy's wife was furious with me for taking her, but I simply had to. And Carrie Lee was in seventh heaven, back with Sarah and me; she never has gotten along too well with Billy's wife. Oh, she goes out there faithfully, on account of Billy and the children. But Billy's wife is different from us—a different breed of cat, altogether, there's no getting around it. I get along fine with her because I mind my own business, but Carrie Lee considers our business her business. And then too, as I said, Carrie Lee is a *finished* servant. She has run my house for months at a time without a word of direction from me. She can plan and put on a formal dinner for twelve without batting an eye. Billy's wife doesn't know anything about good servants. She tells Carrie Lee every day what she wants done that day; and she insulted her, the first time she had a party, by showing her how to set the table.

No doubt there are two sides to the story. I'm sure Billy's wife gets sick of hearing Carrie Lee say, "But Miss Emma don't do it that way." It must be like having an extra mother-in-law. I won't go into that. I know it's the style nowadays not to get along with your mother-in-law, although I don't see why. I never had a breath of trouble with mine.

But I'm wandering again. I want to tell you the wonderful thing Carrie Lee said when she was telling us about her stepdaughter.

The children were taking their naps one afternoon, and Sarah and I were lying down in my room and Carrie Lee was sitting in there talking to us. Sarah was still thrashing around about Wesley. The truth is she wanted to go back to him. She was hollering to Carrie Lee about how he'd betrayed her and how she could never forgive him—just asking somebody please to find a good reason why she should forgive him, if the truth be known. But I wasn't going to help her; I knew it would never work.

Carrie Lee listened a while and thought about it a while and then she said, "Miss Sarah, honey, you know I got a crazy child?"

That took the wind out of Sarah's sails, and she sat up and stopped crying and said, "What?"

I was surprised, too. I didn't know a thing about that crazy girl. When I thought about it, I remembered that Carrie Lee had mentioned her to me once or twice, but at the time I hadn't paid any attention.

"I got a crazy child," Carrie Lee says. "Least, she ain't exactly my child, she old Henry's. But she *sho* crazy."

"I didn't know that, Carrie Lee," I said. "Where does she stay?"

"She stay with me," Carrie Lee says. "Right there in the house with me. Neighbors tend to her in the daytime. I ain't had her with me long—no more than a year or two."

"Well, what do I care? What's it got to do with me?" Sarah said, and she began to cry again. She wasn't herself, or she wouldn't have been so mean.

"This what," Carrie Lee says, "You know why she crazy? A man driv her crazy, that's why. You don't watch out, a man gonna driv you crazy."

Sarah lay back on the bed and kicked her feet like a baby.

"Honey, you want me to tell you how to keep a man from driving you crazy? And not only a man. Howsomever it happens, the day comes when one of God's creatures, young or old, is bound to break your heart. I'll tell you how to bear it."

Sarah shook her head.

"I'm gonna tell you anyhow. Look at me. I'm sixty years old. I looks forty-five. No man never driv me crazy, nor nobody else. I tell you how I keep him from it."

Sarah couldn't help it. She sat up and listened.

"See everything, see nothing," says Carrie Lee. "Hear everything, hear nothing. Know everything, know nothing. Trust in the Lord and love little children. That's how to ease your heart."

Did you ever? Well sir, maybe Sarah would have gone anyway, or maybe she needed Carrie Lee's advice. Anyway, she took the two children soon afterwards and went back to Wesley, and it wasn't until three years later that they got a divorce.

So here we are, Carrie Lee and I, getting old. You might say we've spent our lives together. I reckon I know her better than I would have known my own sister, if I had had one. As Carrie Lee would say, "We've seen some wonderful distressing times."

On Sundays, when she's off, lots of times she bakes me a cake and brings it around and we sit and talk of the old days when Mama and Bill were alive and when the children were little. We talk about the days of the flood, about this year's crop, about the rains in April, and in August the dry weather, about Billy's wife, and Sarah and Billy's grown-up troubles, about the grandchildren, and "all the days we've seen."

If she comes to see me on Sunday, Carrie Lee will tell me something that amuses me the whole week long. Like a couple of weeks ago we were talking about the crop. I'd been worrying all summer about the drought. It looked for a while as if Billy wouldn't make a bale to the acre. And every time I mentioned it to Carrie Lee, she'd say, "Trust in the Lord, Miss Emma." She's still a great one for leaving things to the Almighty.

Then, bless John, the cotton popped open, and, in spite of everything, it's a good year.

"Well, Carrie Lee," I said, "it looks like you were right and I was wrong. Billy's got a fine crop."

And Carrie Lee says (just listen to this), she says, "Miss Emma, if I say a chicken dips snuff, you look under his bill."

Isn't that killing? When I got by myself, I just hollered.

Looking at it another way, though, it isn't so funny. Billy's a man, and a son is never the companion to his mother that a daughter is. You know the old saying, "A son is a son till he gets him a wife, but a daughter's a daughter all of her life." I think if his father had lived, if there were a man in the house, Billy would come to see me more often. If Sarah were here, we would enjoy each other, I know; but she's married again and lives so far away, they seldom come home, and when they do, it's only for a few days.

I've never been a reader, either. I like to visit, to *talk*. I'm an articulate person. And nowadays, instead of visiting, people sit and stare at a television set. Oh, I still play cards and mah-jongg. I have friends here, but we drifted apart during the years I was in Atlanta, and things have never been quite the same since I came back.

So I'm often alone on Sunday afternoon when Carrie Lee comes to see me. That's how it happens we sit so long together, drinking coffee and talking. Late in the afternoon, Billy sometimes comes and brings the children to call, but they never stay for long. They go home to Wildwood because Billy's wife doesn't like to be there alone after dark. Carrie Lee stays on, and we go in the kitchen and she fixes my supper. As I've told you, I'd rather visit with her than with most white folks. She understands me. When I think about it, it sometimes seems to me, with Bill and Mama dead and the children grown and gone, that Carrie Lee is all I have left of my own.

ELLEN DOUGLAS lives in Jackson, Mississippi, and is the author of a collection of short fiction and six novels, of which the most recent is Can't Quit You, Baby. *Her work has been included in the O. Henry Prize Stories collection.*

Artists

L E E S M I T H

IT IS ONE OF THOSE hot Sunday afternoons that seem to stretch out, all green and gauzy and golden, over the length of my childhood; I walk in my grandmother's garden. The others are back on the porch in the curly wicker chairs, talking. Their voices come to me in little waves, musical and nonsensical like the sound of bees in the garden, across the wide green grass. I hear my mother's laugh. I cannot see her, or the others. They are cool up there on the porch, I know it; they have iced tea in the tall skinny glasses, with mint. But I want none of that. I attain the roses and halt before them, self-consciously. *I am transfixed by beauty,* I think. In fact I like the names of the roses perhaps more than I like the roses themselves—Pink Cloud, Peace, Talisman, Queen Elizabeth—the names unfurl across my mind like a silken banner, like the banner the children carry in the processional on Easter Sunday. I held a corner of that banner then. My grandmother taught me these names. I lean forward, conscious of myself leaning forward, to examine a Peace rose more closely. It is perfect: the pale velvety outer petals wide and graceful, then turning, curling and closing inward to its strange deep crimson center. The leaves are profuse, glossy, and green. There are thorns. I draw back. What I really perfer is the baby's breath along this border, the riot of pinks by the fountain, the snapdragons like a sassy little army at my feet. But my grandmother told me that these roses are the pride of her heart. And she grows no common flowers here—no zinnias, no marigolds. This baby's breath is so fragile I can see through it and beyond, to where a lizard flashes shining across a stone and is gone in the phlox. I suck in my breath, feeling dizzy. The sun is so hot on my head and my feet hurt a lot in my patent leather pumps with the straps—because I have nearly outgrown them, I guess, just like my mother says. She says it is time for me to buy some more grown-up shoes, but I have been resisting this, finding excuses not to shop. I like these shoes; I hope that the pain will make me a better person and improve my soul.

For I am all soul these days. I have not missed Sunday School in four years, not even on the occasions when my mother hauls me off to Tucson or Florida and I have to attend strange churches where I ask pastors with funny names to sign affidavits concerning my presence. I mail these documents back to Mr. Beech at the First Methodist Church, so that nothing will mar my record. I have earned so many gold bars for good attendance and special merit that they clink when I walk and Daddy says I look like a major general. I have gone forward to the altar so many times during summer revivals that my mother, embarrassed by my zeal, refuses to let me attend them any more unless I make a solemn pledge that I will not rededicate my life.

"Religious," then, I am also prone to fears and tremblings of a more general nature, and just about anything can set me off: my father when he's in a hurry; my black-headed first cousin Scott who is up in that big old sycamore tree right now, gathering a collection of sycamore balls; anything at all about cripples, puppies, or horses. For instance I had to go to bed for three days after my aunt Dora foolishly read me "The Little Match Girl" a couple of winters ago. I am "sensitive," "artistic," and "delicate," and everybody knows this is how I am, because my grandmother has laid down the law. Rarely does she lay down the law in such definite terms, preferring that her wishes be intuited, but now she has and this is it: *Do not tease Jennifer. Do not cut her hair.*

I wear a white piqué dress in my grandmother's garden this Sunday, a dress my mother ordered from Miller and Rhoads in Richmond, and I love it because I think it makes me look even thinner than I am. I want to be Peter Pan. I also want to be a ballerina, a detective, a missionary among the savages. My pale blond hair, pulled back by a white velvet bow, hangs down to my waist. My bars for good attendance and special merit jangle ever so slightly when I walk. They are calling me now from the porch. I pretend not to hear them, crossing the grass to where the

iron marker has been placed near the thicket of willow trees at the edge
of the creek. This marker reads

> The Scent of the Rose for Pardon
> The Song of the Birds for Mirth
> I am Closer to God in my Garden
> Than Anywhere Else on Earth

I stop and run my fingers over the raised iron lettering, hot from the sun.
"Rose for Pardon" blazes into my palm, and in the back of my mind I see
myself in fifteen years or so on a terrible gory battlefield somewhere or
maybe it is a dingy tenement, pardoning a man both elegant and
doomed—a *rake*. I think he has tuberculosis.

"Jennifer!" My mother stands beside the rose garden, shading her eyes
with her hand. "Come on! Your father is ready to go."

My mother wears a red linen dress and black-and-white spectator
shoes. She likes golf, bridge, and dancing to jazz music. She hates these
Sunday dinners. I follow her back to the porch, pretending not to see
Scott, who throws his sycamore balls down with great skill so that they
land silently in the grass just close enough to annoy me, too far away for
me to complain. Scott is one of the crosses I have to bear. It's too soon for
me to tell whether Sammy, my own little brother, will turn out to be such
a cross or not; sometimes he exhibits certain promise, I think. Other times
he is awful. When he had a virus, for instance, he threw up all over my
diary, eliminating February. Sammy is already in the car when we reach
the porch. I can see his blond head bobbing up and down in the rear
window. My father stands by the gate in his seersucker suit, waiting for
us.

"Let's go!" he calls.

"Hurry and make your manners, now," my mother tells me in an
undertone."I can't wait to get out of this damn dress."

I ignore her vulgarity and head for the porch, as full of relatives as it is
every Sunday, where I have to wait for my uncle Carl—my great-uncle,
actually—to finish telling a story. The other people on the porch are my
cousin Virginia, Scott's pretty older sister, whom I hate; my aunt Lucia,
Scott's mother, who holds a certain interest for me because of a nervous
breakdown she is rumored to have had in her twenties; Scott's boring
father, Bill; my maiden aunts Dora and Fern; my grandfather, sweet and

bent over in his chair, whittling; and my grandmother, of course, imperious as a queen in the glider, moving ever so slightly back and forth as if pushed by a personal breeze. My grandmother wears a pink brocade suit and a rhineshone sunburst pin, which I consider beautiful. Her hair, faintly blue, is piled into wispy curls that float above her wide white forehead, above her pale blue milky eyes, which look away from them all and across the river to the mountains where the sun goes down.

"And so I hollered, 'Well, John, start it up,' and John started his up, and I got in and started mine—" my uncle Carl is a famous storyteller even in Richmond, where he is in the Legislature, and he will not be hurried. The story he is telling now is one I've heard about a million times before, but it's one of Grandaddy's favorites, all about how Uncle Carl and Grandaddy were the first people in this county to consider automobiles, how they went to Richmond on the train and bought themselves an automobile apiece and drove them home, and then—the climax of the story—how they, the owners of the only two cars in the county at that time, went out driving with their new young wives one Sunday ("in the springtime of our lives," as my uncle Carl always put it) and had a head-on collision on the hairpin curve at the bend of the Green River.

Grandaddy claps his knees with both hands and doubles over laughing, scattering wood chips all over the porch. He is the best-humored man in town—everybody says so—and everybody loves him. He could have been in politics himself, like Uncle Carl, if he had had the ambition. But he did not. He laughs so hard he coughs, and then he can't stop coughing. The wood chips fly all over the porch.

"What a display, Mr. Morris," my grandmother says without moving her mouth.

"Daddy, are you all right?" My own father moves from his place at the gate, starts up the concrete walk. My aunt Lucia stands up by her chair.

"Sure, sure," Grandaddy wheezes and laughs. "But do you remember how those cars *looked*, Carl, how they looked all nosed into each other thataway? And old man Rob Pierce asked if we was trying to mate them."

Daddy grins, on the step below, but Grandmother leans forward to examine the undersides of the fern in the pot by her feet.

"Don't you remember that, Mother?" Daddy asks her.

My grandmother sits up very straight. "Oh yes," she says in her whispery voice. "Oh, yes. I was cast into the river," she says, her head turned away from us all. The glider moves back and forth with the slightest of motions so that in her pink brocade suit she appears to shimmer, tiny and iridescent before us, like a rainbow on the verge of disappearing.

"Now, hell, Flo, that didn't happen at all!" Grandaddy says. "We were right there on the curve where Stinson's store is now. Nobody went in the water."

"Cast into the rushing stream," my grandmother says, looking off.

Uncle Carl guffaws, Grandaddy slaps his knee, and everybody else laughs and laughs.

"Come on now, Jenny," my mother calls. She gets in the car.

"Thank you so much for dinner," I say.

"Oh can't she stay, Roy?" My grandmother suddenly springs to life. "Can't she?"

"Well, sure, I guess so," my daddy says, with an uneasy look back at the car. "That is, if she—"

"Oh please, Daddy, please, please, please!" I run down the steps and cling to his hand and beg him.

"Have you met my daughter, Sarah Bernhardt?" my mother says to nobody in particular.

"Please," I beg.

"Well, I suppose so, Jenny, but—" my father says.

My mother closes her door.

"I'll bring her home in the morning," Grandaddy calls from the porch. He stands up to wave as they pull off down the long dirt driveway. Sammy sticks his thumbs in his ears and wiggles his fingers, and grins out the car's back window. They round the bend beyond the willows, almost out of sight. I know that right now inside our car, my mother and father are lighting cigarettes; I know that they will go home and sit on wrought-iron chairs in the yard with gin and tonic, and Sammy will play with the hose. I wave. When the blue Buick has disappeared, I enter my grandmother's house where it is always cool, always fragrant with something like potpourri, where even the air is cool and dense, and the pictures of people I never knew stare out of the gloom at me from the high dark walls.

My grandmother was famous in our town, and her character was widely discussed. Her dedication to what she referred to as the "finer things of life" was admired by many people and ridiculed by others who found her affected or even laughable. I had heard Mrs. Beech, the preacher's wife, refer to her passionately as a "great lady." I had seen my mother's sister Trixie hold her sides laughing as she and my mother recalled incident after incident in which grandmother played the role of a comic figure, "putting on airs."

In any case everyone knew her. For at least forty years she had been a fixture in the First Methodist Church, taking her place each Sunday in the third row from the front, left hand side, directly beneath a stained glass window that depicted Jesus casting the moneylenders out of the temple in a fury of vermilion and royal blue. She had headed the Methodist Ladies' Auxiliary and the Garden Club until all the ladies died who had voted for her year after year and these groups were overrun by younger women with pantsuits and new ideas. She still wrote long, complicated letters to local newspapers on the subjects of town beautification, historic preservation, and the evils of drink; she wore hats and white gloves on every possible occasion. Her manner of dress had changed so little over the years that even I could recognize its eccentricity. She *dressed up* all the time. I never saw her in my life without her pale voile or silk or brocade dresses, without her stockings, without her feet crammed into elegant shoes at least two sizes too small for her, so that at the end her feet were actually crippled. I never saw her without her makeup or the flashing rhinestone earrings and brooches and bracelets that finally she came to believe—as I believed then—were real.

I never ate dinner in her kitchen, either. Meals were served in the octagonal dining room with its dark blue velvet draperies held back by the golden tassels, its wallpaper featuring gods and goddesses and nymphs. Meals there were interminable and complicated, involving courses intended to be brought in and taken away by that long procession of servants my grandmother hired and then dispensed of, big hardy dough-faced country women who could hoe all day but didn't know what to do next when she rang that silver bell. I was present at the table when one of them, after a fatal error that escapes me now, threw her white apron entirely up over her head crying out "Lord God" in a strangled voice, and fled forever out the back door as fast as her feet would take her. (Some people, my grandmother informed me solemnly after this memorable meal, cannot be taught anything and are best left down in the mire.) Of course I looked up "mire." Of course I remember everything on that table, to this day: the roses in the center, in a silver bowl; the pale pink crystal water goblets, beaded with icy drops, sitting on their cut-glass coasters; pale pink linen napkins and mats or maybe pale green ones and on special occasions the white Irish lace tablecloth; the silver salt and peppers, shaped like swans; the little glass basket, wonderfully wrought, which held pickles or mints or nuts. My grandmother declared the round mahogany table itself to be a family heirloom, then an antique, then a priceless antique from France. In any case it was large, dark, and shining, supported by horrible clawed feet with talons three or four inches long. The knowledge of these cruel taloned feet, right there beneath the table, added greatly to my enjoyment of these meals.

One ate only at the table in that house. Sometimes, though, I let my bestial elements get the best of me and snuck down into the kitchen for a snack after I was sure she was asleep. Once I surprised my grandaddy doing the same thing. The light from the refrigerator turned him light blue in his long flannel nightshirt and he broke into a delighted cackle at the sight of me. We ate cold fried chicken and strawberry ice cream together at the kitchen table and he told me about how he had traded a pony for a bicycle one time when he was a boy and how he tried and tried to get it back after his sprocket chain broke. We laughed a lot. I washed our dishes and he dried them and put them away and kissed me goodnight. His moustache tickled my cheek and I loved him so much at that moment; yet I felt disloyal, too. I climbed up the long stairs in shame.

Grandaddy called my grandmother Flo, but everyone else called her Florence. "Flo," she said severly, "has connotations." I did not know what those were, nor did I inquire. I called her Grandmother, as instructed. Grandmother called Grandaddy "Mr. Morris" in public all her life. Yet despite her various refinements, my grandmother was a country woman herself, born right in this county. Her father had started the First Methodist Church by importing a circuit rider to preach beneath the big sycamore tree, before the house was built. Her father had been by all accounts a hard, dangerous kind of a man, too, who had made a lot of money and had carried a pistol with him at all times. He had not believed in the education of women, so my grandmother never went to school. Eventually he was murdered, but no one ever mentioned this fact in front of my grandmother. She had married my grandaddy when she was only fifteen years old, but we didn't mention this fact either. Grandaddy was a carpenter who refused to elevate himself; he loved his work and he worked only as much as he had to. At least she had inherited the house.

All her ideas of refinement had come from books and from the self-improvement courses she took by mail, many of these deriving from a dubious institution known as the LaGrande University of Correspondence, which figured largely in my mother's and Trixie's glee. My grandmother knew all about these, among other things: Christianity, including particularly the lives of the saints; Greek mythology; English country houses; etiquette; Japanese flower arranging; Henry VIII and all his wives; crewel embroidery; and the Romantic poets. She wrote poetry herself and locked it away in a silver filigree box. She made Japanese flower arrangements for everyone, strange flat affairs usually involving one large dried flower, a considerable array of sticks, and little porcelain Oriental men with huge sacks on their backs. She had ordered dozens of these little men for her arrangements. My grandmother had read the entire *Encyclopaedia Britannica* cover to cover, or claimed to have read it; even my mother found this admirable, although Trixie did not.

The primary cross my grandmother had to bear was Grandaddy, who steadfastly refused to be drawn into the rarefied world of the finer things in life. He stayed there, in act, only long enough to eat. Otherwise he was whittling, smoking cigars out back, cracking jokes, drinking coffee in the Rexall drugstore downtown, building cabinets occasionally. He liked to drink bourbon and go hunting with his friends Mr. J.O. McCorkle and Mr. Petey Branch. My grandmother seemed to amuse him, I would say, more than anything else: he liked to "get her going," as he said. My father did not even like to "get her going"; but he was her son, too, in many ways, consumed by all that ambition my grandfather lacked, a man eaten up with the romance of making money. He made a great deal of money, luckily, since my mother was an expensive wife. Very early in their marriage she developed delicate health and terrible sinus allergies that required her removal, for months at a time, to Tuscon, where Trixie lived, or to Coral Gables, Florida, where my father bought her a house. My father encouraged these illnesses, which got us out of town, and in retrospect I can see that they broadened my horizons considerably. At the time, of course, I never wanted to go. I wanted to stay with my grandmother, and sometimes I was allowed to and sometimes not.

I am in the parlor while my grandmother works on a watercolor at her easel in the garden (her newest enthusiasm) and Grandaddy is off to the barber shop. I love this parlor, mine now; I love the gloom. I love the blackish gnarled voluptuous roses in the patterned carpet, the tufted velvet chairs and the horsehair sofa; I don't care how uncomfortable anything is. I love the doilies on the tables and the stiff antimacassars on the arms and the backs of the chairs, the *Leaves of Gold* book of poems on the table. I consider this the most beautiful room in the world. I move from portrait to portrait—mostly old daguerrotypes—along the walls, looking. There is stern-faced old Willie Lloyd Morris, her father, staring down his hatchet nose at me across the years. *Murdered.* A delicious chill travels from the top of my head down the length of my spine. There is my grandmother herself, a young girl with a face like a flower, seated primly in a wing chair before a painted backdrop of mountains and stormy clouds. She wears white. I see countless babies, my father among them, in stiff embroidered dresses and little caps. My aunt Lucia gazes soulfully out of her gold-leaf frame at me with strangely glistening dark eyes, like a movie star. My father stands at attention in high boots and the uniform he had to wear at military school, a wonderful uniform with at least a hundred shiny buttons on it. He looks furious. I pause before a family portrait that must have been taken just after my father finished at the University and swept my mother off her feet at a debutante ball in Richmond: it includes my aunts Dora and Fern, young then; my uncle Carl with a pipe in his mouth; my grandaddy grinning broadly, his thumbs locked in his suspenders; my grandmother standing slightly to one side; my father, young and impossibly dashing; and my mother with her hair all a tangle of curls. Then it hits me: *I am not there.* I am not anywhere at all in this picture. Looking at this picture is like being *dead.*

"Gotcha." Scott gooses me.

I whirl around, absolutely furious, mainly because I don't know how long he's been in this room. I don't know how long he's been watching me. I jump on him and we fall in a tangle onto the rose-figured carpet; I kick him in the nose until it bleeds.

"Hey," Scott keeps saying. "Hey."

We lie on our backs breathing hard.

"What's the matter with you?" Scott says.

"You can't just come in here like this," I say. "You can't." I start to cry.

Emboldened by my weakness, Scott sits up. "What do you do in here all the time?" he asks. He scoots closer. He looks like an Indian, having inherited my aunt Lucia's dark exotic charm.

"Nothing."

"Come on, Jenny," Scott moves closer still. *He exerts a certain fascination for her,* I think. *Jennifer succumbs to his appeal.*

"It's just so pretty," I falter. "I like to look at everything."

"Like what?" His black eyes shine through the shadows, close to mine.

"Well, like that table over there, like all the stuff on it." In my confusion I indicate what is in truth my favorite piece of furniture in the room, a multi-tiered mahogany stand that holds my grandmother's figurine collection, a wondrous array of angels, whistling boys, soldiers, Colonial ladies, cardinals and doves, unicorns—a whole world, in fact, topped by her "pièce de résistance" as she calls it, a white porcelain replica of Michelangelo's *David* displayed alone on the top tier. She ordered it from the Metropolitan Museum of Art in New York City. I love the *David* best of all because he seems entirely noble as well as beautiful, his left leg thrust forward in pursuit of justice in some doomed and luminous cause.

"I know why you like that one," Scott sneers.

"What one?"

"That one on the top. That naked guy."

"That's not a naked guy, Scott." I am enraged. "That is Michelangelo's famous statue *David.* It's a work of Art, if you know anything about Art, which you don't, of course." I do not forget to pronounce the statue's name *Daveed.*

"You don't know anything about art either," Scott hollers. "You just like to look at him because he hasn't got any clothes on, that's all."

I stand up shakily. "I'm going to tell Grandmother," I announce.

Scott stands up too. "Go on them. Tell her," he says. "Just go on and tell her. She's even crazier than you are. She's so crazy because Grandaddy has a girlfriend, that's what my mother says. She says it's a good thing Grandmother has an outlet—"

Even in my horror I recognize a certain terrible authenticity in Scott's words; he sounds like his mother, who uses psychological terms with great aplomb—something I have, in fact, admired about my aunt Lucia in the past.

Now I hate her.

"That's a *lie!*" I scream. "Get out of here!"

Instead, Scott grabs me by the shoulders and pulls me to him and kisses me on the mouth until I get my senses together and push him away. "Yuck!" I wipe my mouth with the back of my hand.

Scott is laughing, doubled up with laughing in my grandmother's parlor. "You're crazy, Jenny," he says. "I'm the best kisser in the eighth grade. Everybody says so."

Still laughing he goes out the front door and gets on his bike and rides off down the curving drive. I go upstairs and brush my teeth. Then I go in the bedroom, fling myself down on the bed, and wait to have a nervous breakdown. *In anguish she considers the violation of her person,* I think.

After a while I went out into the garden and asked Grandmother if I could try painting a rose. "Why yes, Jennifer," she said. Her pale blue eyes lit up. She sent me into the house for more paper, a glass of water, and the lap desk, so that my paper might remain, as she told me, absolutely stationary.

"Anything worth doing is worth doing well," she said severely. "Now then." She dipped her brush into the water and I did the same. "Not too much," she cautioned. "There now."

We painted all that afternoon, until the sun was gone. I did three and a half roses. Then we gathered up all our materials and put them away just so. I went ahead of her, carrying the lap desk and the easel into the hall. I came back out to the porch and found that Grandmother had spread my roses out on the glider. She was studying them. I thought they were pretty good, considering. We stood together and looked at them for some time as they glided ever so gently back and forth.

Grandmother turned to me and clasped me violently against her, smashing me into the spiky sunburst brooch on her bosom. "Jennifer, Jennifer," she said. She had grown little and frail by then and we were almost the same size; I couldn't see her face, but I was lost in her lavender perfume. "Jennifer, Jennifer," she was sobbing. "You must live your life, my darling. You must not get caught up in the press of circumstance; you must escape the web of fate."

I couldn't breathe and I had no idea what "web of fate" she referred to, but I felt as though I had received a solemn commission. "I *will,*

Grandmother," I said. "I *will.*"

"Hello, ladies!" It was my grandaddy, stumbling a bit on the steps. Mr. J.O. McCorkle stood behind him, grinning broadly. They both appeared to be in a wonderful humor.

"Oh, Mr. Morris, you gave me such a turn!" Grandmother whirled around; seeing Mr. J.O. McCorkle, her eyes narrowed. "Well, Mr. Morris!" she said with a certain significance. She swept up my three and a half roses and vanished mysteriously into the house.

"Now Flo, don't you Mr. Morris me!" Grandaddy called after her. He and Mr. McCorkle laughed. Grandaddy came up on the porch and gave me a whiskery kiss. "How about some checkers?" he asked me.

"Not right now." *Jennifer said meaningfully,* I thought. I turned and went into the house.

This was the first indication of my Talent. Spurred on by my grandmother's enthusiasm, I painted more roses and at length a morning glory. I ventured into daisies, then columbine; I mastered Swedish ivy and attempted, at last, a Still Life. This proved somewhat more difficult because Sammy kept eating the apples and spoiling my arrangement. "Never mind," Grandmother told me when I rode my bicycle over to her house to weep after one such disaster. "Never mind. Great art requires great suffering," my grandmother said.

The second indication of my Talent came from school, where I had written a sonnet, which my English teacher, Miss Hilton, praised extravagantly. This sonnet compared life to a carousel ride, in highly symbolic terms. It was named "The Ride of Life." Miss Hilton sent "The Ride of Life" to the local newspaper, which printed it on the book page. My mother drummed her fingers on the tabletop, reading it. "For heaven's sake!" she said, staring at me. My grandmother clipped it and had it framed. I was suddenly so artistic that my only problem came from trying to decide in which direction to focus my Talent. I did not forget to suffer, either, lying on my bed for a while each afternoon in order to do so.

It didn't surprise me at all, consequently, when I came down with a virus, which all turned into bronchitis, then pneumonia. For a long time I was so sick that they thought I might die. The doctor came every day for a while, and everyone tiptoed. A spirit lamp hissed night and day in my bedroom, casting out a wispy blue jet of steam that formed itself into the camphorous blue haze that still surrounds my entire memory of that illness. Grandaddy came every day, bringing little wooden animals and people carved from pine. Once he brought a little chest of drawers he had made for me. It was incredibly intricate; each drawer opened and shut. I dozed in my blue cloud holding the chest in my hand. Every now and then, when I awakened, I would open and close the drawers. Once when I woke up I saw my mother, in tears, standing beside the bed. This shocked me. I asked for Coca-Cola and drank it; then I sat up and ate some soup; and at the end of that illness it was Grandaddy, not me, who died.

He had a heart attack in the Post Office; after examining him, the hospital doctors said there was nothing they could do and sent him home, where he lived for three more days. During this time, my grandmother's house was filled with people—all our relatives, all his friends—in and out. The kitchen was full of food. My grandmother did not enter his bedroom, as she had not entered mine. Illness made her faint and she had always said so; nobody expected her to. She stayed in the Florida room, painting cardinals and doves, while my aunts sat on the divan and watched her.

From the time they brought Grandaddy home, my own father sat by his bed. I have never, before or since, seen my father as upset—*distraught,* actually, is the word—as he was then. On the morning of the second day, Grandaddy raised his head from the pillow and rolled his eyes around the room. Daddy came forward and bent over him, taking his hand. Grandaddy made a horrible gargling kind of noise in his throat; he was trying to talk. Daddy bent closer. Grandaddy made the noise again. The veins in his forehead stood out, awful and blue. Daddy listened. Then he stood up straight and cleared his own throat.

"By God, I'll do it!" my father announced in a ringing voice, like somebody in a movie. He turned and left the room abruptly, and all of the people remaining looked at one another. My grandfather continued to stare wildly around the room, with his breath rattling down in his throat.

Twenty minutes later my father came back bringing Mollie Crews, the woman who had been my grandaddy's lover for twenty-five years. Mollie Crews was a large, heavy woman with curly and obviously dyed red hair; she was a beautician, with a shop over the Western Auto store downtown.

Mollie Crews wore her white beautician's uniform, an orange cardigan sweater, and white lace-up shoes with thick crepe soles. Her hands flew up to her face when she saw Grandaddy, and her big shoulders shook. Then she rushed over to take the chair at the side of his bed, dropping her purse on the floor. "Oh, Buddy," she sobbed. *Buddy?* I was stunned. Grandaddy's eyes fastened on her and an expression like a smile came to his face. He sank back into the pillow, closing his eyes. The rattle of his breathing softened. Still firmly holding his hand, Mollie Crews took off her cardigan—awkwardly, with her free hand—and slung it over the back of the chair. She reached down and fumbled around in her purse and got a cigarette and lit it with a gold lighter. She exhaled, crossing her legs, and settled down into the chair. My father brought her an ashtray. Aunt Lucia stood up abruptly, flashing her black eyes at everyone. She started to speak and then did not. Aunt Lucia exited theatrically, jerking me from the room along with her. My cousin Virginia followed. The hall outside Grandaddy's room was full of people, and Aunt Lucia pulled me straight through them all, sailing out of the house. Scott was in the front yard. "What did I tell you?" he said. "What did I tell you?"

Aunt Lucia never returned to Grandaddy's room, nor did my Uncle Bill or my cousin Virginia or my old maid aunts. Uncle Carl came back from Richmond that night and stayed with him until the end. So did my father, and my mother was in and out. The whole family had to take sides. I went in and sat dutifully with Grandmother, working at her easel in the Florida room. "This is a woodpecker," she said once, exhibiting her latest. "Note the pileations." But I couldn't stay away from Grandaddy's room either, where I was mesmerized by Mollie Crews with her generous slack mouth and her increasingly rumpled beautician's uniform. She looked like a nurse. *A fallen woman,* I told myself, and I watched her sit there hour after hour holding his hand, even when he was in a coma and no longer knew she was there. *A Jezebel,* I thought, watching her. I wondered whether she would go to hell.

When my grandfather actually died, everyone left the room except Mollie Crews, and after a long while she came out too, shaking her curls and throwing her head back as she opened the door. We were crowded into the hall. She looked at all of us, and then for some reason she came back to me. "He was a fine man," Mollie Crews said. She was not crying. She looked at everyone again and then she walked out of the house as abruptly as she had come and sat on the front porch until somebody in a battered sky blue Oldsmobile picked her up, and then she was completely and finally gone.

Mollie Crews was the only person in town who did not attend the funeral. Grandmother wore her black silk suit with a hat and a veil. She came in like royalty and sat between Daddy and Aunt Lucia, never lifting her veil, and she stood straight with my mother and me under a black umbrella when they buried Grandaddy in the church cemetery afterward, in a fine gray drizzle that started then and went on for days. Everyone in town paid a call on my grandmother in the week after that, and she sat in her parlor on the tufted sofa beside the tiered table and received them. But her blue eyes had grown mistier, paler than ever, and sometimes the things she said did not connect.

I am walking by the ocean, alone, on the beach near my mother's house in Florida. It is a bright, clear morning. Sometimes I bend down to pick up a shell. Other times I pause and gaze dramatically out to sea, but this Florida sea is not as I would have it: not tempest-tossed, not filled with drowning nobility clutching at shards of ships. This is a shiny blue Florida sea, determinedly cheerful. The waves have all been choreographed. They arch and break like clockwork at my feet, bringing me perfect shells. The weather is perfect, too. Everything in Florida is hot and easy and tropical and I hate it. My mother has yanked Sammy and me out of school and brought us down here to humor her famous allergies, but I can't see that she has any allergies: all she does in Florida is shop and play bridge. I feel like a deserter from a beautiful sinking ship. I have deserted my grandmother, just when she needs me most.

My mother has arranged for me to have a Cuban tutor who is supposed to teach me Spanish as well as other things. This Cuban tutor is named Dominica Colindres. She is a plump, dark young woman with greasy hair and big sagging bosoms and pierced ears. She sweats under her arms. I hate Dominica Colindres. I refuse to learn anything she tries to teach me, and I refuse to have anything at all to do with any of the other children my age who try to befriend me on the beach. I walk the shoreline, picking up shells. I think about sin, art, heaven, and hell. Since my arrival in Florida I have written two poems I am rather proud of, although no one else has seen them. One is a poem about the ocean, named "The Sea of

Life." The other is named "Artifacts of Existence," about shells.

The sun is hot on my back, even through my long-sleeved shirt, so I pick up one last shell and walk back up the beach to our house. I wear a hat and long pants, too, wet now below the knee: I refuse to get a tan.

My mother is entertaining our next-door neighbors, Mr. and Mrs. Donlevy from Indiana, on the patio. She wears a yellow sundress, looks up and smiles. Mr. and Mrs. Donlevy smile. I do not smile, and my mother raises her eyebrows at Mr. and Mrs. Donlevy in a significant manner. I know they've been talking about me. They are drinking bloody marys and reading the morning paper. The hibiscus around the patio is pink and gaudy in the sun.

I go into my room to work on my shell collection. I have classified my shells as to type, and arranged each type in gradations of hue. This means that every time I find a good shell, I have to move *everything,* in order to put the new shell into its proper place. I take a certain pleasure in the difficulty of this arrangement. I am hard at work when the bells begin to ring, and then, of course, it hits me. *Sunday!* Mother and the Donlevys were reading the Sunday *Times!* It's the first time I've missed Sunday school in four years; my perfect attendance record is broken.

I put my last shell, a *Tellina lineata,* carefully in place. I leave my room. Mother is telling Mr. and Mrs. Donlevy goodbye at the front door. It's already hot; the air conditioner clicks on. I cross the white carpet in the living room, the red tile kitchen floor. Once on the patio, I rush toward the round glass table with its striped umbrella and push it violently, overturning it onto the flagstone. The whole glass top shatters. The umbrella crushes the hibiscus. The frosted bloody mary glasses are flung into the grass, and one of them breaks.

I go back in the kitchen and find Sammy, who has just gotten up, eating Wheaties at the kitchen table. He has made a little mess of his own, fixing his cereal, and this gives me extra satisfaction.

"I had a funny dream," Sammy says.

"What was it about?" I sit down with Sammy at the kitchen table. My mother comes through the kitchen humming and goes out into the patio.

"It was real funny," Sammy says. Milk dribbles down his chin.

"But what was it *about?*" I ask. Out on the patio, my mother has started to shriek.

"I can't remember what it was about." Sammy looks at me with his big blue eyes. "But the name of it was 'The Secret of the Seven Arrows.'"

I get up and hug Sammy as hard as I can, laughing. He *is* cute. Maybe he won't be a cross after all. Then I start to cry. I cry for two hours as hard as I can, and then after that I feel fine and my mother takes Sammy and me out to a fancy restaurant for dinner.

My mother never said a word to me about the broken table, although I knew—in the way children know things, almost like osmosis—that she *knew*. Workmen in overalls came the next day and replaced it. The new umbrella was lime green, with a flowered lining. My mother took me shopping and we bought new bathing suits for both of us; eventually I acquired a tan. I even learned a little Spanish, and on the day before we left, Dominica Colindres pierced my ears.

The day we came back—this was in February—I went straight over to my grandmother's house, of course, riding my bicycle through the falling snow; but even though Daddy had told me how it would be there, I was not prepared. Grandmother had "failed considerably"—those were his words—in the eight weeks we had been gone. Daddy had hired two practical nurses to stay with her, one at night and one in the daytime, and he had turned the dining room into a downstairs bedroom since Grandmother could no longer manage the steps. When I arrived, Grandmother was sitting in the tufted rose velvet wing chair where she always sat in the winter, but she seemed to have shrunk by one or two feet. Or maybe I had grown. In any case Grandmother was so small that she looked lost in the chair, and her feet dangled above the floor. She was dressed as carefully as always, though, and this reassured me at first as I stood in the dark hall pulling off my gloves, my boots, my coat. Noise from the television blared out into the hall: this was very unusual, since Grandmother hated television and said it had been invented to amuse people who needed such amusements. The parlor looked all different somehow, lit primarily by the glow of the TV. A tall thin woman stood up from where she sat in the rocking chair. "You must be Jennifer," she said. "I'm Mrs. Page." Mrs. Page wore her hair in a bun; she was crocheting a brown and white afghan.

"It's so nice to meet you." *Jennifer said mechanically like a windup doll,* I thought as I crossed the flowered carpet to take my grandmother's hand. Her hand was little and frail, her bones like the bones of birds. She would not look at me.

"Grandmother!" I said. "Grandmother! It's me, Jennifer." Grandmother watched the TV. I noticed that she wore three of her huge rhinestone brooches in an uneven row on the front of her dress. "Grandmother," I said.

"Excuse me, miss, but she doesn't know anybody right now. She just doesn't. It takes them that way sometimes." Mrs. Page looked up from her afghan and smiled.

"Well, this is my grandmother and she will know *me!*" I snapped.

But she didn't.

The only response she made came later, in that same awful afternoon. I had been sitting on a footstool beside her while it grew darker outside and more snow fell and the bluish-white light of the television danced off the bones of her face. The program had changed again; this time it was a stock car race, and it seemed to interest her. She leaned forward and said something under her breath.

"Do you like this, Grandmother?" I asked.

"Listen," Mrs. Page said. "She just likes it all. She doesn't even know what she's watching."

This infuriated me. "What are you watching, Grandmother?" I asked. On the television screen, the cars went round and round the track, and one of them turned over and burst into flames.

"Serves him right for driving that thing," Mrs. Page remarked.

"Grandmother," I said.

Grandmother turned to face me, fully, for the first time. Her light blue eyes seemed to have grown larger. They shone in the pale bony planes of her face. In front of her, the numbered cars went around a track somewhere in Georgia. Grandmother opened her mouth and stared back and forth from me to the television screen.

"What are you watching, Grandmother?" I asked again.

"Art," she said. "I'm watching art, Jennifer."

The cars went around and around on the television, and after watching them for a while longer I put on all my things and rode my bike home through the snow. The road had been scraped but it was still icy in spots, and a fine mist of snow covered the asphalt. I should have been careful, riding, but I was not. I pedaled as hard as I could, gulping huge mouthfuls of cold air and falling flakes of snow. I was moving so fast that the snow seemed to rush straight at me, giving me an odd sense of weightlessness, as if I were somehow suspended between the earth and the sky.

This feeling of suspension—a kind of not belonging, a sense of marking time—hung on even after my grandmother died, which happened a few weeks after our return. Her house was bought by a young attorney. Everything in the house was parceled out among the relatives, who insisted that I should have all the art supplies and the entire figurine collection, including *David*. These things sat in two cardboard boxes in my room for a long time, while I remained suspended. Then one Saturday morning in early May, I knew exactly what I wanted to do. I hauled both boxes out to the tool shed, placing them neatly beside the garden tools. I closed the tool shed door. I went inside and took the saved-up allowance money out of my jewelry box; then I got on my bike and rode straight downtown, parking my bicycle in front of the Western Auto store. Mollie Crews cut my hair off in a page boy, which curled softly under my ears. It looked terrific. Then I rode my bike over to see Scott, who turned out to be—exactly as he had promised—a good kisser. So I grew up. And I never became an artist, although my own career has certainly had its ups and downs, like most careers. Like most lives. Now I keep my grandmother's figurine collection on a special low table for my own children, who spend long hours arranging and rearranging all the little figures in their play.

LEE SMITH *teaches at North Carolina State University in Raleigh. She has published one collection of stories and seven novels, including her most recent,* Fair and Tender Ladies.

Old Frank and Jesus

LARRY BROWN

MR. PARKER'S ON THE couch, reclining. He's been there all morning, almost, trying to decide what to do.

Things haven't gone like he's planned. They never do.

The picture of his great-grandpa's on the mantel looking down at him, a framed old dead gentleman with a hat and a long beard who just missed the Civil War. The picture's fuzzy and faded, with this thing like a cloud coming up around his neck.

They didn't have good photography back then, Mr. P. thinks. That's why the picture looks like it does.

Out in the yard, his kids are screaming. They're just playing, but to Mr. P. it sounds like somebody's killing them. His wife's gone to the beauty parlor to get her hair fixed. There's a sick cow in his barn, but he hasn't been down to see about her this morning. He was up all night with her, just about. She's got something white and sticky running out from under her tail, and the vet's already been out three times without doing her any good. He charges for his visits anyway, though, twenty-five smacks a whack.

That's...seventy-five bucks, he thinks, and the old white stuff's just pouring out.

Mr. P clamps his eyes shut and rolls over on the couch, feels it up. He had cold toast four hours ago. He needs to be up and out in the cotton patch, trying to pull the last bolls off the stalks, but the bottom's dropped out because foreign rayon's ruined the market. He guesses that somewhere across the big pond, little Japanese girls are sewing pants together and getting off from their jobs and meeting boyfriends for drinks and movies after work, talking about their supervisors. Maybe they're eating raw fish. They did that on Okinawa after they captured the place and everything settled down. He was on Okinawa. Mr. P. got shot on Okinawa.

He reaches down and touches the place, just above his knee. They were full of shit as a Christmas turkey. Eight hundred yards from the beach under heavy machine-gun fire. No cover. Wide open. They could have gotten some sun if they'd just been taking a vacation. They had palm trees. Sandy beaches. No lotion. No towels, no jamboxes, no frosty cool brewskies. They waded through water up to their necks and bullets zipped in the surf around them killing men and fish. Nobody had any dry cigarettes. Some of their men got run over by their own carriers and some of the boys behind shot the boys in front. Mr. P. couldn't tell who was shooting whom. He just shot. He stayed behind a concrete barrier for a while and saw some Japanese symbols molded into the cement, but he couldn't read them. Every once in a while he'd stick his head out from behind the thing and just shoot.

He hasn't fired a shot in anger in years now, though. But he's thinking seriously about shooting a hole in the screen door with a pistol. Just a little hole.

He knows he needs to get up and go down to the barn and see about that cow, but he just can't face it today. He knows she won't be any better. She'll be just like she was last night, not touching the water he's drawn up in a barrel for her, not eating the hay he's put next to her. That's how it is with a cow when they get down, though. They just stay down. Even the vet knows that. The vet knows no shot he can give her will make her get up, go back on her feed. The vet's been to school. He's studied anatomy, biology. Other things, too. He knows all about animal husbandry and all.

But Mr. P. thinks him not much of a vet. The reason is, last year, Mr. P. had a stud colt he wanted cut, and he had him tied and thrown with a blanket over his head when the vet came out, and Mr. P. did most of the cutting, but the only thing the vet did was dance in and out with advice because he was scared of getting kicked.

The phone rings and Mr. P. stays on the couch and listens to it ring. It's probably somebody calling with bad news. That's about the only thing a phone's good for anyway, Mr. P. thinks, to let somebody get ahold of you with some bad news. He knows people just can't wait to tell bad news. Like if somebody dies, or if a man's cows are out in the road, somebody'll be sure to pick up the nearest phone and call somebody else and tell him or her all about it. And they'll tell other things, too. Personal things. Mr. P. thinks it'd probably be better to just not have a phone. If you didn't have a phone, they'd have to come over to your house personally to give you bad news, either drive over or walk. But with a phone, it's easy to give it to you. All they have to do's just pick it up and call, and there you are.

But on second thought, he thinks, if your house caught on fire and you needed to call up the fire department and report it, and you didn't have a phone, there you'd be again.

Or the vet.

The phone's still ringing. It rings eight or nine times. Just ringing ringing ringing. There's no telling who it is. It could be the FHA. They hold the mortgage on his place. Or, it could be the bank. They could be calling again to get real shitty about the note. He's borrowed money from them for seed and fertilizer and things and they've got a lien. And, it could be the county forester calling to tell him, Yes, Mr. Parker, it's just as we feared: your whole 160-acre tract of pine timber is heavily infested with Southern pine beetle and you'll have to sell all your wood for stumpage and lose your shirt on the whole deal. It rings again. Mr. P. finally gets up from the couch and goes over to it. He picks it up. "Hello," he says.

"Hello?"

"Yes," Mr. P. says.

"Mr. Marvin Parker," the phone says.

"Speaking," says Mr. P.

"Jim Lyle calling, Mr. Parker. Amalgamated Pulpwood and Benevolent Society? Just checking our records here and see you're a month behind on your premium. Just calling to check on the problem, Marv."

They always want their money, Mr. P. thinks. They don't care about you. They wouldn't give a damn if you got run over by a bush hog. They just want your money. Want you to pay that old premium.

"I paid," Mr. P. says. He can't understand it. "I pay by bank draft every month."

A little cough comes from the phone.

"Well yes," the voice says. "But our draft went through on a day when you were overdrawn, Mr. Parker."

Well kiss my ass, Mr. P. thinks.

Mr. P. can't say anything to this man. He knows what it is. His wife's been writing checks at the Fabric Center again. For material. What happened was, the girls needed dresses for the program at church, capes and wings and things. Plus, they had to spend $146.73 on a new clutch and pressure plate for the tractor. Mr. P. had to do all the mechanical stuff, pull the motor and all. Sometimes he couldn't find the right wrenches and had to hunt around in the dirt for this and that. There was also an unfortunate incident with a throw-out bearing.

Mr. P. closes his eyes and leans against the wall and wants to get back on the couch. Today, he just can't get enough of that couch.

"Can I borrow from the fund?" says Mr. P. He's never borrowed from the fund before.

"Borrow? Why...."

"Would it be all right?" Mr. P. says.

"All right?"

"I mean would everything be fixed up?"

"Fixed up? You mean paid?" says the voice over the phone.

"Yes," says Mr. P. "Paid."

"Paid. Why I suppose...."

"Don't suppose," says Mr. P. He's not usually this ill with people like Jim Lyle of APABS. But he's sick of staying up with that cow every night. He's sick of his wife writing checks at the Fabric Center. He's sick of a vet who's scared of animals he's sworn to heal. He doesn't want Jim Lyle of APABS to suppose. He wants him to know.

"Well, yes sir, if that's the way...."

"All right, then," Mr. P. says, and he hangs up the phone.

"Goodbye," he says, after he hangs it up. He goes back to the couch and stretches out quick, lets out this little groan. He puts one forearm over his eyes.

The kids are still screaming at the top of their lungs in the yard. He's worried about them being outside. There's been a rabies epidemic: foaming foxes and rabid raccoons running amuck. Even flying squirrels have attacked innocent people. And just last week, Mr. P. had to take his squirrel dog off, a little feist he had named Frank that was white with black spots over both eyes. He got him from a family of black folks down the road and they all swore up and down that his mama was a good one, had treed as many as sixteen in one morning. Mr. P. raised that dog from a puppy, played with him, fed him, let him sleep on his stomach and in front of the fire, and took him out in the summer with a dried squirrel skin and let him trail it all over the yard before he hung it up in a tree and let him tree it. He waited for old Frank to get a little older and then took him out the first frosty morning and shot a squirrel in front of him, didn't kill it on purpose, just wounded it, and let old Frank get ahold of it and get bitten in the nose because he'd heard all his life that doing that would make a squirrel dog every time if the dog had it in him. And old Frank did. He caught that squirrel and fought it all over the ground, squalling, with the squirrel balled up on his nose, bleeding, and finally killed it. After that he hated squirrels so bad he'd tree every squirrel he smelled. They killed nine opening day, one over the limit. Mr. P. was proud of old Frank.

But last week he took old Frank out in the pasture and shot him in the head with a .22 rifle because his wife said the rabies were getting too close to home.

Now why did I do that? Mr. P. wonders. Why did I let her talk me into shooting old Frank? I remember he used to come in here and lay down on my legs while I was watching "Dragnet." I'd pat him on the head and he'd close his eyes and curl up and just seem happy as anything. He'd even go to sleep sometimes, just sleep and sleep. And he wouldn't mess in the house either. Never did. He'd scratch on the door till somebody let him out. Then he'd come back in and hop up here and go to sleep.

Mr. P. feels around under the couch to see if it's still there. It is. He just borrowed it a few days ago, from his neighbor, Hulet Steele. He doesn't even know if it'll work. But he figures it will. He told Hulet he wanted it for rats. He told Hulet he had some rats in his corncrib.

Next thing he knows, somebody's knocking on the front door. Knocking hard, like he can't see the kids out in the yard and send them in to call him out. He knows who it probably is, though. He knows it's probably Hereford Mullins, another neighbor, about that break in the fence, where his cows are out in the road. Mr. P. knows the fence is down. He knows his cows are out in the road, too. But he just can't seem to face it today. It seems like people just won't leave him alone.

He doesn't much like Hereford Mullins anyway. Never has. Not since that night at the high school basketball game when their team won and Hereford Mullins tried to vault over the railing in front of the seats and landed on both knees on the court, five feet straight down, trying to grin like it didn't hurt.

Mr. P. thinks he might just get up and go out on the front porch and slap the shit out of Hereford Mullins. He gets up and goes out there.

It's Hereford, all right. Mr. P. stops inside the screen door. The kids are still screaming in the yard, getting their school clothes dirty. Any other time they'd be playing with old Frank. But old Frank can't play with them now. Old Frank's busy getting his eyeballs picked out right now probably by some buzzards down in the pasture.

"Ye cows out in the road again," says Hereford Mullins. "Thought I'd come up here and tell ye."

"All right," says Mr. P. "You told me."

"Like to hit em while ago," says Hereford Mullins. "I'd git em outa the road if they's mine."

"I heard you the first time," says Mr. P.

"Feller come along and hit a cow in the road," goes on Hereford Mullins, "he ain't responsible. Cows ain't sposed to be in the road. Sposed to be behind a fence."

"Get off my porch," says Mr. P.

"What?"

"I said get your stupid ass off my porch," Mr. P. says.

Hereford kind of draws up, starts to say something, but leaves the porch huffy. Mr. P. knows he'll be the owner of a dead cow within two minutes. That'll make two dead cows, counting the one in the barn not quite dead yet that he's already out seventy-five simoleans on.

He goes back to the couch.

Now there'll be a lawsuit, probably. Herf'll say his neck's hurt, or his pickup's hurt, or something else. Mr. P. reaches under the couch again and feels it again. It's cold and hard, feels scary.

Mr. P.'s never been much of a drinking man, but he knows there's some whiskey in the kitchen cabinet. Sometimes when the kids get colds or the sore throat, he mixes up a little whiskey and lemon juice and honey and gives it to them in a teaspoon. That and a peppermint stick always helps their throats.

He gets the whiskey, gets a little drink, and then gets another pretty good drink. It's only ten o'clock. He should have had a lot of work done by now. Any other time he'd be out on the tractor or down in the field or up in the woods cutting firewood.

Unless it was summer. If it was summer he'd be out in the garden picking butter beans or sticking tomatoes or cutting hay or fixing fences or working on the barn roof or digging up the septic tank or swinging a joe-blade along the driveway or cultivating the cotton or spraying or trying to borrow some more money to buy some more poison or painting the house or cutting the grass or doing a whole bunch of other things he doesn't want to do anymore at all. All he wants to do now's stay on the couch.

Mr. P. turns over on the couch and sees the picture of Jesus on the wall. It's been hanging up there for years. Old Jesus, he thinks. Mr. P. used to know Jesus. He used to talk to Jesus all the time. There was a time when he could have a little talk with Jesus and everything'd be all right. Four or five years ago he could. Things were better then, though. You could raise cotton and hire people to pick it. They even used to let the kids out of school to pick it. Not no more, though. Only thing kids wanted to do now was grow long hair and listen to the damn Beatles.

Mr. P. knows about hair because he cuts it in his house. People come in at night and sit around the fire in his living room and spit tobacco juice on the hearth and Mr. P cuts their hair. He talks to them about cotton and cows and shuffles, clockwise and counterclockwise around the chair they're sitting in, in his house shoes and undershirt and overalls and snips here and there.

Most of the time they watch TV, "Gunsmoke" or "Perry Mason." Sometimes they watch Perry Como. And sometimes, they'll get all involved and interested in a show and stay till the show's over.

One of Mr. P.'s customers—this man who lives down the road and doesn't have a TV—comes every Wednesday night to get his haircut. But Mr. P. can't cut much of his hair, having to cut it every week like that. He has to just snip the scissors around on his head some and make out like he's cutting it, comb it a little, walk around his head a few times, to make him think he's getting a real haircut. This man always comes in at 6:45 P.M. just as Mr. P. and his family are getting up from the supper table.

This man always walks up, and old Frank used to bark at him when he'd come up in the yard. It was kind of like a signal that old Frank and Mr. P. had, just between them. But it wasn't a secret code or anything. Mr. P. would be at the supper table, and he'd hear old Frank start barking, and if it was Wednesday night, he'd know to get up from the table and get his scissors. The Hillbillies always come on that night at seven, and it takes Mr. P. about fifteen minutes to cut somebody's hair.

This man starts laughing at the opening credits of the Hillbillies, and shaking his head when it shows old Jed finding his black gold, his Texas tea, just as Mr. P.'s getting through with his head. So by the time he's finished, the Hillbillies have already been on for one or two minutes. And then, when Mr. P. unpins the bedsheet around this man's neck, if there's nobody else sitting in his living room watching TV or waiting for a haircut, this man just stays in the chair, doesn't get up, and says, "I believe I'll jest set here and watch the Hillbillies with y'all since they already started if y'all don't care."

It's every Wednesday night's business.

Mr. P. doesn't have a license or anything, but he actually does more than a regular barber would do. For one thing, he's got some little teenincy scissors he uses to clip hairs out of folks' noses and ears. Plus, Mr. P.'s cheaper than the barbers in town. Mr. P.'ll lower your ears for fifty cents. He doesn't do shaves, though. He's got shaky hands. He couldn't shave a balloon or anything. He could flat shave the damn Beatles though.

Mr. P.'s wondering when the school bus will come along. It's late today. What happened was, Johnny Crawford got it stuck in a ditch about a mile down the road to dodge one of Mr. P.'s cows. They've called for the wrecker, though, on Mr. P.'s phone. They gave out that little piece of bad news over his phone, and he thinks he heard the wrecker go down the road a while ago. He knows he needs to get up and go down there and fix that fence, get those cows up, but he doesn't think he will. He thinks he'll just stay right here on the couch and drink a little more of this whiskey.

Mr. P. would rather somebody get him down on the ground and beat his ass like a drum than to have to fix that fence. The main thing is, he doesn't have anybody to help him. His wife has ruined those kids of his, spoiled them, until the oldest boy, fourteen, can't even tie his own shoelaces. Mr. P. can say something to him, tell him to come on and help him go do something for a minute, and he'll act like he's deaf and dumb. And if he does go, he whines and moans and groans and carries on about it until Mr. P. just sends him on back to the house so he won't have to listen to it. Mr. P. can see now that he messed up with his kids a long time ago. He's been too soft on them. They don't even know what work is. It just amazes Mr. P. He wasn't raised like that. He had to work when he was little. And it was rough as an old cob back then. Back then you couldn't sit around on your ass all day long and listen to a bunch of long-haired hippies singing a bunch of rock and roll on the radio.

Mr. P.'s even tried paying his kids to get out and help him work, but they won't do it. They say he doesn't pay enough. Mr. P.'s raised such a rebellious bunch of youngsters with smart mouths that they'll even tell him what the minimum wage is.

Even if his oldest boy would help him with the fence, it'd still be an awful job. First off they'd have to move all the cows to another pasture so they could tear the whole fence down and do it right. And the only other pasture Mr. P.'s got available is forty acres right next to his corn patch. They'd probably push the fence down and eat his corn up while he's across the road putting up the new fence, because his wife won't run cows. Mr. P.'s run cows and run cows and tried to get his wife out there to help him run cows and she won't hardly run cows at all. She's not fast enough to head one off or anything. Plus, she's scared of cows. She's always afraid she's going to stampede them and get run over by a crazed cow. About the only thing Mr. P.'s wife is good for when it comes to running cows is just sort of jumping around, two or three feet in any direction, waving her arms, and hollering, "Shoo!"

Mr. P. can't really think of a whole lot his wife is good for except setting his kids against him. It seems like they've fought him at every turn, wanting to buy new cars and drive up to Memphis to shop and getting charge accounts at one place and another and wanting him to loan money to her old drunk brother. Mr. P. doesn't know what the world's coming to. They've got another damn war started now and they'll probably be wanting his boys to go over there in a few more years and get killed or at the very least get their legs blown off. Mr. P. worries about that a good bit. But Mr. P. just worries about everything, really. Just worries all the time. There's probably not a minute that goes by when he's awake that he's not worrying about something. It's kind of like a weight he's carrying around with him that won't get off and can't get off because there's no way for it *to* get off.

The whiskey hasn't done him any good. He hoped it would, but he really knew that it wouldn't. Mr. P. thinks he knows the only thing that'll do him any good, and it won't be good.

He wonders what his wife'll say when she comes in and sees him still on the couch. Just him and Jesus, and grandpa. She's always got something to say about everything. About the only thing she doesn't say too much about is that guy who sells the siding. Mr. P.'s come up out of the pasture on the tractor four or five times and seen that guy coming out of the house after trying to sell some siding to his wife. She won't say much about him, though. She just says he's asking for directions.

Well, there the bus is to get his kids. Mr. P. can hear it pull up and he can hear the doors open. He guesses they got it out of the ditch all right. He could have taken his tractor down there and maybe pulled it out, but he might not have. A man has to be careful on a tractor. Light in the front end like they are, a man has to be careful how he hooks onto something.

Especially something heavy like a school bus. But the school bus is leaving now. Mr. P. can hear it going down the road.

It's quiet in the house now.

Yard's quiet, too.

If old Frank was in here now he'd be wanting out. Old Frank. Good little old dog. Just the happiest little thing you'd ever seen. He'd jump clean off the ground to get a biscuit out of your hand. He'd jump about three feet high. And just wag that stubby tail hard as he could.

Old Frank.

Mr. P. thinks now maybe he should have just shot his wife instead of old Frank when she first started talking about shooting old Frank. Too late now.

Mr. P. gets another drink of the whiskey and sees Jesus looking down at him. He feels sorry for Jesus. Jesus went through a lot to save sinners like him. Mr. P. thinks, Jesus died to save me and sinners like me.

Mr. P. can see how it was that day. He figures it was hot. In a country over there like that, it was probably always hot. And that cross He had to carry was heavy. He wonders if Jesus cried from all the pain they put Him through. Just thinking about anybody being so mean to Jesus that He'd cry is enough to make Mr. P. want to cry. He wishes he could have been there to help Jesus that day. He'd have helped Him, too. If he could have known what he knows now, and could have been there that day, he'd have tried to rescue Jesus. He could have fought some of the soldiers off. But there were probably so many of them, he wouldn't have had a chance. He'd have fought for Him, though. He'd have fought for Jesus harder than he'd ever fought for anything in his life, harder than he fought on the beach at Okinawa. Given his own blood. Maybe he could have gotten his hands on a sword, and kept them away from Jesus long enough for them to get away. But those guys were probably good sword-fighters back then. Back then they probably practiced a lot. It wouldn't have mattered to him, though. He'd have given his blood, all of it, and gladly to help Jesus.

The kids are all gone now. Old Frank's gone. His wife's still at the beauty parlor. She won't be in for a while. He gets another drink of whiskey. It's awful good. He hates to stop drinking it, but he hates to keep on. With Jesus watching him and all.

The clock's ticking on the mantel. The hair needs sweeping off the hearth. He knows that cow's still got that white stuff running out from under her tail. But somebody else'll just have to see about it. Maybe the guy who sells the siding can see about it.

Mr. P. figures he ought to make sure it'll work first, so he pulls it out from under the couch and points it at the screen door in back. Right through the kitchen.

He figures maybe they won't be able to understand that. It'll be a big mystery that they'll never figure out. Some'll say Well he was making sure it'd work. Others'll say Aw it might have been there for years. They'll say What was he doing on the couch? And, I guess we'll have to go to town for a haircut now.

They'll even talk about how he borrowed it from Hulet for rats.

Old Frank has already gone through this. He didn't understand it. He trusted Mr. P. and knew he'd never hurt him. Maybe Mr. P. was a father to him. Maybe Mr. P. was God to him. What could he have been thinking of when he shot his best friend?

What in God's name can he be thinking of now?

Mr. Parker, fifty-eight, is reclining on his couch.

LARRY BROWN is the author of a collection of short stories, Facing the Music, *and a novel,* Dirty Work. *He resides in Tula, Mississippi, where, until recently, he was a captain of the fire department in nearby Oxford.*

Happy Birthday, Billy Boy

RUTH MOOSE

MAMA SETTLES HERSELF in the back seat, twisting her navy pleated skirt like she's smoothing a nest. "If I'd known you were going to be this late," she says, "I could still be fixing my face. I told your daddy to get the camera and come on."

Evanelle doesn't answer. The baby, Billy Buttons, threw up twice and she had to change him skin out, every stitch. Then she had to pick up the cake and flowers. Mama insisted she get silk. "Anything fresh won't last five minutes in that place. They keep it hot as an oven. I took your grandmother an African violet and it didn't live three weeks. *Three weeks!*"

There are roses on the cake. Thirty-six. Evanelle had to wait while they put on every last one of them. And she'd called in her order Friday—decorated. Done everything but spell it. And all the time she ordered, Darren Ravel rubbed her thigh. He kept saying he just *loved* the feel of Arnel. Arnel, her ass. When she told anyone she worked at WKIS, they'd get so excited, their eyes would bulge out and they'd say, "You know D.R. the D.J.?" And she'd say Lord yes, she ought to as long as she worked at KIS. What she didn't say was she knew D.R. more than she wanted to. More than anybody ought to, but that was water over the dam or spilled milk or whatever you wanted to call it.

Billy Buttons sleeps in her arms and Evanelle thinks he is the most beautiful baby in the world. His dark lashes curl up from round cheeks and he sucks air with a pink pucker. He looks stuffed, fat as a frog in his blue terry jumpsuit with anchor buttons and little red sailboats embroidered on the collar. He's growing so fast, no matter what Mama says about bottle babies. It worries Evanelle though when he spits up and that's why she can't say the reason they are late.

Earl pushes in the cigarette lighter, pulls it out again when he remembers he isn't smoking anymore. This is not his idea of a good time. He couldn't have been any slower getting dressed if he tried. Which is another reason they are late. He put on too much musk cologne and Evanelle thinks she may be sick. She feels dizzy, nauseated.

"Let me hold that sweet thing." Mama leans over the front seat, brushes Evanelle's forehead with her stiff hair. Evanelle thinks she feels a red, ugly scratch there. "I never get to hold him," Mama says. "People say I bet you spoil that grandbaby to death, now you finally got one, and I say I don't even have a chance. He's in that awful nursery all the time."

Evanelle would love for Mama to hold the baby. That way if he spit up again Mama would go around the rest of the day smelling soured. "He's asleep," Evanelle says. It almost comes out a sigh.

Mama dangles an earring close to Evanelle's eye and she pulls away from the sharp edges. Mama always said earrings were her weakness. She's got two hundred pair in every color and shape. Drawers of earrings, little trees and cats and birds that hold earrings. When Mama went to get her ears pierced, Evanelle had to hold her hand and it made her feel strange in the middle. There was Billy Buttons kicking her inside...only she didn't know it was him then. Earl kept calling him girl names—Tammy Lynn and Loretta Rae and Crystal Sue—all names of his old girlfriends. And Mama kept pulling her on the outside. It gave her a funny feeling she still thinks about sometimes. A feeling that comes back and grabs her from behind like somebody sneaking up when she was little, playing Hide and Go Seek. Sometimes Evanelle feels her life has been turned upside-down like that game they used to play on rainy days in the sixth grade, Fruitbasket Turnover.

Mama folds her rain bonnet. She rattles it like paper and says, "I don't know what on earth can be keeping your daddy." She says this even though she knows Lester Pedy is not Evanelle's daddy; never was, never will be. She just says that to Evanelle to try to make up to her for remarrying and to make her feel more family. "All he had to do was get the camera and close the door. He was right behind me." Mama fans with her folded bonnet. "How long can it take somebody to close a durn door?

If he'd been any closer behind, he'd been on my heels and we're late enough as it is." She keeps fanning, making little steam sounds with her breath. "And this rain. I'm proud of Earl for driving."

Earl grunts. Evanelle is proud he's even going. That's all. For over two weeks now, Mama has planned this four-generation thing and Evanelle has worried. Worried about taking Billy in that place. Worried he'll catch something. She doesn't know what, just something. Worried that Earl will act up. He said he didn't see any sense in this business. That it didn't amount to a hill of beans. Evanelle said her family wasn't a hill of beans and she didn't appreciate him talking like that. Then he said that was kinda cute, the way she got mad like she used to and he called her "Pepper Pot" and "Red." He used to say she didn't have red hair for nothing. Actually Evanelle could have hair any color she wanted, but this was one she'd gotten used to and so had everybody else. Now it covered the gray that was creeping in a hair at a time. At forty-two she saw it coming and she didn't want to be solid white like Mama and going all Easter egg colors; pink, blue, and lavender. Mama had been going to Eunice Platt all her life. Every Friday. And everybody knew Eunice never measured when she mixed. Evanelle had nightmares that she'd be gray-haired in the hospital and the nurses would say things like, "Why honey, this can't be your first!" or ask wasn't she the baby's grandmother? Or giggle behind her back that at her age she should have known better. Well, she couldn't help it. The baby wasn't something she went out and decided. He just happened. Earl acted more surprised than she did. After twenty-two years you just forget, don't expect. She'd never been in love with the idea of kids in the first place and here she was in the middle of this fourth-generation thing, just so Mama could show up her sister Faith Anne who never liked Evanelle from day one. Faith Anne's three daughters had married and divorced and moved twenty states away so they could stay away as much as they liked. So here goes Evanelle, baby and all, to some party in the nursing home. Grandma wouldn't know any of them and Mama would probably hold the baby right up to her face so both of them would have to fight for breath. She accused Evanelle of being peculiar, then taking him to that day nursery where he was exposed to every kind of germ there was. He was in that place so much, Mama said, he wouldn't know anyplace else. Not his real home, nor who his real mama was. It made Evanelle feel like two cents. She didn't work for the fun of it. Lord, she didn't know what they'd live on every week if it wasn't for her paycheck. Earl's didn't seem to go anywhere. She tried to save, but something always came along.

"Where is that man?" Mama rolled down her window. "How long can it take somebody to pull a door shut?" She was ready to yell when Lester backed onto the porch, settled his hat sideways on his head. He had a wide rear like two brown pillows pushed together, a bald doorknob of a head. In some ways Evanelle felt sorry for him; that he lived with Mama seven days a week, twenty-four hours a day. How does he stand it? How do I? How do any of us stand each other? And somehow we'll go on putting up with each other until they put us off in a bed with sides and chairs with wheels to push like Billy Buttons in his stroller.

"Faith Anne has called me fifty times about that cake," Mama says as Lester gets in. "You got it?"

"Right here." Lester pushes the camera in her face.

"I can see that," Mama says, "I'm talking about the cake."

"In the trunk," Evanelle says quietly. What she doesn't say is the cake has only thirty-six roses instead of the eighty-six Mama wanted. Even after Evanelle telephoned the order. She was going to be mad, but it was too late to do anything. Let her be mad, thought Evanelle. I've got this baby and a job and husband to look after. I can't do everything. The baby snored wetly, wiggled like a puppy and snuggled closer. He was sweet even if he did cry a lot and spit up. When he wasn't crying, his face didn't look so puckered and red.

Earl turned at the light and Lester kept clicking the camera, twirled in a roll of film. It snapped like a beetle or something.

"Is that camera what took you so long?" Mama asks.

"I had to find the film," Lester grunts.

"Well, that didn't have to take you all day."

"It wouldn't if you kept things in the place they ought to be." Earl puts the camera to his eye. "I like to never found the film."

"It was in the linen closet the whole time."

Earl hunts a country/western station on the radio to try to drown out the back seat. All he gets is the Radio Gospel Hour and Ministry of the Air. "I've seen the blind learn to see," some preacher yells, "and the lame throw down their crutches and walk. I've seen drunkards lay their bottles down and never reach for them again." Earl turns the radio off.

Evanelle shifts the heavy baby in her arms. It's a wonder all that door-slamming and fuss hasn't waked him up. He makes a snuffling noise and sucks his fist. She hopes that means he's not going to spit up again.

Lester has rolled down his window and Evanelle hears Mama make a noise like she is going to say something about her hair being blown to shreds and changes her mind.

"I sure like this car," Lester says.

"I'll sell her to you." Earl peels off a breath mint, chews. "Nothing down and a hundred when I catch you."

"Har," laughs Lester, "har. I heard tell of deals like that."

Mama pats the back of the front seat. "This is a nice car, Earl. Yours or the company's?"

Mama loves to rub it in that the only car Evanelle has ever owned is the blue one she bought herself when she still lived at home. And Earl has a different one every week, all belonging to the dealer he works for. It's a wonder he hasn't traded or sold Evanelle's, but that's only because she won't let him.

Sometimes Evanelle thinks she's been married a hundred years. Fifty at least. Her life seems to be running away from her and she can't slow it down. It wasn't good having a baby at her age. Not when she'd shut off her mind to the idea a long time ago. Billy Buttons would grow up with a bald daddy and the oldest mama in the first grade while her own mother was going around saying, "I never thought I'd have a grandbaby in the first place and here you go off leaving it with some stranger every day. Nobody could pay me to be away from the only baby I'd ever have when he was at his sweetest and most precious stage."

When Mama says that, Lester always says, "Hush. Now that Nelle's got started, who says she's going to stop. She and Earl may end up with a baseball team yet."

Earl always blushes and grins, says, "I'm all for it." Then he pokes Evanelle in the ribs like he wants her to laugh.

She doesn't see anything to laugh about. Earl slept right through the midnight feedings and on past 5:00 a.m. when Billy Buttons woke up the day. There wasn't one thing slow about him, even if that's one of the things her doctors worried about at first. Her age. They did the test and everything came back normal. Evanelle knew it would be. Billy Buttons kicked and turned and twisted too much to be the least bit slow.

"If you go slow by here"—Lester leans over the front seat and points for Earl—"right up there. That service station. That's where I found a man with my name once. I tell you that was a crazy feeling."

"I don't know what's crazy about it," Mama snorts. "It's a common name."

"I was selling soap for the car washes and when I walked in that station and saw my name, I like to have backed out. Scared me so." Lester points. "Right there."

The only thing that sits in the spot now is a fruit stand and adult book store. The sign reads "JOY" in big, orange letters. "Tapes, books, records and films."

"It's got so nobody can stay in business anymore," Lester says as they drive past. "Used to be a Gulf station. And the fellow that ran it was honest as they come."

"How you know?" Mama asks. "He buy you out?"

"He didn't buy a thing," Lester says. "But anybody with my same name has got to be an all right fellow."

"Shoot," Mama says. "You're lucky he wasn't a crook. One of the ten most wanted. Picture in the post office. How would you like that?"

"My liking wouldn't have anything to do with it," Lester says. "His face, my name. Now my face in the post office would be a different story. It might just pretty up the place."

"I found my name once." Earl brakes for a light. "In an obituary. Like to have scared me to death."

Then Mama has to tell about the time H.A. (who is Evanelle's real daddy) stopped in a cemetery somewhere in Kansas. "Never been there before nor since—and there was his name big as anything on a tombstone. I tell you if that don't set your mind to thinking, nothing will."

Evanelle has heard the story ten hundred times. She could tell about the time she was scared to death, right recently. When Billy Buttons was born and nobody, nobody was there. Not Earl—he'd gone to Nashville. Not Mama—she'd gone across the river to some outlet store with Gladine Williams and they stopped to look at bedding plants and got to talking and forgot her only daughter in her time of need. Evanelle had called a dozen places from the grocery store to the beauty shop to church and couldn't find one trace of her. Here she was two weeks late and Mama had called every single day for the last month, driving her crazy, asking,

"You gone yet?" Then the one day Mama didn't call, Evanelle's water breaks and she has to call a taxi to get to the hospital. She's never been madder nor more embarrassed in her life. Then the driver didn't have change for a twenty and she'd had to stand in front of the hospital and wait—in her condition. Sometimes she didn't know how she got through half the things she did.

They were nearing The Home now. Seven Oaks, but it was only some bent little pines and seven smooth, gray stumps. The oaks had been cut down to add on to The Home and it was too much trouble to change the name. The Home was long and low like a pink motel without a marquee. It had a porte-cochère with an ambulance parked under it.

"I called here yesterday," Mama says, "and they're supposed to have her up and dressed. Faith Anne is bringing her an orchid. That's what they told me at the florist. She didn't. Yellow. I said orchids aren't orchids unless they're purple, but it's not me buying. It's her money."

"Florist?" Evanelle shifts the sleeping baby. There is a damp spot on her dress and his hair is plastered down. She tries to fluff it. "I got silk," she says. "That's what you told me."

"I know. I know," Mama says. "But I was by the florist and just dropped in. You know how Harmon is. If you're within ten miles and don't stop, he gets his feelings hurt."

There are three flags flying in front of Seven Oaks. The state flag, the regular red, white, and blue one, and the other Evanelle can't figure out. It is purple with some sort of yellow trim and design. She can't think what it stands for. Council on Aging? Presidential Seal of Approval? Duncan Hines rating?

Earl eases into a parking place that looks too small. It is an end one and marked off for a small car. "Foreign," says Earl. "I wish they'd outlaw the things. Not let them in the gates of this country."

"I hate to wake him," Evanelle says to nobody in particular.

"Well, if you want to sit in the parking lot all day," Earl says, "we'll let you." He slicks back his hair with both hands, looks in the mirror. When Evanelle was in the eighth grade and Earl was a senior, she fell all over herself trying to make him notice her. He wore duck tails and white loafers and when he did the twist, it was "locomotion." Everybody said they had never seen anybody who could move so much standing in one place. And she'd been a little bitty thing with a ponytail, but he'd noticed. He even said then that she had more up there than most women would have in a lifetime of wishing. Then he went off to the Navy, never wrote once. When he came back, Evanelle was still there, living in the same house, doing the same things, seeing the same people. She worked after school for the radio station, answering the phone, typing spots.

"I hope I never live long enough to have to go to one of these places," Mama says. Earl hands her the flowers, Lester takes the cake, and they leave Evanelle with the baby, diaper bag, and her handbag. She can't figure out how she's going to carry it all, but they have gone up the walk, past an old man in a sea captain's hat sitting in a wheelchair on the porch.

The baby wakes with a wail and Evanelle shifts him to her shoulder, the diaper bag to the other, and somehow grabs her purse. She doesn't have a free hand to shut the car door, so she gives it a boot with her foot and leaves a print on Earl's fresh wash job. She doesn't care. Serves him right.

She's glad it stopped raining or she'd be getting soaked to her toes and the baby too. He turns his eyes to the sky like he sees something, stares.

The old man in the wheelchair holds the door for her with his cane. There is a beach towel spread across his lap that has pictures of punk rockers and the words, "It's a Wild and Crazy World." Evanelle thinks it sure is. Earl and Mama aren't in sight.

"They brought me here and dumped me and haven't been back since," the old man says. He has stubble on his chin like cactus.

"Who?" Evanelle thinks of Earl and Mama.

"My daughter," he says, "and that good-for-nothing she married. That's who."

Evanelle adjusts the baby on her shoulder. Something has fallen from the diaper bag and she drags it behind her like a tail.

"You're losing something," the old man says, pokes at it with his cane.

"I got too much." Evanelle thrusts the baby onto his lap, where the baby begins threshing his legs and cranking up to cry. The old man pokes a stubby brown finger in Billy Buttons's face. "Dooba, booba doo," he says. "This boy won't turn his old daddy out in the world not caring if he lives or dies. Not this boy. No siree."

Evanelle repacks the diapers. Under the wheelchair she notices a lint-ball big and gray as a mouse. Faith Anne has been saying all the time this place wasn't kept clean.

"Yar," the old man says to the baby, who is sucking in air to let out a sharp, red-faced howl. She takes the baby, gives the old man the diaper bag, and he rolls after her. "Some around here," he says, "got chairs that go by themselves. I like to roll my own, thank you."

When they round the corner, Mama and Earl are nowhere to be seen, but Lester is leaning against the wall next to the Coke machine. "Don't tell your mama," he says, draining the last drop. "Air in this place makes my mouth dry."

Evanelle wonders what Coke does to his diabetes. I must look like a parade, she thinks, with the old man in his wheelchair following her, then Lester in the rear. She feels like a drum majorette with her skirt hiked up in front and her thighs showing. Lord, Faith Anne was right, she thinks. This place almost knocks you out with ammonia. It reeks like a giant diaper pail.

There is a crowd of nurses at the nurses' station, pulling at some flowers brought over from a church service. Evanelle thinks the gladolias look rusty and the mums limp and brown-edged. She feels something bump the back of her knees and the old man says, "I didn't go to do it, honey. It's hard to stop when somebody slows down and you got all geared up to go ahead."

The door to her grandmother's room is open and she hears Mama and Faith Anne rattling paper, moving things around. The bed is completely covered with a display of gifts and the cake they've placed at her grandmother's feet. Her grandmother looks small, plastic as a doll in a box, her silver hair screwed in tight wads like French knots. Mama loves to tell everyone The Home has its own beauty shop and everyone gets their hair done once a week whether they want it or not.

Faith Anne and Mama are taking turns posing with Grandma. "Smile, Mama," Faith Anne says. "It won't hurt you."

Grandma flickers her eyes, but keeps the same stony expression.

"Grandma," Evanelle starts.

"Not now, honey," Mama says, cradling Grandma at the same time she elbows Faith Anne back and smiles for Uncle Frank, who holds the camera. "Hold the thing straight," Mama says. "I don't want you cutting me off. Get both of us in there. Me and Mama."

The baby jumps when the flash goes off, squeezes shut his eyes. He'll probably do that on the picture, Evanelle thinks, but she doesn't care.

Lights probably aren't all that good for his eyes anyway. Not so much at one time.

Faith Anne tries to move closer to her mother and sister, but Mama steps in front. "I don't know how many flashes he's got left"—she motions to Frank—"and we want to get the four generations in. That's what we come for."

Faith Anne makes a face and Evanelle thinks if she'd been any younger she would have stuck her tongue out at Mama. Faith Anne looks that peeved.

"I thought it was birthday," Faith Anne says. "That's what it was supposed to be about. I've had four generations three times and nobody made a fuss."

"Well," Mama says, "this is *my* four-generation." She takes the baby from Evanelle, jostles him upright so that he reaches out both arms like someone has a gun in his back. "Look what I brought," Mama shouts to Grandma. "You ever seen anything so cute?" She props him beside the prone woman. "Now Evanelle, honey, you come get on this side and Frank you get us all in the picture and see if you can not make me look as big as you did the last time." Mama jerks Evanelle around close to the bed.

Frank shoots three pictures and each time Evanelle blinks when the flash goes off. She is sure the baby does too. That ought to be next week's winner in the *Horsepoint Herald*. Sometimes they put generation pictures on the front page if nobody robbed a branch bank, there wasn't a flash flood or fire, and nobody shot a deer or killed a big rattlesnake.

"I've waited long enough for my turn." Faith Anne squeezes close between Mama and Evanelle. "I got Mama something she's never had before. A happy birthday card from Ronald Reagan—the President. Look, it's got her name right here." She pushes the card under Mama's nose.

"I can read," Mama says. "It's one like they send to everybody who asks for them."

"You got to be over eighty," Faith Anne says, "and you got to write in months ahead of time. Not everybody in this world gets one."

Evanelle looks at the gold-trimmed card. It does have some signature on it that looks real and it says Ronald Reagan.

"What's she going to do with it?" Mama asks. "I've seen prettier cards before. It's got no design, no color, no flowers, no nothing."

"Nothing but the President's signature," Faith Anne says, and waves the card. "She can put it on her bedside table for all the nurses to see"—she props it behind a water pitcher—"or hang it on the wall." Faith Anne holds the card against the wall, then presses it to her chest. "I just might have it framed for her. Myself."

"You do that," Mama says. "Now move over. We got pictures to take here."

The baby lies like he's been stunned and Grandma reaches one old yellow hand toward him, tries to stroke his hair. She makes a deep noise in her throat that comes out like a bird squeak. Evanelle pushes the baby closer and sits on the edge of the bed.

"We've got to have at least one more picture." Mama motions to Frank. "Let's finish out the roll. Where's Earl?" She goes to the door. "We need Earl. Earl," she calls.

"That's okay," Evanelle says, and takes off her shoe, rubs her foot. "He didn't have anything to do with it." But Mama goes down the hall and comes back pulling Earl, who poses at the head of the bed just like he belongs there, which almost makes Evanelle smile. She knows a secret she'll never tell. Not if she lives to be a hundred. Not if Earl behaves himself like he has lately. Not if D.R. the D.J. goes his merry way and keeps going.

When the pictures come back, Evanelle's eyes aren't closed but she's making a funny mouth and her nose looks like she's been crying. Everybody who sees it in the *Horsepoint Herald* says it's a good picture. After a while Evanelle thinks, "Well, it could've been worse." But she knows different.

RUTH MOOSE is the author of two short-story collections, The Wreath-Ribbon Quilt *and* Dreaming in Color. *The recipient of a PEN Award for Short Fiction, she lives in Albemarle, North Carolina.*

Love Life

OPAL LOLLS IN HER recliner, wearing the Coors cap her niece Jenny brought her from Colorado. She fumbles for the remote-control paddle and fires a button. Her swollen knuckles hurt. On TV, a boy is dancing in the street. Some other boys dressed in black are banging guitars and drums. This is her favorite program. It is always on, night or day. The show is songs, with accompanying stories. It's the music channel. Opal never cared for stories—she detests those soap operas her friends watch—but these fascinate her. The colors and the costumes change and flow with the music, erratically, the way her mind does these days. Now the TV is playing a song in which all the boys are long-haired cops chasing a dangerous woman in a tweed cap and a checked shirt. The woman's picture is in all their billfolds. They chase her through a cold-storage room filled with sides of beef. She hops on a motorcycle, and they set up a roadblock, but she jumps it with her motorcycle. Finally, she slips onto a train and glides away from them, waving a smiling goodbye.

On the table beside Opal is a Kleenex box, her glasses case, a glass of Coke with ice, and a cut-glass decanter of liquid that could be just water for the plants. Opal pours some of the liquid into the Coke and sips slowly. It tastes like peppermint candy, and it feels soothing. Her fingers tingle. She feels happy. Now that she is retired, she doesn't have to sneak into the teachers' lounge for a little swig from the jar in her pocketbook. She still dreams algebra problems, complicated quadratic equations with shifting values and no solutions. Now kids are using algebra to program

93

computers. The kids in the TV stories remind her of her students at Hopewell High. Old age could have a grandeur about it, she thinks now as the music surges through her, if only it weren't so scary.

But she doesn't feel lonely, especially now that her sister Alice's girl, Jenny, has moved back here, to Kentucky. Jenny seems so confident, the way she sprawls on the couch, with that backpack she carries everywhere. Alice was always so delicate and feminine, but Jenny is enough like Opal to be her own daughter. She has Opal's light, thin hair, her large shoulders and big bones and long legs. Jenny even has a way of laughing that reminds Opal of her own laughter, the boisterous scoff she always saved for certain company but never allowed herself in school. Now and then Jenny lets loose one of those laughs and Opal is pleased. It occurs to her that Jenny, who is already past thirty, has left behind a trail of men, like that girl in the song. Jenny has lived with a couple of men, here and there. Opal can't keep track of all of the men Jenny has mentioned. They have names like John and Skip and Michael. She's not in a hurry to get married, she says. She says she is going to buy a house trailer and live in the woods like a hermit. She's full of ideas, and she exaggerates. She uses the words "gorgeous," "adorable," and "wonderful" interchangeably and persistently.

Last night, Jenny was here, with her latest boyfriend, Randy Newcomb. Opal remembers when he sat in the back row in her geometry class. He was an ordinary kid, not especially smart, and often late with his lessons. Now he has a real-estate agency and drives a Cadillac. Jenny kissed him in front of Opal and told him he was gorgeous. She said the placemats were gorgeous, too.

Jenny was asking to see those old quilts again. "Why do you hide away your nice things, Aunt Opal?" she said. Opal doesn't think they're that nice, and she doesn't want to have to look at them all the time. Opal showed Jenny and Randy Newcomb the double-wedding-ring quilt, the star quilt, and some of the crazy quilts, but she wouldn't show them the craziest one—the burial quilt, the one Jenny kept asking about. Did Jenny come back home just to hunt up that old rag? The thought makes Opal shudder.

The doorbell rings. Opal has to rearrange her comforter and magazines in order to get up. Her joints are stiff. She leaves the TV blaring a song she knows, with balloons and bombs in it.

At the door is Velma Shaw, who lives in the duplex next to Opal. She has just come home from her job at Shop World. "Have you gone out of your mind, Opal?" cries Velma. She has on a plum-colored print blouse and a plum skirt and a little green scarf with a gold pin holding it down. Velma shouts, "You can hear that racket clear across the street!"

"Rock and roll is never too loud," says Opal. This is a line from a song she has heard.

Opal releases one of her saved-up laughs, and Velma backs away. Velma is still trying to be sexy, in those little color-coordinated outfits she wears, but it is hopeless, Opal thinks with a smile. She closes the door and scoots back to her recliner.

Opal is Jenny's favorite aunt. Jenny likes the way Opal ties her hair in a ponytail with a ribbon. She wears muumuus and socks. She is tall and only a little thick in the middle. She told Jenny that middle-age spread was caused by the ribs expanding and that it doesn't matter what you eat. Opal kids around about "old Arthur"—her arthritis, visiting her on damp days.

Jenny has been in town six months. She works at the courthouse, typing records—marriages, divorces, deaths, drunk- driving convictions. Frequently, the same names are on more than one list. Before she returned to Kentucky, Jenny was waitressing in Denver, but she was growing restless again, and the idea of going home seized her. Her old rebellion against small-town conventions gave way to curiosity.

In the South, the shimmer of the heat seems to distort everything, like old glass with impurities in it. During her first two days there, she saw two people with artificial legs, a blind man, a man with hooks for hands, and a man without an arm. It seemed unreal. In a parking lot, a pit bull terrier in a Camaro attacked her from behind the closed window. He barked, viciously, his nose stabbing the window. She stood in the parking lot, letting the pit bull attack, imagining herself in an arena, with a crowd watching. The South makes her nervous. Randy Newcomb told her she had just been away too long. "We're not as countrified down here now as people think," he said.

Jenny has been going with Randy for three months. The first night she went out with him, he took her to a fancy place that served shrimp flown in from New Orleans, and then to a little bar over in Hopkinsville. They went with Kathy Steers, a friend from work, and Kathy's husband, Bob.

Kathy and Bob weren't getting along and they carped at each other all evening. In the bar, an attractive, cheerful woman sang requests for tips, and her companion, a blind man, played the guitar. When she sang, she looked straight at him, singing to him, smiling at him reassuringly. In the background, men played pool with their girlfriends, and Jenny noticed the sharp creases in the men's jeans and imagined the women ironing them. When she mentioned it, Kathy said she took Bob's jeans to the laundromat to use the machine there that puts knifelike creases in them. The men in the bar had two kinds of women with them: innocent-looking women with pastel skirts and careful hairdos, and hard-looking women without makeup, in T-shirts and jeans. Jenny imagined that each type could be either a girlfriend or a wife. She felt odd. She was neither type. The singer sang "Happy Birthday" to a popular regular named Will Ed, and after the set she danced with him, while the jukebox took over. She had a limp, as though one leg were shorter than the other. The leg was stiff under her jeans, and when the woman danced Jenny could see that the leg was not real.

"There, but for the grace of God, go I," Randy whispered to Jenny. He squeezed her hand, and his heavy turquoise ring dug into her knuckle.

"Those quilts would bring a good price at an estate auction," Randy says to Jenny as they leave her aunt's one evening and head for his real-estate office. They are in his burgundy Cadillac. "One of those star quilts used to bring twenty-five dollars. Now it might run three hundred."

"My aunt doesn't think they're worth anything. She hides all her nice stuff, like she's ashamed of it. She's got beautiful dresser scarves and starched doilies she made years ago. But she's getting a little weird. All she does is watch MTV."

"I think she misses the kids," Randy says. Then he bursts out laughing. "She used to put the fear of God in all her students! I never will forget the time she told me to stop watching so much television and read some books. It was like an order from God Almighty. I didn't dare not do what she said. I read *Crime and Punishment*. I never would have read it if she hadn't shamed me into it. But I appreciated that. I don't even remember what *Crime and Punishment* was about, except there was an ax murderer in it."

"That was basically it," Jenny says. "He got caught. Crime and punishment—just like any old TV show."

Randy touches some controls on the dashboard and Waylon Jennings starts singing. The sound system is remarkable. Everything Randy owns is quality. He has been looking for some land for Jenny to buy—a couple of acres of woods—but so far nothing on his listings has met with his approval. He is concerned about zoning and power lines and frontage. All Jenny wants is a remote place where she can have a dog and grow some tomatoes. She knows that what she really needs is a better car, but she doesn't want to go anywhere.

Later, at Randy's office, Jenny studies the photos of houses on display, while he talks on the telephone to someone about dividing up a sixty-acre farm into farmettes. His photograph is on several certificates on the wall. He has a full, well-fed face in the pictures, but he is thinner now and looks better. He has a boyish, endearing smile, like Dennis Quaid, Jenny's favorite actor. She likes Randy's smile. It seems so innocent, as though he would do anything in the world for someone he cared about. He doesn't really want to sell her any land. He says he is afraid she will get raped if she lives alone in the woods.

"I'm impressed," she says when he slams down the telephone. She points to his new regional award for the fastest-growing agency of the year.

"Isn't that something? Three branch offices in a territory this size—I can't complain. There's a lot of turnover in real estate now. People are never satisfied. You know that? That's the truth about human nature." He laughs. "That's the secret of my success."

"It's been two years since Barbara divorced me," he says later, on the way to Jenny's apartment. "I can't say it hasn't been fun being free, but my kids are in college, and it's like starting over. I'm ready for a new life. The business has been so great, I couldn't really ask for more, but I've been thinking—Don't laugh, please, but what I was thinking was if you want to share it with me, I'll treat you good. I swear."

At a stoplight, he paws at her hand. On one corner is the Pepsi bottling plant, and across from it is the Broad Street House, a restaurant with an old-fashioned statue of a jockey out front. People are painting the black faces on those little statues white now, but this one has been painted bright green all over. Jenny can't keep from laughing at it.

"I wasn't laughing at you—honest!" she says apologetically. "That statue always cracks me up."

"You don't have to give me an answer now."

"I don't know what to say."

"I can get us a real good deal on a house," he says. "I can get any house I've got listed. I can even get us a farmette, if you want trees so bad. You won't have to spend your money on a piece of land."

"I'll have to think about it." Randy scares her. She likes him, but there is something about his energy and optimism. Everyone around her seems to be bursting at the seams, like that pit bull terrier.

"I'll let you think about it," he says, pulling up to her apartment. "Life has been good to me. Business is good, and my kids didn't turn out to be dope fiends. That's about all you can hope for in this day and time."

Jenny is having lunch with Kathy Steers at the Broad Street House. The iced tea is mixed with white grape juice. It took Jenny a long time to identify the flavor, and the Broad Street House won't admit it's grape juice. Their iced tea is supposed to have a mystique about it, probably because they can't sell drinks in this dry county. In the daylight, the statue out front is the color of the Jolly Green Giant.

People confide in Jenny, but Jenny doesn't always tell things back. It's an unfair exchange, though it often goes unnoticed. She is curious, eager to hear other people's stories, and she asks more questions than is appropriate. Kathy's life is a tangle of deceptions. Kathy stayed with her husband, Bob, because he had opened his own body shop and she didn't want him to start out a new business with a rocky marriage, but she acknowledges now it was a mistake.

"What about Jimmy and Willette?" Jenny asks. Jimmy and Willette are the other characters in Kathy's story.

"That mess went on for months. When you started work at the office, remember how nervous I was? I thought I was getting an ulcer." Kathy lights a cigarette and blows at the wall. "You see, I didn't know what Bob and Willette were up to, and they didn't know about me and Jimmy. That went on for two years before you came. And when it started to come apart—I mean, we had *hell!* I'd say things to Jimmy and then it would get back to Bob because Jimmy would tell Willette. It was an unreal circle. I was pregnant with Jason and you get real sensitive then. I thought Bob was screwing around on me, but it never dawned on me it was with

Willette."

The fat waitress says, "Is everything all right?"

Kathy says, "No, but it's not your fault. Do you know what I'm going to do?" she asks Jenny.

"No, what?"

"I'm taking Jason and moving in with my sister. She has a sort of apartment upstairs. Bob can do what he wants to with the house. I've waited too long to do this, but it's time. My sister keeps the baby anyway, so why shouldn't I just live there?"

She puffs the cigarette again and levels her eyes at Jenny. "You know what I admire about you? You're so independent. You say what you think. When you started work at the office, I said to myself, 'I wish I could be like that.' I could tell you had been around. You've inspired me. That's how come I decided to move out."

Jenny plays with the lemon slice in the saucer holding her iced-tea glass. She picks a seed out of it. She can't bring herself to confide in Kathy about Randy Newcomb's offer. For some reason, she is embarrassed by it.

"I haven't spoken to Willette since September third," says Kathy.

Kathy keeps talking, and Jenny listens, suspicious of her interest in Kathy's problems. She notices Kathy is enjoying herself. Kathy is looking forward to leaving her husband the same way she must have enjoyed her fling with Jimmy, the way she is enjoying not speaking to Willette.

"Let's go out and get drunk tonight," Kathy says cheerfully. "Let's celebrate my decision."

"I can't. I'm going to see my aunt this evening. I have to take her some booze. She gives me money to buy her vodka and peppermint schnapps, and she tells me not to stop at the same liquor store too often. She says she doesn't want me to get a reputation for drinking! I have to go all the way to Hopkinsville to get it."

"Your aunt tickles me. She's a pistol."

The waitress clears away the dishes and slaps down dessert menus. They order chocolate pecan pie, the day's special.

"You know the worst part of this whole deal?" Kathy says. "It's the years it takes to get smart. But I'm going to make up for lost time. You can bet on that. And there's not a thing Bob can do about it."

Opal's house has a veranda. Jenny thinks that verandas seem to imply a history of some sort—people in rocking chairs telling stories. But Opal doesn't tell any stories. It is exasperating, because Jenny wants to know about her aunt's past love life, but Opal won't reveal her secrets. They sit on the veranda and observe each other. They smile, and now and then roar with laughter over something ridiculous. In the bedroom, where she snoops after using the bathroom, Jenny notices the layers of old wallpaper in the closet, peeling back and spilling crumbs of gaudy ancient flower prints onto Opal's muumuus.

Downstairs, Opal asks, "Do you want some cake, Jenny?"

"Of course. I'm crazy about your cake, Aunt Opal."

"I didn't beat the egg whites long enough. Old Arthur's visiting again." Opal flexes her fingers and smiles. "That sounds like the curse. Girls used to say they had the curse. Or they had a visitor." She looks down at her knuckles shyly. "Nowadays, of course, they just say what they mean."

The cake is delicious—an old-fashioned lemon chiffon made from scratch. Jenny's cooking ranges from English-muffin minipizzas to brownie mixes. After gorging on the cake, Jenny blurts out, "Aunt Opal, aren't you sorry you never got married? Tell the truth, now."

Opal laughs. "I was talking to Ella Mae Smith the other day—she's a retired geography teacher?—and she said,'I've got twelve great-great grandchildren, and when we get together I say, "Law me, look what I started!" ' " Opal mimics Ella Mae Smith, giving her a mindless, chirpy tone of voice. "Why, I'd have to use quadratic equations to count up all the people that woman has caused," she goes on. "All with a streak of her petty narrow-mindedness in them. I don't call that a contribution to the world." Opal laughs and sips from her glass of schnapps. "What about you, Jenny? Are you ever going to get married?"

"Marriage is outdated. I don't know anybody who's married and happy."

Opal names three schoolteachers she has known who have been married for decades.

"But are they really happy?"

"Oh, foot, Jenny! What you're saying is why are *you* not married and why are *you* not happy. What's wrong with little Randy Newcomb? Isn't that funny? I always think of him as little Randy."

"Show me those quilts again, Aunt Opal."

"I'll show you the crazies but not the one you keep after me about."

"O.K., show me the crazies."

Upstairs, her aunt lays crazy quilts on the bed. They are bright-colored patches of soft velvet and plaids and prints stitched together with silky embroidery. Several pieces have initials embroidered on them. The haphazard shapes make Jenny imagine odd, twisted lives represented in these quilts.

She says, "Mom gave me a quilt once, but I didn't appreciate the value of it and I washed it until it fell apart."

"I'll give you one of these crazies when you stop moving around," Opal says. "You couldn't fit it in that backpack of yours." She polishes her glasses thoughtfully. "Do you know what those quilts mean to me?"

"No, what?"

"A lot of desperate old women ruining their eyes. Do you know what I think I'll do?"

"No, what?"

"I think I'll take up aerobic dancing. Or maybe I'll learn to ride a motorcycle. I try to be modern."

"You're funny, Aunt Opal. You're hilarious."

"Am I gorgeous, too?"

"Adorable," says Jenny.

After her niece leaves, Opal hums a tune and dances a stiff little jig. She nestles among her books and punches her remote-control paddle. Years ago, she was allowed to paddle students who misbehaved. She used a wooden paddle from a butter churn, with holes drilled in it. The holes made a satisfying sting. On TV, a 1950s convertible is out of gas. This is one of her favorites. It has an adorable couple in it. The girl is wearing bobby socks and saddle oxfords, and the boy has on a basketball jacket. They look the way children looked before the hippie element took over. But the boy begins to grow cat whiskers and big cat ears, and then his face gets furry and leathery, while the girl screams bloody murder. Opal sips some peppermint and watches his face change. The red and gold of his basketball jacket are the Hopewell school colors. He chases the girl. Now he has grown long claws.

The boy is dancing energetically with a bunch of ghouls who have escaped from their coffins. Then Vincent Price starts talking in the background. The girl is very frightened. The ghouls are so old and ugly. That's how kids see us, Opal thinks. She loves this story. She even loves the credits—scary music by Elmer Bernstein. This is a story with a meaning. It suggests all the feelings of terror and horror that must be hidden inside young people. And inside, deep down, there really are monsters. An old person waits, a nearly dead body that can still dance.

Opal pours another drink. She feels relaxed, her joints loose like a dancer's now.

Jenny is so nosy. Her questions are so blunt. Did Opal ever have a crush on a student? Only once or twice. She was in her twenties then, and it seemed scandalous. Nothing happened—just daydreams. When she was thirty, she had another attachment to a boy, and it seemed all right then, but it was worse again at thirty-five, when another pretty boy stayed after class to talk. After that, she kept her distance.

But Opal is not wholly without experience. There have been men, over the years, though nothing like the casual affairs Jenny has had. Opal remembers a certain motel room in Nashville. She was only forty. The man drove a gray Chrysler Imperial. When she was telling about him to a friend, who was sworn to secrecy, she called him "Imperial," in a joking way. She went with him because she knew he would take her somewhere, in such a fine car, and they would sleep together. She always remembered how clean and empty the room was, how devoid of history and association. In the mirror, she saw a scared woman with a pasty face and a shrimpy little man who needed a shave. In the morning he went out somewhere and brought back coffee and orange juice. They had bought some doughnuts at the new doughnut shop in town before they left. While he was out, she made up the bed and put her things in her bag, to make it as neat as if she had never been there. She was fully dressed when he returned, with her garter belt and stockings on, and when they finished the doughnuts she cleaned up all the paper and the cups and wiped the crumbs from the table by the bed. He said, "Come with me and I'll take you to Idaho." "Why Idaho?" she wanted to know, but his answer was vague. Idaho sounded cold, and she didn't want to tell him how she disliked his scratchy whiskers and the hard powdery doughnuts. It seemed unkind to her, but if he had been nicer-looking, without such a demanding dark beard, she might have gone with him to Idaho in that shining Imperial. She hadn't even given him a chance, she thought later.

She had been so scared. If anyone from school had seen her at that motel, she could have lost her job. "I need a woman," he had said. "A woman like you."

On a hot Saturday afternoon, with rain threatening, Jenny sits under a tent on a folding chair while Randy auctions off four hundred acres of woods on Lake Barkley. He had a road bulldozed into the property, and he divided it up into lots. The lakefront lots are going for as much as two thousand an acre, and the others are bringing up to a thousand. Randy has several assistants with him, and there is even a concession stand, offering hot dogs and cold drinks.

In the middle of the auction, they wait for a thundershower to pass. Sitting in her folding chair under a canopy reminds Jenny of graveside services. As soon as the rain slacks up, the auction continues. In his cowboy hat and blue blazer, Randy struts around with a microphone as proudly as a banty rooster. With his folksy chatter, he knows exactly how to work the crowd. "Y'all get yourselves a cold drink and relax now and just imagine the fishing you'll do in this dreamland. This land is good for vacation, second home, investment—heck, you can just park here in your camper and live. It's going to be paradise when that marina gets built on the lake and we get some lots cleared."

The four-hundred-acre tract looks like a wilderness. Jenny loves the way the sun splashes on the water after the rain, and the way it comes through the trees, hitting the flickering leaves like lights on a disco ball. A marina here seems farfetched. She could pitch a tent here until she could afford to buy a used trailer. She could swim at dawn, the way she did on a camping trip out West, long ago. All of a sudden, she finds herself bidding on a lot. The bidding passes four hundred, and she sails on, bidding against a man from Missouri who tells people around him that he's looking for a place to retire.

"Sold to the young lady with the backpack," Randy says when she bids six hundred. He gives her a crestfallen look, and she feels embarrassed.

As she waits for Randy to wind up his business after the auction, Jenny locates her acre from the map of the plots of land. It is along a gravel road and marked off with stakes tied with hot-pink survey tape. It is a small section of the woods—her block on the quilt, she thinks. These are her trees. The vines and underbrush are thick and spotted with raindrops.

She notices a windfall leaning on a maple, like a lover dying in its arms. Maples are strong, she thinks, but she feels like getting an ax and chopping that windfall down, to save the maple. In the distance, the whining of a speedboat cuts into the day.

They meet afterward at Randy's van, his mobile real-estate office, with a little shingled roof raised in the center to look rustic. It looks like an outhouse on wheels. A painted message on the side says, REALITY IS REAL ESTATE. As Randy plows through the mud on the new road, Jenny apologizes. Buying the lot was like laughing at the statue at the wrong moment—something he would take the wrong way, an insult to his attentions.

"I can't reach you," he says. "You say you want to live out in the wilderness and grow your own vegetables, but you act like you're somewhere in outer space. You can't grow vegetables in outer space. You can't even grow them in the woods unless you clear some ground."

"I'm looking for a place to land."

"What do I have to do to get through to you?"

"I don't know. I need more time."

He turns onto the highway, patterned with muddy tire tracks from the cars at the auction. "I said I'd wait, so I guess I'll have to," he says, flashing his Dennis Quaid smile. "You take as long as you want to, then. I learned my lesson with Barbara. You've got to be understanding with the women. That's the key to a successful relationship." Frowning, he slams his hand on the steering wheel. "That's what they tell me, anyhow."

Jenny is having coffee with Opal. She arrived unexpectedly. It's very early. She looks as though she has been up all night.

"Please show me your quilts," Jenny says. "I don't mean your crazy quilts. I want to see that special quilt. Mom said it had the family tree."

Opal spills her coffee in her saucer. "What is wrong with young people today?" she asks.

"I want to know why it's called a burial quilt," Jenny says. "Are you planning to buried in it?"

Opal wishes she had a shot of peppermint in her coffee. It sounds like a delicious idea. She starts toward the den with the coffee cup rattling in its saucer, and she splatters drops on the rug. Never mind it now, she thinks, turning back.

"It's just a family history," she says.

"Why's it called a burial quilt?" Jenny asks.

Jenny's face is pale. She has blue pouches under her eyes and blue eye shadow on her eyelids.

"See that closet in the hall?" Opal says. "Get a chair and we'll get the quilt down."

Jenny stands on a kitchen chair and removes the quilt from beneath several others. It's wrapped in blue plastic and Jenny hugs it closely as she steps down with it.

They spread it out on the couch, and the blue plastic floats off somewhere. Jenny looks like someone in love as she gazes at the quilt. "It's gorgeous," she murmurs. "How beautiful."

"Shoot!" says Opal. "It's ugly as homemade sin."

Jenny runs her fingers over the rough textures of the quilt. The quilt is dark and somber. The backing is a heavy gray gabardine, and the nine-inch-square blocks are pieced of smaller blocks of varying shades of gray and brown and black. They are wools, apparently made from men's winter suits. On each block is an appliquéd off-white tombstone—a comical shape, like Casper the ghost. Each tombstone has a name and date on it.

Jenny recognizes some of the names. Myrtle Williams. Voris Williams. Thelma Lee Freeman. The oldest gravestone is "Eulalee Freeman 1857-1900." The shape of the quilt is irregular, a rectangle with a clumsy foot sticking out from one corner. The quilt is knotted with yarn, and the edging is open, for more blocks to be added.

"Eulalee's daughter started it," says Opal. "But that thing has been carried through this family like a plague. Did you ever see such horrible old dark colors? I pieced on it some when I was younger, but it was too depressing. I think some of the kinfolks must have died without a square, so there may be several to catch up on."

"I'll do it," says Jenny. "I could learn to quilt."

"Traditionally, the quilt stops when the family name stops," Opal says. "And since my parents didn't have a boy, that was the end of the Freeman line on this particular branch of the tree. So the last old maids finish the quilt." She lets out a wild cackle. "Theoretically, a quilt like this could keep going till doomsday."

"Do you care if I have this quilt?" asks Jenny.

"What would you do with it? It's too ugly to put on a bed and too morbid to work on."

"I think it's kind of neat," says Jenny. She strokes the rough tweed. Already it is starting to decay, and it has moth holes. Jenny feels tears start to drip down her face.

"Don't you go putting my name on that thing," her aunt says.

Jenny has taken the quilt to her apartment. She explained that she is going to study the family tree, or that she is going to finish the quilt. If she's smart, Opal thinks, she will let Randy Newcomb auction it off. The way Jenny took it, cramming it into the blue plastic, was like snatching something that was free. Opal feels relieved, as though she has pushed the burden of that ratty old quilt onto her niece. All those miserable, cranky women, straining their eyes, stitching on those dark scraps of material.

For a long time, Jenny wouldn't tell why she was crying, and when she started to tell, Opal was uncomfortable, afraid she'd be required to tell something comparable of her own, but as she listened she found herself caught up in Jenny's story. Jenny said it was a man. That was always the case, Opal thought. It was five years earlier. A man Jenny knew in a place by the sea. Opal imagined seagulls, pretty sand. There were no palm trees. It was up North. The young man worked with Jenny in a restaurant with glass walls facing the ocean. They waited tables and collected enough tips to take a trip together near the end of the summer. Jenny made it sound like an idyllic time, waiting on tables by the sea. She started crying again when she told about the trip, but the trip sounded nice. Opal listened hungrily, imagining the young man, thinking he would have had handsome, smooth cheeks, and hair that fell attractively over his forehead. He would have had good manners, being a waiter. Jenny and the man, whose name was Jim, flew to Denver, Colorado, and they rented a car and drove around out West. They visited the Grand Canyon and Yellowstone and other places Opal had heard about. They grilled salmon on the beach, on another ocean. They camped out in the redwoods, trees so big they hid the sky. Jenny described all these scenes, and the man sounded like a good man. His brother had died in Vietnam and he felt guilty that he had been the one spared, because his brother was a swimmer and could have gone to the Olympics. Jim wasn't athletic. He had a bad knee and hammertoes. He slept fitfully in the tent, and Jenny said soothing things to him, and she cared about him, but by the time they had curved northward and over to Yellowstone the trip was becoming unpleasant. The romance wore off. She loved him, but she couldn't deal with his needs. One of the last nights they spent together, it rained all night long. He told her not to touch the tent material, because somehow the pressure of a finger on the nylon would make it start to leak at that spot. Lying there in the rain, Jenny couldn't resist touching a spot where the water was collecting in a sag in the top of the tent. The drip started then, and it grew worse, until they got so wet they had to get in the car. Not long afterward, when they ran short of money, they parted. Jenny got a job in Denver. She never saw him again.

Opal listened eagerly to the details about grilling the fish together, about the zip-together sleeping bags and setting up the tent and washing themselves in the cold stream. But when Jenny brought the story up to the present, Opal was not prepared. She felt she had been dunked in the cold water and left gasping. Jenny said she had heard a couple of times through a mutual friend that Jim had spent some time in Mexico. And then, she said, this week she had begun thinking about him, because of all the trees at the lake, and she had an overwhelming desire to see him again. She had been unfair, she knew now. She telephoned the friend, who had worked with them in the restaurant by the sea. He hadn't known where to locate her, he said, and so he couldn't tell her that Jim had been killed in Colorado over a year ago. His four-wheel-drive had plunged off a mountain curve.

"I feel some trick has been played on me. It seems so unreal." Jenny tugged at the old quilt, and her eyes darkened. "I was in Colorado, and I didn't even know he was there. If I still knew him, I would know how to mourn, but now I don't know how. And it was over a year ago. So I don't know what to feel."

"Don't look back, hon," Opal said, hugging her niece closely. But she was shaking, and Jenny shook with her.

Opal makes herself a snack, thinking it will pick up her strength. She is very tired. On the tray, she places an apple and a paring knife and some milk and cookies. She touches the remote-control button, and the picture blossoms. She was wise to buy a large TV, the one listed as the best in the consumer magazine. The color needs a little adjustment, though. She eases up the volume and starts peeling the apple. She has a little bump on one knuckle. In the old days, people would take the family Bible and bust a cyst like that with it. Just slam it hard.

On the screen, a Scoutmaster is telling a story to some Boy Scouts around a campfire. The campfire is only a fireplace, with electric logs. Opal loses track of time, and the songs flow together. A woman is lying on her stomach on a car hood in a desert full of gas pumps. TV sets crash. Smoke emerges from an eyeball. A page of sky turns like a page in a book. Then, at a desk in a classroom, a cocky blond kid with a pack of cigarettes rolled in the sleeve of his T-shirt is singing about a sexy girl with a tattoo on her back who is sitting on a commode and smoking a cigarette. In the classroom, all the kids are gyrating and snapping their fingers to wild music. The teacher at the blackboard with her white hair in a bun looks disapproving, but the kids in the class don't know what's on her mind. The teacher is thinking about how, when the bell rings, she will hit the road to Nashville.

BOBBIE ANN MASON, a native of Mayfield, Kentucky, holds a Ph.D. from the University of Connecticut and lives in Pennsylvania. She is the author of two novels and two collections of stories, of which the first, Shiloh and Other Stories, *won the PEN/Hemingway Award in 1983.*

Leaving

S H I R L E Y   C O C H R A N E

EVERY MORNING WHEN she came downstairs her son was sitting in front of the television set. She never knew whether he had gotten up early or never gone to bed.

"Do you sit there watching the station signal too? Just sit there, all night, waiting for the early-early, after watching the late-late?"

He sighed. *Always begins in on me first thing,* she could hear him thinking.

He rose, went over to fiddle with the color knob. The panelists turned pea green, then bubble-gum pink, then Indian-red; finally, normal. There was nothing you could do about the screen's being cut off an inch at top and bottom. Like living in a low-ceilinged room.

He was twenty-five, her oldest; born in the first happiness of marriage. There had been no more babies for seven years; then suddenly, three more boys in eighteen months—twins, then a singleton. He had minded them on the street, translated their twin-talk. *I used him,* she thought, *I used him up.*

Her twin sons were in communes, going to night school, the youngest doing poorly in preparatory school, but still, *away.* Her oldest son had helped launch them; then collapsed. Sometimes she thought this way, sometimes she thought there was a malevolence to his staying—an unconscious punishment of her. It made her want to open an upstairs window and push him—a giant, wildly flapping baby bird—*out.*

She said to him now: "Look: Every time I go in the bathroom I find the soggy bath-mat on the floor. I feel I have to pick it up, but with my bum back..." This speech had disintegrated into whine. Not the sustained anger she had determined on.

He looked at her mildly, giving her his polite attention but indicating he had not quite caught her words.

"You missed a good show last night," he said amiably. *"The Graduate."*

"For God's sake, I get a chance to go *out* and you tell me I should have stayed home and watched some tv show? Besides, I saw it when it first came out. It was good but not *that* good."

"The Simon and Garfunkel music was great."

He got up, walked to the stereo, stopping to turn the tv volume down. Barbara Walters mouthed silently on.

Tall, blond, bearded, he wore (as he did most of the time now) a wine-dark terry-cloth robe, too short. She had expected his fine body to go either to fat or bone sitting around the house all the time. But it had done neither. Nor had his brain deteriorated, as she had feared.

"Listen to this." He pointed a long finger in the direction of the stereo. The words came; beautiful when sung, maybe ordinary when spoken.

"You could write words as good as that," she told him. "Better, maybe."

He turned from her, sullen. He had a poet's profile, fitting the poet she had hoped he would become. Recently she had collected all his scribbled verse, typed it up, sent it out to literary magazines. The effort had brought one acceptance and a detailed critique with an invitation to submit more. Furious, he had hurled objects about the room, one nearly hitting the tv—a missed blessing. Then he'd stomped away for two days—to his father's, she supposed.

He looked at her now, intently. "Listen," he commanded.

The lyrics eased themselves into her consciousness. Tingles shot from her ear lobes down into her torso, stirring the pelvic region like a quickening of life. He saw her pleasure and smiled, suddenly the ghost of his youthful father.

She rose quickly, feeling like a girl caught in a boy's room back in the days when this was forbidden. Often there was this suggestion of courtship between them.

"Haven't had my coffee yet," she said, then went into the kitchen.

The image of his father persisted. She did not often think of him now. In the last years of their marriage she had thought of their original love as still intact—recoverable, like a prized letter under the welter of magazines on the coffee table. Now she suspected it had been concocted out of World War II songs and movies.

Early one morning her husband had come down while she was making coffee and told her about the girl. How he had tried to give her up, could not. *Then go,* she had said, wanting to be done with it immediately.

The kettle now sounded its insistent note. She poured hot water over the beads of instant coffee, stirred the sleeping giant Caffeine to life. She took a yogurt from the refrigerator—prune whip, last choice.

Simon and Garfunkel gave way to the suicide song from *M*A*S*H,* an old terror to her. Played constantly during the early days of her son's depression, she had taken it as a signal of intent. Bad as he still was, *then* he had been worse—a stubbled horror, barely speaking, turning night into day. He had refused to see a psychiatrist. His father had come at her request, taken him home with him for a week, brought him back, pronounced sane. She could make no dent in that paternal complacency.

She took her breakfast into the living room. He had turned off the tv, sat drowning in music.

"I want to *talk* to you," she said.

Eyes closed, he pretended not to hear.

"Shut it off!" she shouted.

He rose slowly, slowly complied.

"Look," she said. "All these tv dramas you must have watched? Family patternings? *Quality,* not soap operas. *You* know?"

"The Subject was Rutabagas? Long Day's Journey into Nothing?" The polite inquiry of a clerk to an indecisive customer.

"That's the idea."

"So?"

She told him about the dream she had had the night before. In it she had watched one of these dramas. Black and white, huge screen, almost like the movie screens of her youth. Maybe she had been in an old movie house. Anyway, in the final scene a mother and son danced in a turn-of-the-century kitchen. Waist-high wooden walls, plates set around an edging at the top, a tiny door for the garbage. Brooklyn? She wasn't sure. Anyway, they had danced, mother flirting up at son. Then the camera had moved in slowly for the final shot. "And I saw they had our faces," she told her son. "Yours and mine. It was *us.*"

"A real nightmare, huh?" She watched him strain out all emotion, present the blandly smiling social face.

"What I'm trying to tell you is, you think these dramas happen to other people. But it's happening to *us*. We're one of those sick mother-son teams. After awhile I might accept it, then *depend* on it. "

They would live like some mismatched married couple. Go grocery-shopping together, lugging bags up the steps, quarreling.

"Mud," he reverted to an old pet name. "You're dramatizing things. We're not like that." He reached for her hand; she jerked it away.

"Don't you hear what I'm saying?" she shouted. "Get out of here before I start hanging onto you!"

He looked at her steadily for a moment, his eyes unbearably sad. "I'm making plans," he said.

He had said this before.

"*This* time, we'll set a date." She went to her desk, scratched for her calendar, circled the date exactly one month from that day, filled in an index card—day, month, year. His full name across the top, her signature at the bottom. She wrote with marking pencil redder than her own blood.

In Walt Disney's nature series the sight of bear cubs sniffing a hollow log, looking for the mother who had deserted them, used to make her weep. Now she understood the necessity of abandonment. Otherwise, they'd grow into great lumbering hulks, lounging about the den, still nursing the mother—a sort of rape. Nature made its alternatives clear.

She handed him the card. He accepted it, pocketed it in his robe, then went upstairs. There was a fierce pride to his going—a boy unjustly sent to his room. Some mother-memory in her wailed its grief.

Phone calls began coming to the house. All day the phone rang. He would lunge for it, call out: "I'll get it." He began to dress, make trips out. The phone calls that came while he was gone were puzzling. Something about an ad. For work, she supposed. One caller mentioned California. She would put each phone message on a separate index card and stack them on the tv table.

Three things kept repeating in her memory. Her husband making his good-bye speech in the dawn-cold kitchen. Her grandmother urging her grandfather to take a trip on the 6:09: "You go down to watch it like some religious observance," she told him. "Some day, just get *on* it. Take you a trip." One day he had done exactly that, never returning. The third memory was of her uncle, goose-fat from excess mother-love, struggling away from his mother's embrace: "Don't leave me, don't leave me, don't leave me!" her grandmother had cried, for all the world like a deserted mistress.

Mothers binding their sons in ransom for their husbands. Had *she* done this to *her* son? Was this the cause of his inertia? She could not let herself think along these lines. They shared a house now: lodger and landlady. He did not even eat the evening meal at home.

The tv set was out of order. When you turned it on it went into kaleidoscopic color patterns, emitted hissing noises. He took his stereo up to his room, played records behind the closed door. Music from his new record floated down the stairwell. Something about a trip: the word *ticket* repeated, with endless sound-plays on it.

Two days before eviction date she came down to find his bank book on the kitchen table, displayed for her to see. The account closed out. No note. Upstairs one of his suitcases was missing; only a few clothes.

She waited a few days, then called his father. No, he had not seen him, heard from him. *The boy's going to be all right,* he told her. She hung up softly midway through the second repeating of this well-worn message.

A steady melancholy set in; as though her son had left his depression behind for her to catch. She called a tv repairman. The estimate was too high; better apply that amount to a new one.

"I've got it *some* better," the repairman told her as he left.

The sound, at least, worked better. Sometimes she turned it on, only to turn it off again. It sat, black and mute, like a faithful dog mourning its dead master.

One of her twin sons, breaking up his commune, sent her a calico cat to care for. A female (which she immediately had spayed), the cat gave the illusion of having on a worn cheap fur coat, ill-fitting about the shoulders and lapels and a matching fur hat badly angled on its head. Its appearance suggested a respectable but impoverished woman who each winter reemerged in her moth-balled furs.

The letter accompanying the cat (delivered by ten young people in a smoking truck) had warned: "She craps on the floor." She put food out; the cat ate it. That was the extent of their association. The cat would sit out on the rock wall and let passers-by pet it. The same people came by daily, making the cat-petting ritual a part of their day.

Going to the grocery store she would notice a portion of sidewalk with her four sons' initials carved in it, alongside the hand prints of the youngest three. The date, almost fifteen years before. She visualized her oldest son stooping, patiently guiding each small hand, then lettering in the initials with a stick. It was as though all four had died; this inscribed block of cement their gravestone.

To combat her depression she made herself see friends. She told them about evicting her son. What else could you do? women would ask over coffee. Some day he'll thank you for it, couples would say over highballs. Old friends, from early marriage; the ones she had kept custody of.

They told her to take an adult education course, get a new hair-style, find a part-time job, take yoga lessons. She did all these things. And began having love affairs. Men caught in bad marriages, in facade marriages, in dissolving marriages. She discovered in herself a hunger for men. Like a middle-aged Miranda, she looked at them with wonder, with awe. The timbre of their voices, their honest smells, their strong hands. Even their possessions: tobacco pouches, key rings, sometimes Boy Scout knives. They could talk on anything: a history of the bright-tobacco industry, statistics on highway construction since 1925, the passenger pigeon and its extinction. Knowledge stored up from boyhood.

Father loss. This diagnosis came to her once in the hour of early-waking, when she would lie in bed trying to figure out her life. Her father, dying young, had abandoned her to matriarchy. He was memorialized in:

1. *Marginalia.* His library was packed in boxes in the attic. She had always meant to have shelves built, put out all his books.

2. *A corpse-portrait.* Posthumously painted from photographs, it too was packed away in the attic, swathed in layers of heavy brown wrapping paper. It had hung over the mantel in his study all her childhood, the eyes following her wherever she went in that room.

3. *Artifacts.* Gold cuff links, tie clips, pongee handkerchiefs, fine silk scarves, fringed; pipes out of a Sherlock Holmes movie. Most were now divided among her sons. Lost, probably.

4. *Photographs*. These she brought out to reexamine. They all looked like pictures of her son, clean-shaven and re-costumed in World War I uniform or in clothes of the twenties. She had never noticed this strong resemblance before.

Each of her love affairs was intense but soon over. Periods of elation alternated with periods of near-despair. In the high periods she felt wonderfully young again. Like the second sister or the roommate in a World War II movie. Star of the sub-plot.

In the periods of letdown between love affairs she felt the chill of age move through her bones. She would remember her grandmother in her nursing-home crib, raised up by nurses. A rag doll with seamed mouth. Always, there were the generations of women—like a set of nested Russian dolls, each opening in the middle, birthing a smaller one; on down to the final indivisible embryo: herself. And now the process reversed: She carried them, re-nested, within herself, the tiny embryo of some distant ancestor.

Her son had been gone for over nine months now. Regularly she called her husband to see if he had heard. He had not, or else was not telling her. Now she called once more. Always the same: the voice of Wife III (he had divorced his second wife a year ago and remarried), a long pause, muffled talk, then her husband's voice. Resonant. Modulated. She had fallen in love with the voice first; afterwards, with the man. The voice had not changed. She suspected that the man had not either.

This time he reported he had had a letter.

"Where is he?" she asked.

"He wrote in transit, I believe. From one city to the other."

"*Where?*" If you pushed him too hard, he retreated into silence. She tried again: "You have no idea where he's settled?"

"I think you could say that he is of no fixed address."

She could see him, blandly smiling into the phone. She hung up.

Late one afternoon a tiny boy walked boldly into the yard. Watching him from the kitchen window she stood frozen like a fling-the-statue player. He looked just like her son had once looked: even to the lederhosen, even to the duck-tail at the back of his neck. The late afternoon cold had appled his cheeks. She turned off the coffee water and went to the door, throwing her son's old sheep-lined corduroy coat across her shoulders.

The boy was not the least bit dismayed when she came outside. He clearly belonged there; she could share the yard with him if she chose. He carried a paper bag, screwed at the top.

"Kitty!" he said to her. The cat had come to rub against his legs.

Seeing him close, she saw that he did not resemble her son as strongly as she had first thought. No more, perhaps, than one small blond boy resembles another.

Perhaps he had been kidnapped, released far from home after the ransom was received. Or abandoned...She would call the authorities, report he had been found, then offer to board him. It would take a long time to trace his parents. Meanwhile, he would stay with her. Abruptly she stopped fantasizing, shocked at this mother-hunger in her.

"Where's your mommy?" she asked him.

Enthralled by the cat, he did not answer. "Kitty *like* me," he shouted to the street.

She walked to the edge of the yard. A tall man was sauntering toward them. He was almost shockingly handsome. Blond, like the child. He looked thirty-five, maybe older; not a young father. He seemed preoccupied, touched with melancholy. A scholar?

"Go ahead, Lance, feed the kitty." He spoke with low-keyed impatience; like a mother, not a father. Then to her: "I hope you don't mind. We take a walk every afternoon and he's made friends with your cat. Today at nursery school he saved part of his lunch for it. Maybe I should have checked with you first."

He came into the yard and took the paper bag from his son, untwisting it to look inside. "No chicken bones," he said.

The boy was in a frenzy, climbing up his father's leg. "*Me* feed him! *Me feed him!*" he cried—an agony of sobs.

"All right, all right." The father handed him back the bag.

There was something martyred in his manner, as though he had had too much child-care. Maybe he had full-time charge of his son. A widower? Deserted? He would take the boy to a day-care center on his way to work, pick him up coming home. No life of his own.

The boy placed meat scraps, a boiled potato, a quarter of an apple, in front of the cat. "He's *eated* it!" he squealed as the cat lifted a piece of meat, mincing it like a woman of genteel poverty come in the cafeteria's off-hours to take advantage of lowered prices.

"Are you new to the neighborhood?" she asked the father.

"Just a few weeks," he answered. "I had one *devil* of a time finding a house."

No mention of a wife. Her mind shot inside her house, to highball glasses, the bottle of good saved Scotch, the living room cleaned that morning. A fire laid. She would work through the boy: ask him in to see the "play-toys" still kept in the barrel under the stairwell, handy for young visitors.

"Look, Daddy, he eated it!" the boy repeated.

"Yes," he answered. "Now we have to go."

Don't leave me, don't leave me, don't leave me! the mother-voice inside her wailed.

The boy was stroking the cat, lifting it gently by the tail until its back feet were off the ground. The cat patiently endured this. The father said: "Lance, come *on*. Mommy's waiting." The boy stooped, tried to force-feed the apple to the cat, then ran after his father. "Good-bye!" he shouted back, not to her but to the cat.

It struck her that neither father nor son had looked her in the face.

The boy's father scooped him up, deposited him on his shoulder. She watched them down the street, the boy's high-running laughter carried back to her. Something strangely like hatred stirred inside her. She walked back inside. To the clean living room, the laid fire, the toys stored beneath the stairwell.

The phone call from her son came almost exactly one year from the day she had given him his eviction notice.

"Mud?" The voice strong, clear. (She knew it was long distance—person-to-person, the operator had come on first. A needless expense.)

She spoke his name; the sound of it stirred a need to weep.

"Look, Mud," he said, almost brusquely. "Get a pencil and write this down. In *exactly* three minutes, there is to be a tv program. Education channel...let's see..." He *um*ed as though consulting something. "Channel 29. Got that? A special education series. 'Pebbles,' it's called. Experimental. Also I guess you could say experiential." He paused, admiring his pedantry. "Now I want you to go turn it on. *Now!*"

"You called me up just to tell me about some tv program?"

"*Watch* it!" he commanded. Then more tenderly: "Good-bye, Mud."

She hung up the phone and went to the tv, found the U, then the right channel; fiddled with the antenna. Kaleidoscopings. Shrieks of red. Green rain. But the sound worked. She heard music, haunting-sweet, stirring memories. The words sung by some young Burl Ives; words somehow familiar.

Through color shocks she could see the figure of a boy, knapsacked, walking down a road. Names slid down the screen—a piece of her son's name. She squinted the rest into focus—his full name! It slid down into oblivion before she could make out the credit. She dealt the top of the set a hammer blow. It shuddered, almost focused, then subsided, hissing ominously.

She raced to the door, grabbing her son's coat. The cat, unfed, was huddled just outside. It shot in, nearly losing its tail in the slam. Outside, she stood looking at the locked door, remembering too late her keys, the tv still on and hissing. She would come home to a blazing house, ignited by color tv, kindled by accumulated newspapers. The cat trapped inside. Spared this, there were lesser horrors to be faced. Meat left to thaw on the drainboard: cat-gnawed. Cat pee all over the house, smelling for days.

She stood on the porch, feeling herself dissolve into vagueness—a floating Chagall figure searching down the street for something lost. Cold seeped around the corduroy coat. She came to. Let the house burn! Let it stink! She paused just long enough to pick the most likely house, the best-functioning tv set, then raced out to the sidewalk and down the street.

SHIRLEY COCHRANE grew up in Chapel Hill, North Carolina, and lives in Washington, D.C., and teaches at Georgetown University. Her work has appeared in many anthologies and periodicals, and she has written two books of poetry.

Everyday Use

A L I C E   W A L K E R

I WILL WAIT FOR HER in the yard that Maggie and I made so clean and wavy yesterday afternoon. A yard like this is more comfortable than most people know. Is is not just a yard. It is like an extended living room. When the hard clay is swept clean as a floor and the fine sand around the edges lined with tiny, irregular grooves, anyone can come and sit and look up into the elm tree and wait for the breezes that never come inside the house.

Maggie will be nervous until after her sister goes: she will stand hopelessly in corners, homely and ashamed of the burn scars down her arms and legs, eying her sister with a mixture of envy and awe. She thinks her sister has held life always in the palm of one hand, that "no" is a word the world never learned to say to her.

You've no doubt seen those TV shows where the child who has "made it" is confronted, as a surprise, by her own mother and father, tottering in weakly from backstage. (A pleasant surprise, of course: What would they do if parent and child came on the show only to curse out and insult each other?) On TV mother and child embrace and smile into each other's faces. Sometimes the mother and father weep, the child wraps them in her arms and leans across the table to tell how she would not have made it without their help. I have seen these programs.

Sometimes I dream a dream in which Dee and I are suddenly brought together on a TV program of this sort. Out of a dark and soft-seated limousine I am ushered into a bright room filled with many people. There I meet a smiling, gray, sporty man like Johnny Carson who shakes my hand and tells me what a fine girl I have. Then we are on the stage and Dee is embracing me with tears in her eyes. She pins on my dress a large orchid, even though she has told me once that she thinks orchids are tacky flowers.

In real life I am a large big-boned woman with rough, man-working hands. In the winter I wear flannel nightgowns to bed and overalls during the day. I can kill and clean a hog as mercilessly as a man. My fat keeps me hot in zero weather. I can work outside all day, breaking ice to get water for washing; I can eat pork liver cooked over the open fire minutes after it comes steaming from the hog. One winter I knocked a bull calf straight in the brain between the eyes with a sledge hammer and had the meat hung up to chill before nightfall. But of course all this does not show on television. I am the way my daughter would want me to be: a hundred pounds lighter, my skin like an uncooked barley pancake. My hair glistens in the hot bright lights. Johnny Carson has much to do to keep up with my quick and witty tongue.

But that is a mistake. I know even before I wake up. Who ever knew a Johnson with a quick tongue? Who can even imagine me looking a strange white man in the eye? It seems to me I have talked to them always with one foot raised in flight, with my head turned in whichever way is farthest from them. Dee, though. She would always look anyone in the eye. Hesitation was no part of her nature.

"How do I look, Mama?" Maggie says, showing just enough of her thin body enveloped in pink skirt and red blouse for me to know she's there, almost hidden by the door.

"Come out into the yard," I say.

Have you ever seen a lame animal, perhaps a dog run over by some careless person rich enough to own a car, sidle up to someone who is ignorant enough to be kind to him? That is the way my Maggie walks. She has been like this, chin on chest, eyes on ground, feet in shuffle, ever since the fire that burned the other house to the ground.

Dee is lighter than Maggie, with nicer hair and a fuller figure. She's a woman now, though sometimes I forget. How long ago was it that the other house burned? Ten, twelve years? Sometimes I can still hear the flames and feel Maggie's arm sticking to me, her hair smoking and her dress falling off her in little black papery flakes. Her eyes seem stretched open, blazed open by the flames reflected in them. And Dee. I see her standing off under the sweet gum tree she used to dig gum out of; a look of concentration on her face as she watched the last dingy gray board of the house fall in toward the red-hot brick chimney. Why don't you do a dance around the ashes? I'd wanted to ask her. She had hated the house that much.

I used to think she hated Maggie, too. But that was before we raised the money, the church and me, to send her to Augusta to school. She used to read to us without pity; forcing words, lies, other folks' habits, whole lives upon us two, sitting trapped and ignorant underneath her voice. She washed us in a river of make-believe, burned us with a lot of knowledge we didn't necessarily need to know. Pressed us to her with the serious way she read, to shove us away at just the moment, like dimwits, we seemed about to understand.

Dee wanted nice things. A yellow organdy dress to wear to her graduation from high school; black pumps to match a green suit she'd made from an old suit somebody gave me. She was determined to stare down any disaster in her efforts. Her eyelids would not flicker for minutes at a time. Often I fought off the temptation to shake her. At sixteen she had a style of her own: and knew what style was.

I never had an education myself. After second grade the school was closed down. Don't ask me why: in 1927 colored asked fewer questions than they do now. Sometimes Maggie reads to me. She stumbles along good-naturedly but can't see well. She knows she is not bright. Like good looks and money, quickness passed her by. She will marry John Thomas (who has mossy teeth in an earnest face) and then I'll be free to sit here and I guess just sing church songs to myself. Although I never was a good singer. Never could carry a tune. I was always better at a man's job. I used to love to milk till I was hooked in the side in '49. Cows are soothing and slow and don't bother you, unless you try to milk them the wrong way.

I have deliberately turned my back on the house. It is three rooms, just like the one that burned, except the roof is tin; they don't make shingle roofs any more. There are no real windows, just some holes cut in the sides, like the portholes in a ship, but not round and not square, with rawhide holding the shutters up on the outside. This house is in a pasture, too, like the other one. No doubt when Dee sees it she will want to tear it down. She wrote me once that no matter where we "choose" to live, she will manage to come see us. But she will never bring her friends. Maggie and I thought about this and Maggie asked me, "Mama, when did Dee ever *have* any friends?"

She had a few. Furtive boys in pink shirts hanging about on washday after school. Nervous girls who never laughed. Impressed with her they worshiped the well-turned phrase, the cute shape, the scalding humor that erupted like bubbles in lye. She read to them.

When she was courting Jimmy T she didn't have much time to pay to us, but turned all her faultfinding power on him. He *flew* to marry a cheap city girl from a family of ignorant flashy people. She hardly had time to recompose herself.

When she comes I will meet—but there they are!

Maggie attempts to make a dash for the house, in her shuffling way, but I stay her with my hand. "Come back here," I say. And she stops and tries to dig a well in the sand with her toe.

It is hard to see them clearly through the strong sun. But even the first glimpse of leg out of the car tells me it is Dee. Her feet were always neat-looking, as if God himself had shaped them with a certain style. From the other side of the car comes a short, stocky man. Hair is all over his head a foot long and hanging from his chin like a kinky mule tail. I hear Maggie suck in her breath. "Uhnnnh," is what it sounds like. Like when you see the wriggling end of a snake just in front of your foot on the road. "Uhnnnh."

Dee next. A dress down to the ground, in this hot weather. A dress so loud it hurts my eyes. There are yellows and oranges enough to throw back the light of the sun. I feel my whole face warming from the heat waves it throws out. Earrings gold, too, and hanging down to her shoulders. Bracelets dangling and making noises when she moves her arm up to shake the folds of the dress out of her armpits. The dress is loose and flows, and as she walks closer, I like it. I hear Maggie go "Uhnnnh" again. It is her sister's hair. It stands straight up like the wool on a sheep. It is black as night and around the edges are two long pigtails that rope about like small lizards disappearing behind her ears.

"Wa-su-zo-Tean-o!" she says, coming on in that gliding way the dress makes her move. The short stocky fellow with the hair to his navel is all grinning and he follows up with "Asalamalakim, my mother and sister!" He moves to hug Maggie but she falls back, right up against the back of my chair. I feel her trembling there and when I look up I see the perspiration falling off her chin.

"Don't get up," says Dee. Since I am stout it takes something of a push. You can see me trying to move a second or two before I make it. She turns, showing white heels through her sandals, and goes back to the car. Out she peeks next with a Polaroid. She stoops down quickly and lines up picture after picture of me sitting there in front of the house with Maggie cowering behind me. She never takes a shot without making sure the house is included. When a cow comes nibbling around the edge of the yard she snaps it and me and Maggie *and* the house. Then she puts the Polaroid in the back seat of the car, and comes up and kisses me on the forehead.

Meanwhile Asalamalakim is going through motions with Maggie's hand. Maggie's hand is as limp as a fish, and probably as cold, despite the sweat, and she keeps trying to pull it back. It looks like Asalamalakim wants to shake hands but wants to do it fancy. Or maybe he don't know how people shake hands. Anyhow, he soon gives up on Maggie.

"Well," I say. "Dee."

"No, Mama," she says. "Not 'Dee,' Wangero Leewanika Kemanjo!"

"What happened to 'Dee'?" I wanted to know.

"She's dead," Wangero said. "I couldn't bear it any longer, being named after the people who oppress me."

"You know as well as me you was named after your aunt Dicie," I said. Dicie is my sister. She named Dee. We called her "Big Dee" after Dee was born.

"But who was *she* named after?" asked Wangero.

"I guess after Grandma Dee," I said

"And who was she named after?" asked Wangero.

"Her mother," I said, and saw Wangero was getting tired. "That's about as far back as I can trace it," I said. Though, in fact, I probably could have carried it back beyond the Civil War through the branches.

"Well," said Asalamalakim, "there you are."

"Uhnnnh," I heard Maggie say.

"There I was not," I said, "before 'Dicie' cropped up in our family, so why should I try to trace it that far back?"

He just stood there grinning, looking down on me like somebody inspecting a Model A car. Every once in a while he and Wangero sent eye signals over my head.

"How do you pronounce this name?" I asked

"You don't have to call me by it if you don't want to," said Wangero.

"Why shouldn't I?" I asked. "If that's what you want us to call you, we'll call you."

"I know it might seem awkward at first," said Wangero.

"I'll get used to it," I said. "Ream it out again."

Well, soon we got the name out of the way. Asalamalakim had a name twice as long and three times as hard. After I tripped over it it two or three times he told me to just call him Hakim-a-barber. I wanted to ask him was he a barber, but I didn't really think he was, so I didn't ask.

"You must belong to those beef-cattle peoples down the road," I said. They said "Asalamalakim" when they met you, too, but they didn't shake hands. Always to busy: feeding the cattle, fixing the fences, putting up salt-lick shelters, throwing down hay. When the white folks poisoned some of the herd the men stayed up all night with rifles in their hands. I walked a mile and a half just to see the sight.

Hakim-a-barber said, "I accept some of their doctrines, but farming and raising cattle is not my style." (They didn't tell me, and I didn't ask, whether Wangero (Dee) had really gone and married him.)

We sat down to eat and right away he said he didn't eat collards and pork was unclean. Wangero, though, went on through the chitlins and corn bread, the greens and everything else. She talked a blue streak over the sweet potatoes. Everything delighted her. Even the fact that we still used the benches her daddy made for the table when we couldn't afford to buy chairs.

"Oh, Mama!" she cried. Then turned to Hakim-a-barber. "I never knew how lovely these benches are. You can feel the rump prints," she said, running her hands underneath her and along the bench. Then she gave a sigh and her hand closed over Grandma Dee's butter dish. "That's it!" she said. "I knew there was something I wanted to ask you if I could have." She jumped up from the table and went over in the corner where the churn stood, the milk in it clabber by now. She looked at the churn and looked at it.

"This churn top is what I need," she said. Didn't Uncle Buddy whittle it out of a tree you all used to have?"

"Yes," I said.

"Uh huh," she said happily. "And I want the dasher, too."

"Uncle Buddy whittle that, too?" asked the barber.

Dee (Wangero) looked up at me.

"Aunt Dee's first husband whittled the dash," said Maggie so low you almost couldn't hear her. "His name was Henry, but they called him Stash."

"Maggie's brain is like an elephant's," Wangero said, laughing. "I can use the churn top as a centerpiece for the alcove table," she said, sliding a plate over the churn, "and I'll think of something artistic to do with the dasher."

When she finished wrapping the dasher the handle stuck out. I took it for a moment in my hands. You didn't even have to look close to see where hands pushing the dasher up and down to make butter had left a kind of sink in the wood. In fact, there were a lot of small sinks; you could see where thumbs and fingers had sunk into the wood. It was beautiful light yellow wood, from a tree that grew in the yard where Big Dee and Stash had lived.

After dinner Dee (Wangero) went to the trunk at the foot of my bed and started rifling through it. Maggie hung back in the kitchen over the dishpan. Out came Wangero with two quilts. They had been pieced by Grandma Dee and then Big Dee and me had hung them on the quilt frames on the front porch and quilted them. One was in the Lone Star pattern. The other was Walk Around the Mountain. In both of them were scraps of dresses Grandma Dee had worn fifty and more years ago. Bits and pieces of Grandpa Jarrell's Paisley shirts. And one teeny faded blue piece, about the size of a penny matchbox, that was from Great Grandpa Ezra's uniform that he wore in the Civil War.

"Mama," Wangero said sweet as a bird. "Can I have these old quilts?"

I heard something fall in the kitchen, and a minute later the kitchen door slammed.

"Why don't you take one or two of the others?" I asked. "These old things was just done by me and Big Dee from some tops your grandma pieced before she died."

"No," said Wangero. "I don't want those. They are stitched around the borders by machine."

"That'll make them last better," I said.

"That's not the point," said Wangero. "These are all pieces of dresses Grandma used to wear. She did all this stitching by hand. Imagine!" She held the quilts securely in her arms, stroking them.

"Some of the pieces, like those lavender ones, come from old clothes her mother handed down to her," I said, moving up to touch the quilts. Dee (Wangero) moved back just enough so that I couldn't reach the quilts. They already belonged to her.

"Imagine!" she breathed again, clutching them closely to her bosom.

"The truth is," I said, "I promised to give them quilts to Maggie, for when she marries John Thomas."

She gasped like a bee had stung her.

"Maggie can't appreciate these quilts!" she said. "She'd probably be backward enough to put them to everyday use."

"I reckon she would," I said. "God knows I been saving 'em long enough with nobody using 'em. I hope she will!" I didn't want to bring up how I had offered Dee (Wangero) a quilt when she went away to college. Then she had told me they were old-fashioned, out of style.

"But they're *priceless!*" she was saying now, furiously; for she has a temper. "Maggie would put them on the bed and in five years they'd be in rags. Less than that!"

"She can always make some more," I said. "Maggie knows how to quilt."

Dee (Wangero) looked at me with hatred. "You just will not understand. The point is these quilts, *these* quilts!"

"Well," I said, stumped. "What would *you* do with them?"

"Hang them," she said. As if that was the only thing you *could* do with quilts.

Maggie by now was standing in the door. I could almost hear the sound her feet made as they scraped over each other.

"She can have them, Mama," she said, like somebody used to never winning anything, or having anything reserved for her. "I can 'member Grandma Dee without the quilts."

I looked at her hard. She had filled her bottom lip with checkerberry snuff and it gave her face a kind of dopey, hangdog look. It was Grandma Dee and Big Dee who taught her how to quilt herself. She stood there with her scarred hands hidden in the folds of her skirt. She looked at her sister with something like fear but she wasn't mad at her. This was Maggie's portion. This was the way she knew God to work.

When I looked at her like that something hit me in the top of my head and ran down to the soles of my feet. Just like when I'm in church and the spirit of God touches me and I get happy and shout. I did something I never had done before: hugged Maggie to me, then dragged her on into the room, snatched the quilts out of Miss Wangero's hands and dumped them into Maggie's lap. Maggie just sat there on my bed with her mouth open.

"Take one or two of the others," I said to Dee.

But she turned without a word and went out to Hakim-a-barber.

"You just don't understand," she said, as Maggie and I came out to the car.

"What don't I understand?" I wanted to know.

"Your heritage," she said. And then she turned to Maggie, kissed her, and said, "You ought to try to make something of yourself, too, Maggie. It's really a new day for us. But from the way you and Mama still live you'd never know it."

She put on some sunglasses that hid everything above the tip of her nose and her chin.

Maggie smiled; maybe at the sunglasses. But a real smile, not scared. After we watched the car dust settle I asked Maggie to bring me a dip of snuff. And then the two of us sat there just enjoying, until it was time to go in the house and go to bed.

ALICE WALKER, a native of Eatonton, Georgia, is the author of fiction, poetry, and numerous essays. Her novel The Color Purple *was awarded the 1983 Pulitzer Prize for fiction and the American Book Award.*

A Christmas Memory

T R U M A N   C A P O T E

IMAGINE A MORNING IN late November. A coming of winter morning more than twenty years ago. Consider the kitchen of a spreading old house in a country town. A great black stove is its main feature; but there is also a big round table and a fireplace with two rocking chairs placed in front of it. Just today the fireplace commenced its seasonal roar.

A woman with shorn white hair is standing at the kitchen window. She is wearing tennis shoes and a shapeless grey sweater over a summery calico dress. She is small and sprightly, like a bantam hen; but, due to a long youthful illness, her shoulders are pitifully hunched. Her face is remarkable—not unlike Lincoln's, craggy like that, and tinted by sun and wind; but it is delicate too, finely boned, and her eyes are sherry-colored and timid. "Oh my," she exclaims, her breath smoking the windowpane, "it's fruitcake weather!"

The person to whom she is speaking is myself. I am seven; she is sixty-something. We are cousins, very distant ones, and we have lived together—well, as long as I can remember. Other people inhabit the house, relatives; and though they have power over us, and frequently make us cry, we are not, on the whole, too much aware of them. We are each other's best friend. She calls me Buddy, in memory of a boy who was formerly her best friend. The other Buddy died in the 1880s, when she was still a child. She is still a child.

"I knew it before I got out of bed," she says, turning away from the window with a purposeful excitement in her eyes. "The courthouse bell sounded so cold and clear. And there were no birds singing; they're gone to warmer country, yes indeed. Oh, Buddy, stop stuffing biscuit and fetch our buggy. Help me find my hat. We've thirty cakes to bake."

It's always the same: a morning arrives in November, and my friend, as though officially inaugurating the Christmas time of year that exhilarates her imagination and fuels the blaze of her heart, announces: "It's fruitcake weather! Fetch our buggy. Help me find my hat."

The hat is found, a straw cartwheel corsaged with velvet roses out-of-doors has faded: it once belonged to a more fashionable relative. Together, we guide our buggy, a dilapidated baby carriage, out to the garden and into a grove of pecan trees. The buggy is mine; that is, it was bought for me when I was born. It is made of wicker, rather unraveled, and the wheels wobble like a drunkard's legs. But it is a faithful object; springtimes, we take it to the woods and fill it with flowers, herbs, wild fern for our porch pots; in the summer, we pile it with picnic paraphernalia and sugarcane fishing poles and roll it down to the edge of a creek; it has its winter uses, too: as a truck for hauling firewood from the yard to the kitchen, as a warm bed for Queenie, our tough little orange and white rat terrier who has survived distemper and two rattlesnake bites. Queenie is trotting beside it now.

Three hours later we are back in the kitchen hulling a heaping buggyload of windfall pecans. Our backs hurt from gathering them: how hard they were to find (the main crop having been shaken off the trees and sold by the orchard's owners, who are not us) among the concealing leaves, the frosted, deceiving grass. Caarackle! A cheery crunch, scraps of miniature thunder sound as the shells collapse and the golden mound of sweet oily ivory meat mounts in the milk-glass bowl. Queenie begs to taste, and now and again my friend sneaks her a mite, though insisting we deprive ourselves. "We mustn't, Buddy. If we start, we won't stop. And there's scarcely enough as there is. For thirty cakes." The kitchen is growing dark. Dusk turns the window into a mirror: our reflections mingle with the rising moon as we work by the fireside in the firelight. At last, when the moon is quite high, we toss the final hull into the fire and, with joined sighs, watch it catch flame. The buggy is empty, the bowl is brimful.

We eat our supper (cold biscuits, bacon, blackberry jam) and discuss tomorrow. Tomorrow the kind of work I like best begins: buying. Cherries and citron, ginger and vanilla and canned Hawaiian pineapple, rinds and raisins and walnuts and whiskey and oh, so much flour, butter, so many eggs, spices, flavorings: why, we'll need a pony to pull the buggy home.

But before these purchases can be made, there is the question of money. Neither of us has any. Except for skinflint sums persons in the house occasionally provide (a dime is considered very big money); or what we earn ourselves from various activities: holding rummage sales, selling buckets of hand-picked blackberries, jars of homemade jam and apple jelly and peach preserves, rounding up flowers for funerals and weddings. Once we won seventy-ninth prize, five dollars, in a national football contest. Not that we know a fool thing about football. It's just that we enter any contest we hear about: at the moment our hopes are centered on the fifty-thousand-dollar Grand Prize being offered to name a new brand of coffee (we suggested "A.M."; and, after some hesitation, for my friend thought it perhaps sacrilegious, the slogan "A.M.! Amen!"). To tell the truth, our only *really* profitable enterprise was the Fun and Freak Museum we conducted in a backyard wood-shed two summers ago. The Fun was a stereopticon with slide views of Washington and New York lent us by a relative who had been to those places (she was furious when she discovered why we'd borrowed it); the Freak was a three-legged biddy chicken hatched by one of our own hens. Everybody hereabouts wanted to see that biddy: we charged grown-ups a nickel, kids two cents. And took in a good twenty dollars before the museum shut down due to the decease of the main attraction.

But one way or another we do each year accumulate Christmas savings, a Fruitcake Fund. These moneys we keep hidden in an ancient bead purse under a loose board under the floor under a chamber pot under my friend's bed. The purse is seldom removed from this safe location except to make a deposit, or, as happens every Saturday, a withdrawal; for on Saturdays I am allowed ten cents to go to the picture show. My friend has never been to a picture show, nor does she intend to: "I'd rather hear you tell the story, Buddy. That way I can imagine it more. Besides, a person my age shouldn't squander their eyes. When the Lord comes, let me see him clear." In addition to never having seen a movie, she has never: eaten in a restaurant, traveled more than five miles from home, received or sent a telegram, read anything except funny papers and the Bible, worn cosmetics, cursed, wished someone harm, told a lie on purpose, let a hungry dog go hungry. Here are a few things she has done, does do: killed with a hoe the biggest rattlesnake ever seen in this county (sixteen rattles), dip snuff (secretly), tame hummingbirds (just try it) till they balance on her finger, tell ghost stories (we both believe in ghosts) so tingling they chill you in July, talk to herself, take walks in the rain, grow the prettiest japonicas in town, know the recipe for every sort of old-time Indian cure, including a magical wart-remover.

Now, with supper finished, we retire to the room in a faraway part of the house where my friend sleeps in a scrap-quilt-covered iron bed painted rose pink, her favorite color. Silently, wallowing in the pleasures of conspiracy, we take the bead purse from its secret place and spill its contents on the scrap quilt. Dollar bills, tightly rolled and green as May buds. Somber fifty-cent pieces, heavy enough to weight a dead man's eyes. Lovely dimes, the liveliest coin, the one that really jingles. Nickels and quarters, worn smooth as creek pebbles. But mostly a hateful heap of bitter-odored pennies. Last summer others in the house contracted to pay us a penny for every twenty-five flies we killed. Oh, the carnage of August: the flies that flew to heaven! Yet it was not work in which we took pride. And, as we sit counting pennies, it is as though we were back tabulating dead flies. Neither of us has a head for figures; we count slowly, lose track, start again. According to her calculations, we have $12.73. According to mine, exactly $13. "I do hope you're wrong, Buddy. We can't mess around with thirteen. The cakes will fall. Or put somebody in the cemetery. Why, I wouldn't dream of getting out of bed on the thirteenth." This is true: she always spends thirteenths in bed. So to be on the safe side, we subtract a penny and toss it out the window.

Of the ingredients that go into our fruitcakes, whiskey is the most expensive, as well as the hardest to obtain: State laws forbid its sale. But everybody knows you can buy a bottle from Mr. Haha Jones. And the next day, having completed our more prosaic shopping, we set out for Mr. Haha's business address, a "sinful" (to quote public opinion) fish-fry and dancing cafe down by the river. We've been there before, and on the same errand; but in previous years our dealings have been with Haha's wife, an iodine-dark Indian woman with brassy peroxided hair and a dead-tired disposition. Actually, we've never laid eyes on her husband, though we've heard that he's an Indian too. A giant with razor scars across his cheeks. They call him Haha because he's so gloomy, a man who never laughs. As we approach this cafe (a large log cabin festooned inside and out with chains of garish-gay naked light bulbs and standing by the river's muddy edge under the shade of river trees where moss drifts through the branches like gray mist) our steps slow down. Even Queenie stops prancing and sticks close by. People have been murdered in Haha's cafe. Cut to pieces. Hit on the head. There's a case coming up in court next month. Naturally these goings-on happen at night when the colored lights cast crazy patterns and the victrola wails. In the daytime Haha's is shabby and deserted. I knock at the door, Queenie barks, my friend calls: "Mrs. Haha, ma'am? Anyone to home?"

Footsteps. The door opens. Our hearts overturn. It's Mr. Haha Jones himself! And he *is* a giant; he *does* have scars; he *doesn't* smile. No, he glowers at us through Satan-tilted eyes and demands to know: "What you want with Haha?"

For a moment we are too paralyzed to tell. Presently my friend half-finds her voice, a whispery voice at best: "If you please, Mr. Haha, we'd like a quart of your finest whiskey."

His eyes tilt more. Would you believe it? Haha is smiling! Laughing, too. "Which one of you is a drinkin' man?"

"It's for making fruitcakes, Mr. Haha. Cooking."

This sobers him. He frowns. "That's no way to waste good whiskey." Nevertheless, he retreats into the shadowed cafe and seconds later appears carrying a bottle of daisy yellow unlabeled liquor. He demonstrates its sparkle in the sunlight and says: "Two dollars."

We pay him with nickels and dimes and pennies. Suddenly, jangling the coins in his hand like a fistfull of dice, his face softens. "Tell you what," he proposes, pouring the money back into our bead purse, "just send me one of them fruitcakes instead."

"Well," my friend remarks on our way home, "there's a lovely man. We'll put an extra cup of raisins in *his* cake."

The black stove, stoked with coal and firewood, glows like a lighted pumpkin. Eggbeaters whirl, spoons spin round in bowls of butter and sugar, vanilla sweetens the air, ginger spices it; melting, nose-tingling odors saturate the kitchen, suffuse the house, drift out to the world on puffs of chimney smoke. In four days our work is done, Thirty-one cakes, dampened with whiskey, bask on window sills and shelves.

Who are they for?

Friends. Not necessarily neighbor friends: indeed the larger share are intended for persons we've met maybe once, perhaps not at all. People who've struck our fancy. Like President Roosevelt. Like the Reverend and Mrs. J.C. Lucey, Baptist missionaries to Borneo who lectured here last winter. Or the little knife grinder who comes through town twice a year. Or Abner Packer, the driver of the six o'clock bus from Mobile, who exchanges waves with us every day as he passes in a dust-cloud whoosh. Or the young Wistons, a California couple whose car one afternoon broke down outside the house and who spent a pleasant hour chatting with us on the porch (young Mr. Wiston snapped our picture, the only one we've ever had taken). Is it because my friend is shy with everyone *except* strangers, that these strangers, and merest acquaintances, seem to us our truest friends? I think yes. Also, the scrapbooks we keep of thank-you's on White House stationery, time-to-time communications from California and Borneo, the knife-grinder's penny postcards, make us feel connected to eventful worlds beyond the kitchen with its view of a sky that stops.

Now a nude December fig branch grates against the window. The kitchen is empty, the cakes are gone; yesterday we carted the last of them to the post office, where the cost of stamps turned our purse inside out. We're broke. That rather depresses me, but my friend insists on celebrating—with two inches of whiskey left in Haha's bottle. Queenie has a spoonful in a bowl of coffee (she likes her coffee chicory-flavored and strong). The rest we divide between a pair of jelly glasses. We're both quite awed at the prospect of drinking straight whiskey; the taste of it brings screwed-up expressions and sour shudders. But by and by we begin to sing, the two of us singing different songs simultaneously. I don't know the words to mine, just: *Come on along, come on along, to the dark-town strutters' ball.* But I can dance: that's what I mean to be, a tap dancer in the movies. My dancing shadow rollicks on the walls; our voices rock the chinaware; we giggle: as if unseen hands were tickling us. Queenie rolls on her back, her paws plough the air, something like a grin stretches her black lips. Inside myself, I feel warm and sparky as those crumbling logs, carefree as the wind in the chimney. My friend waltzes round the stove, the hem of her poor calico skirt pinched between her fingers as though it were a party dress: *Show me the way to go home,* she sings, her tennis shoes squeaking on the floor. *Show me the way to go home.*

Enter: two relatives. Very angry. Potent with eyes that scold, tongues that scald. Listen to what they have to say, the words tumbling together into a wrathful tune: "A child of seven! whiskey on his breath! are you out of your mind? feeding a child of seven! must be loony! road to ruination! remember Cousin Kate? Uncle Charlie? Uncle Charlie's brother-in-law? shame! scandal! humiliation! kneel, pray, beg the Lord!"

Queenie sneaks under the stove. My friend gazes at her shoes, her chin quivers, she lifts her skirt and blows her nose and runs to her room. Long after the town has gone to sleep and the house is silent except for the chimings of the clocks and the sputter of fading fires, she is weeping into a pillow already as wet as a widow's handkerchief.

"Don't cry," I say, sitting at the bottom of her bed and shivering despite my flannel nightgown that smells of last winter's cough syrup, "don't cry," I beg, teasing her toes, tickling her feet, "you're too old for that."

"It's because," she hiccups, "I *am* too old. Old and funny."

"Not funny. Fun. More fun than anybody. Listen. If you don't stop crying you'll be so tired tomorrow we can't go cut a tree."

She straightens up. Queenie jumps on the bed (where Queenie is not allowed) to lick her cheeks. "I know where we'll find real pretty trees, Buddy. And holly, too. With berries big as your eyes. It's way off in the woods. Farther than we've ever been. Papa used to bring us Christmas trees from there: carry them on his shoulder. That's fifty years ago. Well, now: I can't wait for morning."

Morning. Frozen rime lusters the grass; the sun, round as an orange and orange as hot-weather moons, balances on the horizon, burnishes the silvered winter woods. A wild turkey calls. A renegade hog grunts in the undergrowth. Soon, by the edge of knee-deep, rapid-running water, we have to abandon the buggy. Queenie wades the stream first, paddles across barking complaints at the swiftness of the current, the pneumonia-making coldness of it. We follow, holding our shoes and equipment (a hatchet, a burlap sack) above our heads. A mile more of chastising thorns, burrs, and briers that catch at our clothes; of rusty pine needles brilliant with gaudy fungus and moulted feathers. Here, there, a flash, a flutter, an ecstasy of shrillings remind us that not all birds have flown south. Always, the path unwinds through lemony sun pools and pitch vine tunnels. Another creek to cross: a disturbed armada of speckled trout froths the water round us; beaver workmen are building a dam. On the farther shore, Queenie shakes herself and trembles. My friend shivers, too: not with cold but enthusiasm. One of her hat's ragged roses sheds a petal as she lifts her head and inhales the pine-heavy air. "We're almost there; can you smell it, Buddy?" she says, as though we were approaching an ocean.

And, indeed, it is a kind of ocean. Scented acres of holiday trees, prickly-leafed holly. Red berries shiny as Chinese bells: black crows swoop upon them screaming. Having stuffed our burlap sacks with enough greenery and crimson to garland a dozen windows, we set about choosing a tree. "It should be," muses my friend, "twice as tall as a boy. So a boy can't steal the star." The one we pick is twice as tall as me. A brave handsome brute that survives thirty hatchet strokes before it keels with a cracking rending cry. Lugging it like a kill, we commence the long trek out. Every few yards we abandon the struggle, sit down, and pant. But we have the strength of triumphant huntsmen; that and the tree's virile, icy perfume revive us, goad us on. Many compliments accompany our sunset return along the red clay road to town; but my friend is sly and non-committal when passers-by praise the treasure perched in our buggy: what a fine tree and where did it come from? "Yonderways," she murmurs vaguely. Once a car stops and the rich mill owner's lazy wife leans out and whines: "Giveya two-bits cash for that ol tree." Ordinarily my friend is afraid of saying no; but on this occasion she promptly shakes her head: "We wouldn't take a dollar." The mill owner's wife persists. "A dollar, my foot! Fifty cents. That's my last offer. Goodness, woman, you can get another one." In answer, my friend gently reflects: "I doubt it. There's never two of anything."

Home: Queenie slumps by the fire and sleeps till tomorrow, snoring loud as a human.

A trunk in the attic contains: a shoebox of ermine tails (off the opera cape of a curious lady who once rented a room in the house), coils of frazzled tinsel gone gold with age, one silver star, a brief rope of dilapidated, undoubtedly dangerous candy-like light bulbs. Excellent decorations, as far as they go, which isn't far enough: my friend wants our tree to blaze "like a Baptist window," droop with weighty snows of ornament. But we can't afford the made-in-Japan splendors at the five-and-dime. So we do what we've always done: sit for days at the kitchen table with scissors and crayons and stacks of colored paper. I make sketches and my friend cuts them out: lots of cats, fish too (because they're easy to draw), some apples, some watermelons, a few winged angels devised from saved-up sheets of Hershey-bar tin foil. We use safety pins to attach these creations to the tree; as a final touch, we sprinkle the branches with shredded cotton (picked in August for this purpose). My friend, surveying the effect, clasps her hands together. "Now honest, Buddy. Doesn't it look good enough to eat?" Queenie tries to eat an angel.

After weaving and ribboning holly wreaths for all the front windows, our next project is the fashioning of family gifts. Tie-dye scarves for the ladies, for the men a home-brewed lemon and licorice and aspirin syrup to be taken "at the first Symptoms of a Cold and after Hunting." But when it comes time for making each other's gift, my friend and I separate to work secretly. I would like to buy her a pearl-handled knife, a radio, a whole pound of chocolate-covered cherries (we tasted some once, and she always swears: "I could live on them, Buddy, Lord yes I could—and that's not taking Him name in vain"). Instead, I am building her a kite. She would like to give me a bicycle (she's said so on several million occasions: "If only I could, Buddy. It's bad enough in life to do without something *you* want; but confound it, what gets my goat is not being able to give somebody something you want *them* to have. Only one of these days I will, Buddy. Locate you a bike. Don't ask how. Steal it maybe"). Instead, I'm fairly certain that she is building me a kite—the same as last year, and the year before: the year before that we exchanged slingshots. All of which is fine by me. For we are champion kite-fliers who study the wind like sailors; my friend, more accomplished than I, can get a kite aloft when there isn't enough breeze to carry clouds.

Christmas Eve afternoon we scrape together a nickel and go to the butcher's to buy Queenie's traditional gift, a good gnawable beef bone. The bone, wrapped in funny paper, is placed high in the tree near the silver star. Queenie knows it's there. She squats at the foot of the tree staring up in a trance of greed: when bedtime arrives she refuses to budge. Her excitement is equaled by my own. I kick the covers and turn my pillow as though it were a scorching summer's night. Somewhere a rooster crows: falsely, for the sun is still on the other side of the world.

"Buddy, are you awake?" It is my friend, calling from her room, which is next to mine; and an instant later she is sitting on my bed holding a candle. "Well, I can't sleep a hoot," she declares. "My mind's jumping like a jack rabbit. Buddy, do you think Mrs. Roosevelt will serve our cake at dinner?" We huddle in the bed, and she squeezes my hand I-love-you. "Seems like your hand used to be so much smaller. I guess I hate to see you grow up. When you're grown up, will we still be friends?" I say always. "But I feel so bad, Buddy. I wanted so bad to give you a bike. I tried to sell my cameo Papa gave me. Buddy"—she hesitates, as though embarrassed—"I made you another kite." Then I confess that I made her one, too; and we laugh. The candle burns too short to hold. Out it goes, exposing the starlight, the stars spinning at the window like a visible caroling that slowly, slowly daybreak silences. Possibly we doze; but the beginnings of dawn splash us like cold water: we're up, wide-eyed and wandering while we wait for others to waken. Quite deliberately my friend drops a kettle on the kitchen floor. I tap-dance in front of closed doors. One by one the household emerges, looking as though they'd like to kill us both; but it's Christmas, so they can't. First a gorgeous breakfast: just everything you can imagine—from flapjacks and fried squirrel to hominy grits and honey-in-the-comb. Which puts everyone in a good humor except my friend and me. Frankly, we're so impatient to get at the presents we can't eat a mouthful.

Well, I'm disappointed. Who wouldn't be? With socks, a Sunday-school shirt, some handkerchiefs, a hand-me-down sweater, and a year's subscription to a religious magazine for children. *The Little Shepherd.* It makes me boil. It really does.

My friend has a better haul. A sack of Satsumas, that's her best present. She is proudest, however, of a white wool shawl knitted by her married sister. But she *says* her favorite gift is the kite I built her. And it *is* very beautiful; though not as beautiful as the one she made me, which is blue and scattered with gold and green Good Conduct stars; moreover, my name is painted on it, "Buddy".

"Buddy, the wind is blowing."

The wind is blowing, and nothing will do till we've run to a pasture below the house where Queenie has scooted to bury her bone (and where, a winter hence, Queenie will be buried, too). There, plunging through the healthy waist-high grass, we unreel our kites, feel them twitching at the string like sky fish as they swim into the wind. Satisfied, sun-warmed, we sprawl in the grass and peel Satsumas and watch our kites cavort. Soon I forget the socks and hand-me-down sweater. I'm as happy as if we'd already won the fifty-thousand-dollar Grand Prize in that coffee-naming contest.

"My, how foolish I am!" my friend cries, suddenly alert, like a woman remembering too late she has biscuits in the oven. "You know what I've always thought?" she says in a tone of discovery, and not smiling at me but a point beyond. "I've always thought a body would have to be sick and dying before they saw the Lord. And I imagined that when He came it would be like looking at the Baptist window: pretty as colored glass with the sun pouring through, such a shine you don't know it's getting dark. And it's been a colored glass with the sun pouring through, such a spooky feeling. But I'll wager it never happens. I'll wager at the very end a body realizes the Lord has already shown Himself. That things as they are"—her hand circles in a gesture that gathers clouds and kites and grass and Queenie pawing earth over her bone—"just what they've always seen, was seeing Him. As for me, I could leave the world with today in my eyes."

This is our last Christmas together.

Life separates us. Those who Know Best decide that I belong in a military school. And so follows a miserable succession of bugle-blowing prisons, grim reveille-ridden summer camps. I have a new home too. But it doesn't count. Home is where my friend is, and there I never go.

And there she remains, puttering around the kitchen. Alone with Queenie. Then alone ("Buddy dear," she writes in her wild hard-to-read script, "yesterday Jim Macy's horse kicked Queenie bad. Be thankful she didn't feel much. I wrapped her in a Fine Linen sheet and rode her in the buggy down to Simpson's pasture where she can be with all her Bones..."). For a few Novembers she continues to bake her fruitcakes single-handed; not as many, but some: and, of course, she always sends me "the best of the batch." Also, in every letter she encloses a dime wadded in toilet paper: "See a picture show and write me the story." But gradually in her letters she tends to confuse me with her other friend, the Buddy who died in the 1880s; more and more thirteenths are not the only days she stays in bed: a morning arrives in November, a leafless birdless coming of winter morning, when she cannot rouse herself to exclaim: "Oh my, it's fruitcake weather!"

And when that happens, I know it. A message saying so merely confirms a piece of news some secret vein had already received, severing from me an irreplaceable part of myself, letting it loose like a kite on a broken string. That is why, walking across a school campus on this particular December morning, I keep searching the sky. As if I expect to see, rather like hearts, a lost pair of kites hurrying toward heaven.

TRUMAN CAPOTE was born in 1924 and grew up in Monroeville, Alabama. He died in 1984 and is best remembered for Breakfast at Tiffany's, *an early work of fiction, and for his "nonfiction novel,"* In Cold Blood, *which paved the way for the true-crime genre.*

Spittin' Image of a Baptist Boy

NANCI KINCAID

I DO NOT LOOK ONE THING like Mother. Maybe just have some of her face. How her cheeks sit out there like little round biscuits of flesh that got put on last, as an afterthought, after the rest of the face was finished. My cheeks did like that too. Sat out there all by themselves, looking added on. And my hands and feet were like Mother's. Very square and neat. No fat looking fingers or toes. Trim and square. We could pick up most anything as good with our toes as with our fingers. A marble. A thumbtack. Mother could be holding two arms full of grocery sacks and pick up the car keys off the ground with her toes, bend up her knee and hand them to Roy. It was a natural thing. Walter said it was amazing and that Mother must have some monkey in her. But I could do it too.

I had some of Mother's ways, but not much of her looks. It was Roy that had those. Brown Roy with his black, shiny, almost wavy hair. Roy who could have dirt all over his hands and face and it wouldn't even be noticeable hardly. Not on his brown self.

It was funny how we were. Roy brown like Mother. Me golden like our real Daddy, which is not what somebody said, but I just saw that. How he had this straight yellow hair like me. And we had those blue eyes and those white eyebrows that go away, invisible, all summer long and come back some in the fall and winter. And then Benny looks like Walter. Kind of, he really does. He's like me and our real Daddy about his white hair and skin and all. But like Walter in his build which is big. Thick. Husky. And like Walter in his quietish ways. And it was not unusual at all for folks to say, "Lord, that boy takes after his Daddy." Meaning Walter. People that didn't know would say that. "You sure can't be denying that child, Walter Sheppard!" People could see it. Even Mother could.

When folks got to telling Walter how Benny was exactly like him, just him made over, Walter would smile and say, "That's one lucky boy there. Damn lucky." And he'd wink at Mother. And it was just generally recognized how Benny was Walter's spittin' image.

Walter's people lived in Valdosta. That's in Georgia, not too far off. There's a bunch of Sheppards there, a slew of them. Walter said he has more cousins than you could shake a stick at. Walter said every other person you'd meet on the street in Valdosta was a Sheppard, or married to one, or lived next door to one. He said there is such a thing as too much of a good thing. He said that's why he came down to Tallahassee. That, and because he had a chance at a right good job with the highway department.

None of us ever laid eyes on any of Walter's people. Not a one. He never did say that much about any of them. Just his brother Hugh. Hugh Henry Sheppard. He was Walter's little brother, grown and all now. Walter liked the heck out of ole Hugh. But that was about all.

Mrs. Sheppard, Walter's mother, was very disappointed that Walter didn't make a better marriage. She called Mother 'the divorcee.' When Walter was fixing to marry Mother and he called Mrs. Sheppard to tell her about the wedding to see if she could come or not, she could not. Mrs. Sheppard couldn't come because it plum broke her heart, Walter marrying a divorcee. And one with kids. She said Walter deserved his own flesh and blood kids. And here he was going to be bringing his hard-earned paycheck home to somebody else's left over wife and another man's kids. And it plum broke her heart. And there wasn't any need in her coming clear down to Tallahassee to cry her eyes out at a terrible mistake of a wedding like that. She wasn't up to it. Walter was just gon have to understand that. So Mrs. Sheppard had never even seen Mother, or any of us. We didn't think she ever wanted to. Walter said we were not missing one thing. He said he'd seen enough of the woman for all of us.

And then one day out of the blue she calls up Walter and says she is coming to visit. She's taking a Trailways bus down to Tallahassee and can he pick her up down there at the bus station. She says her conscience cannot rest until she sees Walter, meets his divorcee wife and all. She just has to come because she can't rest until she does. Walter was married to Mother almost a year by then—and his poor Mother can't rest.

Mother went into a frenzy over the idea. Not mad exactly, just a nervous wreck, worrying about what to fix for dinner. Does your Mama like this or that? Does she like biscuits better than cornbread? Does she like sweet pickles in her potato salad? And then Mother wished we could go on and paint my bedroom. It had been needing it so she wished we could paint it. She wanted Walter to mow the grass, and wash the car and his highway truck, and fix the tear in the screen door. She wanted Roy and Benny to get them a haircut. She wanted to clip our fingernails—and our toenails. She did speeches on us acting nice, stuff about not just yes ma'am, no ma'am, please and thank-you. But also about chew with your mouth closed, put your napkin in your lap. Do not pick your nose. Keep quiet. Don't scratch. Say excuse me. Be polite. No fighting and yelling. No slamming the screen door. No grabbing food. Smile. Say nice-to-meet-you. Walter's mother coming was not one thing like when our Granddaddy came.

We kind of had the feeling we were in a contest to see if we could be nice enough to win Mrs. Sheppard so she might want to be like our grandmother or something. Like she was the Grand Prize if we won the niceness contest. If we could be good enough.

Walter tried to calm Mother down because she was about to wear herself out, and us too. And Walter said it wasn't the Queen of England coming, just his mother, Emma Jean Sheppard. And there wasn't no sense in trying so hard to please her. No sense at all. But you couldn't tell Mother that. On the day Mrs. Sheppard was coming Mother changed clothes a half a dozen times. Brushed the curl right out of her hair. Got all the rest of us nervous too. She burned the first batch of homemade dinner rolls she put in the oven. Walter told me to go on up to Melvina's and get her. Mother did not know one thing about dinner rolls. He said to get Melvina in the kitchen before it was too late. So Mother went on in the bathroom and brushed her hair some more. Melvina got in the kitchen mumbling all kinds of this and that.

When Mrs. Sheppard finally came walking in the house with Walter one step behind her carrying her suitcase she was not exactly what we were expecting because we didn't know what we were expecting. Walter standing there behind his Grand Prize Mother. Everybody, including Melvina, gathered up around her and stared like she was some outer-space creature or something. Mrs. Sheppard in her little pill box hat with the flowers on it, with her silver blue curled hair and her seashell earbobs. She was a pretty regular grandmother type we thought. She didn't look so bad.

Walter said, "Mama, I want you to meet Sarah here. My wife, Sarah."

Mother reached out her hand and said, "Mighty glad to meet you, Mrs. Sheppard. Walter has told me an awful lot about you."

Mrs. Sheppard did not go to shake hands with Mother, but just looked her over some. Just stood there with her hands folded across her stomach and let her eyes fix on Mother. "You are a pretty thing. I'll say so. Walter, she is a pretty thing. How is it a pretty girl like you come to be a divorcee?"

"Mrs. Sheppard, meet the children," Mother said, putting her arms around us. "This here is Lucy...and Roy...and little Benny..." She didn't add that at that moment we were the three squeakiest clean children in Tallahassee. But she could have. She did not say, "Look here, Mrs. Sheppard, look behind these kids' ears, clean as a whistle. See that?" She did not make us show our teeth, how toothpaste white they were, or make us hold out our hands for Mrs. Sheppard to check how our fingernails were clipped so nice and all. She didn't do it, but she could have.

We said, "Glad to meet you." Then Mrs. Sheppard told Walter she sure was tired and thought she would like to lie down and rest some. No howdy-do or nothing. And that was how the visit started. And it never got better.

Mrs. Sheppard was a right peculiar woman. She went and laid down on the bed in my room—with her flower hat still on her head and all. She laid on her back with her hands still folded over her stomach, her shoes still on her feet. She looked like somebody waiting to get buried in a grave.

Mother went and put on a Tennessee Ernie Ford religious record on the record player. She thought some music would help Mrs. Sheppard rest better and it would drown out any noise me and Roy and Benny made, which wasn't much. Mother told Melvina she could go on home, since supper was under control and everything. But Melvina didn't want to. She said she ain't come clear down here for nothing and she's gon wait til after we eat supper. That was because if there was something good left over from this company dinner she was gon take it home with her. She always did like that. Fix her a big plate and take it up to her house. Meanwhile she was gon sit in the kitchen with a flyswatter in her hand and wait.

Most of the afternoon passed with Mrs. Sheppard laying up in my bed. Finally Walter went in there and woke her up to come eat supper. Mother made him do it because she didn't know how much longer the three of us could keep up with being so good. It was like she was afraid our good behavior was going to run out just about the time Mrs. Sheppard woke up and we sat down to eat, and Roy and me would go to chewing with our mouths open and grabbing food. And Benny would start crying and rub jello in his hair. She wanted to get supper over with before our goodness ran completely out.

When we were all seated at the table, Benny in his highchair by Mother and all, then we bowed our heads and Mother asked the blessing, like she always did. Sometimes she would let me or Roy ask the blessing, but on an occasion like this with Mrs. Sheppard eating with us, then Mother said it herself. And she meant every word of it, you could tell.

We started up passing the food around in a quiet way and Mrs. Sheppard looked at Mother and said, "What church do you go to?"

Walter made this noise in his throat.

"Well," Mother said, "I was raised Methodist and I'm raising the children Methodist."

"What is the name of your Methodist church?"

"It's right in downtown Tallahassee," she said. "A big ole church. Trinity Methodist. It's a very nice church."

"Walter was raised a Baptist," Mrs. Sheppard said. "Been a Baptist all his life. My boys were raised Baptist. I saw to that."

Walter kept on eating.

"Walter never missed a day of Sunday School or church growing up. Did you, Walter? If the doors were open the Sheppard family was there. Walter's Daddy was a deacon, rest his soul. Walter's been a Baptist all his life."

"There's not too much difference between Methodist and Baptist,"

Mother said. "They're pretty close."

"World of difference," Mrs. Sheppard said, putting spoonsful of sugar in her already sweetened tea. "World of difference. I know because I've been a Baptist my whole life and raised my boys Baptist. If it was good enough for John the Baptist, then it is good enough for me. Baptizing is. Real baptizing, like the Bible says. Dunking yourself clean underwater, head and all, washing away those sins, being reborn right on the spot. Wet as a newborn baby. Baptized and reborn."

"Mama," Walter said, in his please-don't-get-started-with-this voice. The same one he used on Mother sometimes.

"It's so," She said. "It is so. Methodists might think sprinkling a little dab of water on their heads is baptizing. But they're wrong. The Bible says that. Sprinkling is not baptizing. It is sprinkling. God does not care one thing about a few drops of water on your head—not even enough to mess up your hair. He wants wet. He wants hold-your-breath, underwater, soaking wet. That's baptizing. Nobody ever got born again over a little sprinkle of water on their heads. There's a world of difference."

Mother acted like she needed to be cutting up Benny's pork chop for him and wiping off his mouth with a napkin and all. We could just tell she was biting her tongue.

"Walter is baptized proper. Aren't you, Walter? Didn't I take you and Hugh Henry and get y'all baptized? I certainly did. Because if the Bible says it, then I believe it."

Mother was looking at Walter eat. Her eyes were beating on him. If her legs could reach him she would have kicked the daylights out of him as a signal for him to say something. It looked like she was chewing her food, but really she was biting her tongue. And beating on Walter with her eyes.

We all ate quietly for a few minutes. Me and Roy had not said one word. And we had not spilled our milk or dropped food in our laps. Since we did not know much about grandmothers we just sat there watching Mrs. Sheppard. She was our first close-up look at a real grandmother.

"So," she said to Mother, "where is your first husband?" Mrs. Sheppard was mashing her jello square with the back of her fork. That jello was shaking like crazy. "Your first husband. Where is he?"

Mother darted her eyes at Walter and then said, "Mrs. Sheppard, we ought not to talk about this at the dinner table with the children and all."

Mother looked at Walter again.

"Sarah don't have a first husband and a second husband, Mama. All she's got is one husband, and that's me."

"I am just asking a harmless question, Walter. It is normal for a Mother to have some curiosity about her boy's wife. It's perfectly normal."

"We're not gon talk about this now, Mama."

It was quiet a long time, us sitting at the table eating. Us using nice manners. Sometimes somebody said pass this or that and somebody would do it. Sometimes Walter cleared his throat. All there was was knives scraping across plates and forks tapping, and ice-cubes melting some and clanking in the glass. And sometimes somebody said pass the butter please. Then Mother started saying did anybody want some dessert? Me and Roy did. Everybody did. So Mother starts fussing around the table moving the plates and all.

Mrs. Sheppard put her hand on Walter's arm, "Son, it's normal for a Mother to have some curiosity about her boy's wife. It's normal."

"Don't the Bible say something about curiosity, Mama? It's bound to say something on the subject."

Mrs. Sheppard looked at Walter in a mean way. "Well, I'll tell you one thing, Walter Sheppard, the Bible says plenty about a divorced woman. It says submit unto your husband, which means your one and only husband. It doesn't say one thing about trade this one in for that one."

Mother went carrying the dinner plates into the kitchen, they were all piled up with forks poking out between them and they rattled when she walked, like skeleton bones banging together. She closed the door with her foot.

Walter pushed back his chair from the table and it made this loud scraping noise. Walter made some loud scraping noises of his own saying, "Let me tell you what!" He was about to speak to his Mother, but then looked at me and Roy with our wide-open eyes and Benny, with jello in his hair, and he stopped. "Lucy, you and Roy take Benny on out in the yard a while. You'll get your dessert later on."

We didn't like the idea.

"Right now I said!" And we could tell Walter meant it. So we got Benny out of his highchair and went on outside. We got up under the dining-room window as quiet as we could be—like we did when Melvina came to see Mother cause old Alfonso beat her up. We got up there by the window because we wanted to hear.

"Let me tell you something, Mama," Walter started. "This here is my house. You're in my house. And Sarah is my wife. This can be any kind of house I want it to be and I want it to be a Methodist house. You hear me? And if you and John the Baptist don't like it it's plain too bad!"

We could hear Mrs. Sheppard sniffling. We wanted to look in the window so bad and see if Walter was making her cry. "And another thing, Mama. You cannot come in my house acting like it is your house. You cannot be talking that divorced woman trash to Sarah. Do you hear me?"

"Walter," Mrs. Sheppard was crying her words. "You never used to talk to me like this...not before you married her."

"For Lord's sake, Mama!" It was Walter's maddest voice.

Mrs. Sheppard kept up the crying. "I just want what's best for you, Walter. That's all. That's all I ever wanted. For you a Christian home with a wife of your own and kids of your own. You can't blame a mother for that. I just want you to have a good wife that appreciates you."

"Mama," Walter said in a calm way, "I'm gon be picking out my wife, not you. And I picked Sarah. And she ain't making me into a Methodist any more than you made a Baptist out of me."

Mrs. Sheppard blew her nose.

"You don't know one thing about Sarah, Mama. Not one thing she's been through and you ain't never gon know because it ain't your damn business."

"Walter..." she cried, "you never used to talk like that."

Then it got quiet. Just Walter sitting there and his Mama crying into her paper napkin. Minutes passed with her sniffling and sobbing. "Do you think I'm blind? Do you, Walter?" Mrs. Sheppard said. "Do you think I was born yesterday?"

"Mama, what are you talking about?"

"When I got here this afternoon and your wife said meet the children—and I saw that baby. Walter I cannot tell you. I can't tell you what it did to me."

"What the..."

"It was like you standing there, Walter. Why he couldn't be any more yours if you named him Walter Sheppard Junior. Did you think I wasn't gon notice that? That little baby looking like your spitting image."

Walter sort of chuckled.

"Don't Mama me. I'm no fool, Walter. I wasn't born yesterday. It just come to me this afternoon, standing there seeing that little baby—you made over. It come to me."

"What did?"

"Why you married that divorcee."

"Mama..."

"Don't deny it. I know you, Walter. I know you like a book. You're an honorable man about a thing like that. And then I just laid in yonder on that bed there, thinking how it was me that raised you that way. Honorable and all. You from a good Baptist home. Some men would be long gone when a divorcee comes up expecting a baby. But not you, Walter. Not one of my honorable boys."

Me and Roy were in the flower bed up under the window. We did not know what to think about crazy Mrs. Sheppard.

"You're dead wrong, Mama. Do you hear me? Dead wrong. This is my house and I'm saying you're dead wrong."

Mother opened up the kitchen door. Her and Melvina had been listening to every word said, they were listening in the kitchen same as we were listening in the flower bed. And so here comes Mother carrying Walter and Mrs. Sheppard plates of pound cake and ice-cream. She set Walter's down in front of him and when she went to set Mrs. Sheppard's down Mrs. Sheppard said, "I'm sorry but I do not believe I can eat this. I have just lost my appetite. I think I'll just go back in yonder and lay down a while. Excuse me." And she got up with her balled up paper napkin pressed against her nose and went in my room and laid on the bed. Again.

Mother sat down at the table with Walter who was eating his dessert like on any ordinary day. Putting a spoonful of ice-cream in his mouth and letting it sit there and slowly melt. "Is she all right?" Mother asked.

"She's okay."

"Should we do something?"

"Nope."

"It seems like we should do something, Walter."

"Like what?"

"I don't know, go in there and talk to her or something. Get this thing straight."

Walter was eating his pound cake and ice-cream slow, like he was enjoying the heck out of it. Like it was one million times more important than his Mother laying like a corpse, crying like she had come down with some fatal truth.

"Well, we can't have her go around thinking Benny is yours and I tricked you, Walter, I don't want her to think that. I'm no tramp. And it bothers me, Walter. It does."

"Look on the good side," Walter said. "It's not you being a tramp so much as it is her Baptist boy being one hell of a lover."

"Walter..." Mother smiled at him like she did when he would not take a serious thing serious. Like it could be the end of the world and Walter would sit and eat a plate of cake and ice-cream, slow and relaxed. Like bombs were going off and Walter would sit still and feel good about himself.

In a minute he got up from the table and walked by Mother, patting her shoulder. "Good supper," he said. "Good supper for a Methodist divorcee." He walked on into the living room and sat in his regular chair over by the picture window.

When me and Roy and Benny came back in for our dessert we saw that Mother was crying, with her hands over her face, and Melvina patting her like Mother was a child. She turned her face from us when we came into the room and then hurried down the hall to her bedroom. Mother back in her room crying and crying, and Mrs. Sheppard laying in my bed doing the same. Some people would probably say that Walter didn't have much of a way with women.

Nothing can take away a child's appetite like a mother crying her eyes out. Me and Roy sat at the table sort of jabbing at our cake, but not eating any of it. Melvina came in and stood by us, saying very quietly, "Y'all allow your Mama to be sad, now, you hear? Don't she allow you to be sad when you need to?"

We looked at Melvina, and she reached out both hands and took our serious faces in them. Her hands were soft and warm and wrapped most nearly from ear to ear under our chins. "God wouldn't have give folks no teardrops if he hadn't of meant for them to cry some. Now would he?"

We nodded our heads no.

"And Melvina wouldn't of give y'all no dessert if she didn't expect y'all to eat it." We half smiled at her. She smiled too, and gave our faces a squeeze. "See can you eat your ice-cream for it melts all over the table."

The next day Walter took his Mother back to the Trailways bus so she could get on home to Valdosta. We said good-by and nice to meet you like Mother told us to say. We felt disappointed for Mother because she wanted us a grandmother so bad and could not get us one no matter what. Me and Roy tried to tell Mother we did not need a grandmother. Not some blue haired woman who just sleeps all the time with her shoes on. It was sort of like when you enter into a contest and try your absolute hardest to win, and then find out that the prize is something you never have wanted in your life. Just some contraption that's gon stay broken and tore up, and don't work good when it's fixed. We told Mother never mind about Mrs. Sheppard, but seems like that made her sadder than ever.

Later on when Walter saw how funeralish we were acting he said his Mother would not know a good kid if one bit her. In fact, he said, if she ever came back that's what me and Roy should do. Bite her. Bite her right on the leg. Me and Roy laughed our heads off. Walter is so funny.

NANCI KINCAID lives in Tuscaloosa, Alabama, where she recently completed the M.F.A. program at the University of Alabama. Her work has appeared in New Stories from the South *(1988) and in several periodicals.*

Kin

EUDORA WELTY

"MINGO?" I REPEATED, and for the first moment I didn't know what my aunt meant. The name sounded in my ears like *something* instead of *somewhere*. I'd been making a start, just a little start, on my own news when Rachel came in in her stately way with the letter.

My aunt was bridling daintily at the unopened envelope in her hand. "Of course you'll be riding out there Sunday, girls, and without me."

"Open it—what does she say now?" said Kate to her mother. "Ma'am? If Uncle Felix—"

"Uncle Felix! Is *he* still living?"

Kate went "Shh!"

But I had only arrived the day before yesterday; and we had of course had so much to catch up with, besides, necessarily, parties. They expected me to keep up in spite of being gone almost my whole life, except for visits—I was taken away from Mississippi when I was eight. I was the only one in Aunt Ethel's downstairs bedroom neither partially undressed nor, to use my aunt's word, "reclining."

"Of course he is," said Aunt Ethel, tearing open the envelope at once, and bringing out an old-fashioned "correspondence card" filled up on both sides with a sharp, jet-black hand, and reading the end. Uncle Felix was her uncle, only my great-uncle. "He is," she said to Kate.

"*Still* this, *still* that," murmured Kate, looking at me sidelong. She was up on the bed too. She leaned lightly across her mother, who was in pink negligée, read ahead of her for an instant, and plucked the last piece of

153

the city candy I had brought from the big shell dish Rachel had seen fit to put it in.

Uncontrite, I rocked. However, I did see I must stop showing what might be too much exuberance in Aunt Ethel's room, since she was old and not strong, and take things more as they came. Kate and I were double first cousins, I was the younger, and neither married yet, but *I* was not going to be an old maid! I was already engaged up North; though I had not yet come to setting a date for my wedding. Kate, though, as far as I could tell, didn't have anybody.

My little aunt, for her heart's sake, had to lie propped up. There inside her tester bed she sometimes looked out as if, I thought, she were riding in some old-fashioned carriage or litter. Now she had drawn that card and its envelope both to her pillowed face. She was smelling them. Mingo, of course, was the home place. It was miles from anywhere, and I saw that she was not to go there any more.

"Look at the gilt edge," she said, shining it. "Isn't it *remarkable* about Sister Anne? I wonder what drawer she went into to find *that* to favor us with?...'Had to drop—' watch?—no, 'water on his tongue—yesterday so he could talk...Must *watch* him—day and night,' underlined. *Poor* old man. She insists, you know, Dicey, that's what she does."

"Buzzard," said Kate.

"Who," I signed, for I thought she had said "sister," and there was no sister at all left of my Aunt Ethel's. But my mind had wandered for a moment. It was two-thirty in the afternoon, after an enormous dinner at which we had company—six girls, chattering almost like ready-made bridesmaids—ending with wonderful black, bitter, moist chocolate pie under mountains of meringue, and black, bitter coffee. We could hear Rachel now, off in the distance, peacefully dropping the iced-tea spoons into the silver drawer in the pantry.

In this little courthouse town, several hours by inconvenient train ride from Jackson, even the cut grass smelled different from Northern grass. (Even by evidence of smell, I knew that really I was a stranger in a way, still, just at first.) And the spring was so much farther advanced—the birds so busy you turned as you would at people as they plunged by. Bloom was everywhere in the streets, wistaria, just ending, Confederate jasmine beginning. And down in the gardens!—they were deep colored as old rugs in the morning and evening shade. Everybody grew some of the best of somebody else's flowers; by the way, if you thank a friend for a flower, it will not grow for you. Everywhere we went calling, Kate brought me out saying, "Here she is! Got off the train talking, and hasn't stopped yet." And everywhere the yawning, inconvenient, and suddenly familiar rooms were as deep and inviting and compelling as the yawning big roses opening and shattering in one day in the heating gardens. At night, the moths were already pounding against the screens.

Aunt Ethel and Kate, and everybody I knew here, lived as if they had never heard of anywhere else, even Jackson—in houses built, I could judge now as a grown woman and a stranger, in the local version of the 1880's—tall and spread out at the bottom, with porches, and winged all over with awnings and blinds. As children, Kate and I were brought up across the street from each other—they were her grandfather's and my grandmother's houses. From Aunt Ethel's front window I could see our chinaberry tree, which Mother had always wanted to cut down, standing in slowly realized bloom. Our old house was lived in now by a family named Brown, who were not very much, I gathered—the porch had shifted, and the screens looked black as a set of dominoes.

Aunt Ethel had gone back to the beginning of her note now. "Oh-oh. Word had penetrated even Mingo, Miss Dicey Hastings, that you're in this part of the world! The minute you reached Mississippi our little paper had that notice you laughed at, that was all about your mother and me and your grandmother, so of course there's repercussions from Sister Anne. Why didn't we tell her! But honestly, she might be the remotest kin in the world, for all you know when you're well, but let yourself get to ailing, and she'd show up in Guinea, if that's where you were, and *stay*. Look at Cousin Susan, 'A year if need be' is the way she put it about precious Uncle Felix."

"She'll be coming to you next if you don't hush about her," said Kate, sitting bolt upright on the bed. She adored her mother, her family. What she had was company-excitement. And I guess I had trip-excitement—I giggled. My aunt eyed us and tucked the letter away.

"But who is she, pure and simple?" I said.

"You'd just better not let her *in*," said Aunt Ethel to Kate. "That's what. Sister Anne Fry, dear heart. Declares she's wild to lay eyes on you. I *should* have shown you the letter. Recalls your sweet manners toward your elders. Sunday's our usual day to drive out there, you remember, Dicey, but I'm inclined to think—I feel now—it couldn't be just your coming brought on this midweek letter. Uncle Felix was taken sick on Valentine's Day and she got there by Saturday. Kate, since you're not working this week—if you're going, you'd better go on today."

"Oh, curses!" cried Kate to me. Kate had told them at the bank she was not working while I was here. We had planned something.

"Mama, what is she?" asked Kate, standing down in her cotton petticoat with the ribbon run in. She was not as tall as I. "I may be as bad as Dicey but I don't intend to go out there today without you and not have her straight."

Aunt Ethel looked patiently upwards as if she read now from the roof of the tester, and said, "Well, she's a remote cousin of Uncle Felix's, to begin with. Your third cousin twice removed, and your Great-aunt Beck's half-sister, my third cousin once removed and my aunt's half-sister, Dicey's—"

"Don't tell me!" I cried. "I'm not that anxious to claim kin!"

"She'll claim you! She'll come visit you!" cried Kate.

"I won't be here long enough." I could not help my smiles.

"When your mother was alive and used to come bringing you, visits were different," said my Aunt Ethel. "She stayed long enough to make us believe she'd fully got here. There'd be time enough to have alterations, from Miss Mattie, too, and transplant things in the yard if it was the season, even start a hook-rug—do a morning glory, at least—even if she'd never really see the grand finale.... Our generation knew more how to visit, whatever else escaped us, not that I mean to criticize one jot."

"Mama, what do you *want?*" said Kate in the middle of the floor. "Let me get you something."

"I don't want a thing," said her mother. "Only for my girls to please themselves."

"Well then, tell me who it was that Sister Anne one time, long time ago, was going to marry and stood up in the church? And she was about forty years old!" Kate said, and lightly, excitedly, lifted my hat from where I'd dropped it down on the little chair some time, to her own head—bare feet, petticoat, and all. She made a face at me.

Her mother was saying, "Now *that* is beyond me at the moment, perhaps because it didn't come off. Though he was some kind of off-cousin, too, I seem to recall...I'll have it worked out by the time you girls get back from where you're going.—Very becoming, dear."

"Kate," I said, "I thought Uncle Felix was old beyond years when I was a child. And now *I'll* be old in ten years, and so will you. And he's still alive."

"He *was* old!" cried Kate. "He *was!*"

"Light somewhere, why don't you," said her mother.

Kate perched above me on the arm of my chair, and we gently rocked. I said, "He had red roses on his suspenders."

"When did he ever take his coat off for you to see that?" objected my aunt. "The whole connection always went out there for *Sundays,* and he was a very strict gentleman all his life, you know, and made us be ladies out there, more even than Mama and Papa did in town."

"But I can't remember a thing about Sister Anne," I said. "Maybe she was too much of a lady."

"Foot," said my aunt.

Kate said in a prompting, modest voice, "She fell in the well."

I cried joyously, "And she came out! Oh, I remember her fine! Mournful! Those old black drapey dresses, and plastered hair."

"That was just the way she looked when she came out of the well," objected Kate.

"Mournful isn't exactly the phrase," said my aunt.

"Plastered black hair, and her mouth drawn down, exactly like that aunt in the front illustration of your *Eight Cousins,*" I told Kate. "I used to think that was who it was."

"You're so bookish," said my aunt flatly.

"This is where all the books *were!*"—and there were the same ones now, no more, no less.

"On purpose, I think she fell," continued Kate. "Knowing there were plenty to pull her out. That was her contribution to Cousin Eva's wedding celebrations, and snitching a little of *her* glory. You're joggling me the way you're rocking."

"There's such a thing as being *unfair,* Kate," said her mother. "I always say, *poor* Sister Anne."

"*Poor* Sister Anne, then."

"And I think Dicey just *thinks* she remembers it because she's heard it."

"Well, at least she had something to be poor about!" I said irrepressibly. "Falling in the well, and being an old maid, that's two things!"

Kate cried, "Don't rock so headlong!"

"Maybe she even knew what she was about. Eva's Archie Fielder got drunk every whipstitch for the rest of his life," said Aunt Ethel.

"Only tell me this, somebody, and I'll be quiet," I said. "What poor somebody's Sister Anne was she to begin with?"

Then I held the rocker and leaned against my cousin. I was terrified that I had brought up Uncle Harlan. Kate had warned me again how, ever since his death seventeen years ago, Aunt Ethel could not bear to hear the name of her husband spoken, or to speak it herself.

"Poor Beck's, of course," said Aunt Ethel. "She's a little bit kin on both sides. Since you ask, Beck's *half*-sister—that's why we were always so careful to call her Sister."

"Oh, I thought that was just for teasing," said Kate.

"Well, of course the teasing element is not to be denied," said Aunt Ethel.

"Who began—" My hat was set, not at all rightly, on my own head by Kate—like a dunce cap.

The town was so quiet the doves from the river woods could be heard plainly. In town, the birds were quiet at this hour. Kate and I went on bobbing slowly up and down together as we rocked very gently by Aunt Ethel's bed. I saw us in the pier glass across the room. Looking at myself as the visitor, I considered myself as having a great deal still waiting to confide. My lips opened.

"He was ever so courtly," said my aunt. "Nobody in the family more so."

Kate with a tiny sting pulled a little hair from my neck, where it has always grown too low. I slapped at her wrist.

"But this last spell when I couldn't get out, and he's begun failing, what I remember about him is what I used to be told as a child, isn't that strange? When I knew him all my life and loved him. For instance, that he was a great one for serenading as a young man."

"Serenading!" said Kate and I together, adoring her and her memory. "I didn't know he could sing," said Kate.

"He couldn't. But he *was* a remarkable speller," said my aunt. "A born speller. I remember how straight he stood when they called the word. You know the church out there, like everything else in the world, raised its money by spelling matches. He knew every word in the deck. One time—one time, though!—I turned Uncle Felix down. I was not so bad myself, child though I was. And it isn't..."

"Ma'am?"

"It just isn't fair to have water dropped on your tongue, is it?"

"She ought not to have told you, the old buzzard!"

"The word," said Aunt Ethel, "the word was knick-knack. K-n-i-c-k, knick, hyphen, k-n-a-c-k, knack, knick-knack."

"She only writes because she has nothing else to do, away out yonder in the country!"

"She used to get *dizzy* very easily," Aunt Ethel spoke out in a firm voice, as if she were just waking up from a nap. "Maybe she did well—maybe a girl might do well sometimes *not* to marry, if she's not cut out for it."

"Aunt Ethel!" I exclaimed. Kate, sliding gently off the arm of my chair, was silent. But as if I had said something more, she turned around, her bare feet singing on the matting, her arm turned above her head, in a saluting, mocking way.

"Find me her letter again, Kate, where is it?" said Aunt Ethel, feeling under her solitaire board and her pillow. She held that little gilt-edged card, shook it, weighed it, and said, "All that really troubles me is that I can't bear for her to be on Uncle Felix's hands for so long! He was always so courtly, and his family's all, all in the churchyard now (but us!)—or New York!"

"Mama, let me bring you a drink of water."

"Dicey, I'm going to *make* you go to Mingo."

"But I want to go!"

She looked at me uncomprehending. Kate gave her a glass of water, with ice tinkling in it. "That reminds me, whatever you do, Kate, if you do go today, take that fresh Lady Baltimore cake out to the house—Little Di can sit and hold it while you drive. Poor Sister Anne can't cook and loves to eat. She can *eat* awhile. And make Rachel hunt through the shelves for some more green tomato pickle. Who'll put that up next year!"

"If you talk like that," said Kate, "we're going to go right this minute, right out into the heat. I thought this was going to be a good day."

"Oh, it is! Grand—Run upstairs both, and get your baths, you hot little children. You're supposed to go to Suzanne's, I know it." Kate, slow-motion, leaned over and kissed her mother, and took the glass. "Kate!—If only I could see him one more time. As he was. And Mingo.

Old Uncle Theodore. The peace. Listen: you give him my love. He's *my* Uncle Felix. Don't tell him why I didn't come. That might distress him more than not seeing me there."

"What's Uncle Felix's trouble?" I asked, shyly at last: but things, even fatal thing, did have names. I wanted to know.

Aunt Ethel smiled, looked for a minute as if she would not be allowed to tell me, and then said, "Old age.—I think Sister Anne's lazy, *idle!*" she cried. "You're drawing it out of me. She never cooked nor sewed nor even cultivated her mind! She was a lily of the field." Aunt Ethel suddenly showed us both highly polished little palms, with the brave gesture a girl uses toward a fortune teller—then looked into them a moment absently and hid them at her sides. "She just hasn't got anybody of her own, that's her trouble. And she needs somebody."

"Hush! She *will* be coming here next!" Kate cried, and our smiles began to brim once more.

"She has no inner resources," confided my aunt, and watched to see if I were too young to guess what that meant. "How you girls do set each other off! Not that you're bothering me, I love you in here, and wouldn't deprive myself *of* it. Yes, you all just better wait and go Sunday. Make things as usual." She shut her eyes.

"Look—look!" chanted Kate.

Rachel, who believed in cutting roses in the heat of the day—and nobody could prevent her now, since we forgot to cut them ourselves or slept through the mornings—came in Aunt Ethel's room bearing a vaseful. Aunt Ethel's roses were at their height. A look of satisfaction on Rachel's face was like something nobody could interrupt. To our sighs, for our swooning attitudes, she paraded the vase through the room and around the bed, where she set it on the little table there and marched back to her kitchen.

"*Rachel* wants you to go. All right, you tell Uncle Felix," said Aunt Ethel, turning toward the roses, spreading her little hand out chordlike over them, "—of course he must have these—that *that's* Souvenir de Claudius Pernet—and *that's* Mermaid—Mary Wallace—Silver Moon—those three of course Étoiles—and oh, Duquesa de Penaranda—Gruss an Aachen's of course his cutting he grew for me a thousand years ago—but there's my Climbing Thor! Gracious," she sighed, looking at it. Still looking at the roses she waited a moment. Pressing out of the vase, those roses of hers looked heavy, drunken with their own light and scent, their stems, just two minutes ago severed with Rachel's knife, vivid with pale thorns through cut-glass. "You know, Sundays always *are* hotter than any other days, and I tell you what: I do think you'd better go on to Mingo today, regardless of what you find."

Circling around in her mind like old people—which Aunt Ethel never used to do, she never used to go back!—she got back to where she started.

"Yes'm," said Kate.

"Aunt Ethel, wouldn't it be better for everybody if he'd come in town to the hospital?" I asked, with all my city seriousness.

"He wouldn't consider it. So give Sister Anne my love, and give Uncle Felix my dear love. Will you remember? Go on, naked," said my aunt to her daughter. "Take your cousin upstairs in her city bonnet. You both look right feverish to me. Start in a little while, so you can get your visit over and come back in the cool of the evening."

"These nights now are so bright," said my cousin Kate, with a strange stillness in her small face, transfixed, as if she didn't hear the end of the messages and did not think who was listening to her either, standing with bare arms pinned behind her head, with the black slick hair pinned up, "these nights are so bright I don't mind, I don't care, how long any ride takes, or how late I ever get home!"

I jumped up beside her and said, pleadingly somehow, to them both, "Do you know—I'd *forgotten* the Milky Way!"

My aunt didn't see any use answering that either. But Kate and I were suddenly laughing and running out together as if we were going to the party after all.

Before we set out, we tiptoed back into Aunt Ethel's room and made off with the roses. Rachel had darkened it. Again I saw us in the mirror, Kate pink and me blue, both our dresses stiff as boards (I had gone straight into Kate's clothes) and creaking from the way Rachel starched them, our teeth set into our lips, half-smiling. I had tried my hat, but Kate said, "Leave that, it's entirely too grand for out there, didn't you hear Mama?" Aunt Ethel stayed motionless, and I thought she was bound to look pretty, even asleep. I wasn't quite sure she was asleep.

"Seems mean," said Kate, looking between the thorns of the reddest rose, but I said, "She meant us to."

"Negroes always like them full blown," said Kate.

Out in the bright, "Look! Those crazy starlings have come. They always pick the greenest day!" said Kate.

"Well, maybe because they look so pretty in it," I said.

There they were, feeding all over the yard and every yard, iridescently black and multiplied at our feet, bound for the North. Around the house, as we climbed with our loads into the car, I saw Rachel looking out from the back hall window, with her cheek in her hand. She watched us go, carrying off her cake and her flowers too.

I was thinking, if I always say "still," Kate still says "always," and laughed, but would not tell her.

Mingo, I learned, was only nine miles and a little more away. But it was an old road, in a part the highway had deserted long ago, lonely and winding. It dipped up and down, and the hills felt high, because they were bare of trees, but they probably weren't very high—this was Mississippi. There was hardly ever a house in sight.

"So green," I sighed.

"Oh, but poor," said Kate, with her look of making me careful of what I said. "Gone to pasture now."

"Beautiful to me!"

"It's clear to Jericho. Looks like that cake would set heavy on your knees, in that old tin Christmas box."

"I'm not ever tired in a strange place. Banks and towers of honeysuckle hanging over that creek!" We crossed an iron bridge.

"That's the Hushomingo River."

We turned off on a still narrower, bumpier road. I began to see gates.

Near Mingo, we saw an old Negro man riding side saddle, except there was no saddle at all, on a slow black horse. He was coming to meet us—that is, making his way down through the field. As we passed, he saluted by holding out a dark cloth cap stained golden.

"Good evening, Uncle Theodore," nodded Kate. She murmured, "Rachel's his daughter, did you know it? But she never comes back to see him."

I sighed into the sweet air.

"Oh, Lordy, we're too late!" Kate exclaimed.

On the last turn, we saw cars and wagons and one yellow wooden school bus standing empty and tilted to the sides up and down the road. Kate stared back for a moment toward where Uncle Theodore had been riding so innocently away. Primroses were blowing along the ditches and between the wheelspokes of wagons, above which empty cane chairs sat in rows, and some of the horses were eating the primroses. That was the only sound as we stood there. No, a chorus of dogs was barking in a settled kind of way.

From the gate we could look up and see the house at the head of the slope. It looked right in size and shape, but not in something else—it had a queer intensity for afternoon. Was every light in the house burning? I wondered. Of course, very quietly out front, on the high and sloping porch, standing and sitting on the railing between the four remembered, pale, square cypress posts, was stationed a crowd of people, dressed darkly, but vaguely powdered over with the golden dust of their thick arrival here in mid-afternoon.

Two blackly spherical Cape Jessamine bushes, old presences, hid both gateposts entirely. Such old bushes bloomed fantastically early and late so far out in the country, the way they did in old country cemeteries.

"The whole countryside's turned out," said Kate, and gritted her teeth, the way she did last night in her sleep.

What I could not help thinking, as we let ourselves through the gate, was that I'd either forgotten or never known how *primitive* the old place was.

Immediately my mind remembered the music box up there in the parlor. It played large, giltlike metal discs, pierced with holes—eyes, eyelids, slits, mysterious as the symbols in a lady's dress pattern, but a whole world of them. When the disc was turned in the machine, the pattern of holes unwound a curious, metallic, depthless, cross music, with silences clocked between the notes. Though I did not like especially to hear it, I used to feel when I was here I must beg for it, as you should ask an old lady how she is feeling.

"I hate to get there," said Kate. She cried, "What a welcome for you!" But I said, "Don't say that." She fastened that creaky gate. We trudged up the the straight but uneven dirt path, then the little paved walk toward the house. We shifted burdens, Kate took the cake and I took the flowers—the roses going like headlights in front of us. The solemnity on the porch was overpowering, even at this distance. It was serene, imperturbable, gratuitous: it was of course the look of "good country people" at such times.

On either side of us were Uncle Felix's roses—hillocks of bushes set in hillocks of rank grass and ragged-robins, hung with roses the size of little biscuits; indeed they already had begun to have a baked look, with little carmine edges curled. Kate dipped on one knee and came up with a four-leaf clover. She could always do that, even now, even carrying a three-layer cake.

By the house, wistaria had taken the scaffolding where a bell hung dark, and gone up into a treetop. The wistaria trunk, sinews raised and twined, like some old thigh, rose above the porch corner, above roof and all, where its sheet of bloom, just starting to go, was faded as an old sail. In spite of myself, I looked around the corner for that well: there it was, squat as a tub beneath the overpiece, a tiger-cat asleep on its cover.

The crowd on the porch were men and women, mostly old, some young, and some few children. As we approached they made no motion; even the young men sitting on the steps did not stand up. Then an old man came out of the house and a lady behind him, the old man on canes and the lady tiptoeing. Voices were murmuring softly all around.

Viewing the body, I thought, my breath gone—but nobody here's kin to me.

The lady had advanced to the head of the steps. It had to be Sister Anne. I saw her legs first—they were old—and her feet were set one behind the other, like an "expression teacher's," while the dress she had on was rather girlish, black taffeta with a flounce around it. But to my rising eyes she didn't look half so old as she did when she was pulled back out of the well. Her hair was not black at all. It was rusty brown, soft and unsafe in its pins. She didn't favor Aunt Ethel and Mama and them, or Kate and me, or any of us in the least, I thought—with that short face.

She was beckoning—a gesture that went with her particular kind of uncertain smile.

"What do I see? Cake!"

She ran down the steps. I bore down on Kate's shoulder behind her. Ducking her head, Kate hissed at me. What had I said? "Who pulled her out?"?

"You *surprised* me!" Sister Anne cried at Kate. She took the cake box out of her hands and kissed her. Two spots of red stabbed her cheeks. I was sorry to observe that the color of her hair was the very same I'd been noticing that spring in robins' breasts, a sort of stained color.

"Long-lost cousin, ain't you!" she cried at me, and gave me the same kiss she had given Kate—a sort of reprisal-kiss. Those head-heavy lights of Aunt Ethel's roses smothered between our unequal chests.

"Monkeys!" she said, leading us up, looking back and forth between Kate and me, as if she had to decide which one she liked best, before anything else in the world could be attended to. She had a long neck and that short face, and round, brown, jumpy eyes with little circles of wrinkles at each blink, like water wrinkles after something's popped in; that looked somehow like a twinkle, at her age. "Step aside for the family, please?" she said next, in tones I thought rather melting.

Kate and I did not dare look at each other. We did not dare look anywhere. As soon as we had moved through the porch crowd and were arrived inside the breezeway—where, however, there were a few people too, standing around—I looked and saw the corner clock was wrong. I was deeply aware that all clocks worked in this house, as if they had been keeping time just for me all this while, and I remembered that the bell in the yard was rung each day at straight-up noon, to bring them in out of the fields at picking time. And I had once supposed they rang it at midnight too.

Around us, voices sounded as they always did everywhere, in a house of death, soft and inconsequential, and tidily assertive.

"I believe Old Hodge's mules done had an attack of the wanderlust. Passed through my place Tuesday headed East, and now you seen' em in Goshen."

Sister Anne was saying bodingly to us, "You just come *right* on *through.*"

This was where Kate burst into tears. I held her to me, to protect her from more kisses. "When, when?" she gasped. "When did it happen, Sister Anne?"

"Now when did what happen?"

That was the kind of answer one kind of old maid loves to give. It goes with "Ask me sometime, and I'll tell you." Sister Anne lifted her brow and fixed her eye on the parlor doorway. The door was opened into that room, but the old red curtain was drawn across it, with bright light, looking red too, streaming out around it.

Just then there was a creaking sound inside there, like an old winter suit bending at the waist, and a young throat was cleared.

"Little bit of commotion here today, but I *would* rather you didn't tell Uncle Felix anything about it," said Sister Anne.

"Tell him! Is he alive?" Kate cried wildly, breaking away from me, and then even more wildly, "I might have known it! What sort of frolic are you up to out here, Sister Anne?"

Sister Anne suddenly marched to the other side of us and brought the front bedroom door to with a good country slam. That room—Uncle Felix's—had been full of people too.

"I beg your pardon," said Kate in a low voice in the next moment. We were still just inside the house—in the breezeway that was almost as wide as the rooms it ran between from front porch to back. It was a hall, really, but still when I was a child called the breezeway. Open at the beginning, it had long been enclosed, and papered like the parlor, in red.

"Why, Kate. You all would be the first to *know*. Do you think I'd have let everybody come, regardless of promises, if Uncle Felix had chosen *not* to be with us still, on the day?"

While we winced, a sudden flash filled the hall with light, changing white to black, black to white—I saw the roses shudder and charge in my hands, Kate with white eyes rolled, and Sister Anne with the livid brow of a hostess and a pencil behind one ear.

"That's what you mean," said Sister Anne. "That's a photographer. He's here in our house today, taking pictures. He's *itinerant,*" she said, underlining in her talk. "And he *asked* to use our parlor—we didn't ask *him*. Well—it *is* complete."

"What is?"

"Our parlor. And all in shape—curtains washed—*you know.*"

Out around the curtain came the very young man, dressed in part in a soldier's uniform not his, looking slightly dazed. He tiptoed out onto the porch. The bedroom door opened on a soft murmuring again.

"Listen," said Sister Anne, leaning toward it. "Hear them in yonder?"

A voice was saying, "My little girl says she'd rather have come on this trip than gone to the zoo."

There was a look on Sister Anne's face as fond and startling as a lover's. Then out the door came an old lady with side-combs, in an enormous black cotton dress. An old man came out behind her, with a mustache discolored like an old seine. Sister Anne pointed a short strict finger at them.

"We're together," said the old man.

"I've got everything under control," Sister Anne called over her shoulder to us, leaving us at once. "Luckily, I was always able to be in two places at the same time, so I'll be able to visit with you back yonder and keep things moving up front, too. Now, what was your name, sir?"

At the round table in the center of the breezeway, she leaned with the old man over a ledger opened there, by the tray of glasses and the water pitcher.

"But where could Uncle Felix be?" Kate whispered to me. As for me, I was still carrying the roses.

Sister Anne was guiding the old couple toward the curtain, and then she let them into the parlor.

"Sister Anne, where have you got him put?" asked Kate, following a step.

"You just come right on through," Sister Anne called to us. She said, behind her hand, "They've left the fields, dressed up like Sunday and Election Day put together, but I can't say they all stopped long enough to bathe, ha-ha! April's a pretty important time, but having your picture taken beats that! Don't have a chance of that out this way more than once or twice in a lifetime. Got him put back out of all the commotion," she said, leading the way. "The photographer's name is—let me see. He's of the Yankee persuasion, but that don't matter any longer, eh, Cousin Dicey? But I shouldn't be funny. Anyway, traveled all the way from some town somewhere since *February,* he tells me. Mercy, but it's hot as churchtime up there, with 'em so packed in! Did it ever occur to you how vain the human race can be if you just give 'em a chance?"

There was that blinding flash again—curtain or not, it came right around it and through it, and down the hall.

"Smells like gunpowder," said Kate stonily.

"Does," agreed Sister Anne. She looked flattered, and said, "May *be.*"

"I feel like a being from another world," I said all at once, just to the breezeway.

"Come on, then," said Sister Anne. "Kate, leave her alone. Oh, Uncle Felix'll eat you two little boogers up."

Not such small haunches moved under that bell-like skirt; the skirt's hem needed mending where a point hung down. Just as I concentrated and made up my mind that Sister Anne weighed a hundred and forty-five pounds and was sixty-nine years old, she mounted on tiptoe like a little girl, and I had to bite my lip to keep from laughing. Kate was steering me by the elbow.

"Now how could she have *moved* him away back here," Kate marveled. Her voice might have even been admiring, with Sister Anne not there.

"Hold your horses while I look at this cake," said Sister Anne, turning off at the kitchen. "What I want to see is *what kind.*"

She squealed as if she had seen a mouse. She took a lick of the icing on her finger before she covered the cake again and set it on the table. "My favorite. And how is Cousin Ethel?" Then she reached for my roses.

"Your ring!" she cried—a cry only at the last second subdued. "Your ring!"

She took my face between her fingers and thumb and shook my cheeks, as though I could not hear what she said at all. She could do this because we were kin to each other.

With unscratchable hands she began sticking the roses into a smoky glass vase too small for them, into which she'd run too little water. Of course there was plumbing. The well was abandoned.

"Well," she said, poking in the flowers, as though suddenly we had all the time in the world, "The other morning, I was looking out at the road, and along came a dusty old-time Ford with a trunk on the back, real slow, then stopped. Was a man. I wondered. And in a minute, knock knock knock. I changed my shoes and went to the door with my finger to my lips." She showed us.

"He was still there, on the blazing porch—eleven-fifteen. He was a middle-aged man all in hot black, short, but reared back, like a stove handle. He gave me a calling card with a price down in the corner, and leaned in and whispered he'd like to use the parlor. He was an itinerant! That's almost but not quite the same as a Gypsy. I hadn't seen a living person in fourteen days, except here, and he was an itinerant photographer with a bookful of orders to take pictures. I made him open and show me his book. It was chock-full. All kinds of names of all kinds of people from all over everywhere. New pages clean, and old pages scratched out. In purple, indelible pencil. I flatter myself I *don't get* lonesome, but I felt sorry for *him.*"

"I first told him he had taken me by surprise, and then thanked him for the compliment, and then said, after persuasion like that, he *could* use the parlor, *providing* he would make it quiet, because my cousin here wasn't up to himself. And he assured me it was the quietest profession on earth. That he had chosen it because it *was* such quiet, refined work, and also so he could see the world and so many members of the human race. I said I was a philosopher too, only I thought the sooner the better, and we made it today. And he borrowed a bucket of water and poured it steaming down the radiator, and returned the bucket, and was gone. I almost couldn't believe he'd been here.

"Then here today, right after dinner, in they start pouring. There's more people living in and around Mingo community than you can shake a stick at, more than you would ever dream. Here they come, out of every little high road and by road and cover and dell, four and five and six at the time—draw up or hitch up down at the foot of the hill and come up and shake hands like Sunday visitors. Everybody that can walk, and two that can't. I've got one preacher out there brought by a delegation. Oh, it's like Saturday and Sunday put together. The rounds the fella must have made! It's not as quiet as all he said, either. There's those mean little children, he never said a word about them, the spook.

"So I said all right mister, I'm ready for you. I'll show them where they can sit and where they can wait, and I'll call them. I says to them, 'When it's not your turn, please don't get up. If you want anything, ask me.' And I told them that any that had to, could smoke, but I wasn't ready to have a fire today, so mind out.

"And he took the parlor right over and unpacked his suitcase, and put up his lights, and unfolded a camp stool, until he saw the organ bench with the fringe around it. And shook out a big piece of scenery like I'd shake out a bedspread and hooked it to the wall, and commenced pouring that little powder along something like a music stand. "First!" he says, and commenced calling them in. I took over that. He and I go by his book and take them in order one at a time, all fair, honest, and above-board."

"And so what about Uncle Felix!" cried Kate, as if now she had her.

"The niggers helped, to get him back there, but it was mostly my fat little self," said Sister Anne. "Oh, you mean how come he consented? I expect I told him a story." She led us back to the hall, where a banjo hung like a stopped clock, and some small, white-haired children were marching to meet each other, singing "Here Comes the Duke A-Riding, Riding," in flat, lost voices. I too used to think that breezeway was as long as a tunnel through some mountain.

"Get!" said Sister Anne, and clapped her hands at them. They flung to the back, off the back porch into the sun, and scattered toward the barn. With reluctance I observed that Sister Anne's fingers were bleeding from the roses. Off in the distance, a herd of black cows moved in a light of green, the feathery April pastures deep with the first juicy weeds of summer.

There was a small ell tacked onto the back of the house, down a turn of the back porch, leading, as I knew, to the bathroom and the other little room behind that. A young woman and little boy were coming out of the bathroom.

"Look at that," shuddered Sister Anne. "Didn't take them long to find out what *we've* got."

I never used to think that back room was to be taken seriously as part of the house, because apples were kept in it in winter, and because it had an untrimmed, flat board door like a shed door, where you stuck your finger through a rough hole to lift up the latch.

Sister Anne stuck in her finger, opened the door, and we all three crowded inside the little room, which was crowded already.

Uncle Felix's side and back loomed from a featherbed, on an old black iron frame of a bedstead, which tilted downwards toward the foot with the sinking of the whole house from the brow of the hill toward the back. He sat white-headed as one of those escaping children, but not childlike—a heavy bulk, motionless, in a night-shirt, facing the window. A woven cotton spread was about his knees. His hands, turned under, were lying one on each side of him, faded from outdoor burn, mottled amber and silver.

"That's a nigger bed," said Kate, in one tone, one word. I turned and looked straight into her eyes.

"*It—is—not,*" said Sister Anne. Her whole face shook, as if Kate could have made it collapse. Then she bowed her head toward us—that we could go on, now, if that was the spirit we had come in.

"Good evening, sir," said Kate, in a changed voice.

I said it after her.

Uncle Felix's long, mute, grizzly head poked around his great shoulder and, motionless again, looked out at us. He visited this gaze a long time on a general point among the three different feminine faces—if you could call Sister Anne's wholly feminine—but never exactly on any of them. Gradually something left his eyes. Conviction was what I missed. Then even that general focus altered as though by a blow, a rap or a tap from behind, and his old head swung back. Again he faced the window, the only window in the house looking shadeless and shameless to the West, the glaring West.

Sister Anne bore the roses to the window and set them down on the window sill in his line of sight. The sill looked like the only place left where a vase could safely be set. Furniture, odds and ends, useless objects were everywhere, pushed by the bed even closer together. There were trunks, barrels, chairs with the cane seats hanging in a fringe. I remembered how sometimes in winter, dashing in here where the window then blew icily upon us, we would snatch an apple from the washed heap on the floor and run slamming out before we would freeze to death; that window always stayed open, then as now propped with a piece of stovewood. The walls were still rough boards with cracks between. Dust had come in everywhere, rolls of dust or lint or cottonwood fuzz hung even from the ceiling, glinting like everything else in the unfair light. I was afraid there might be dirt-daubers' nests if I looked. Our roses glared back at us as garish as anything living could be, almost like paper flowers, a magician's bouquet that had exploded out of a rifle to shock and amaze us.

"We'll enjoy our sunset from over the pasture this evening, won't we, Uncle Felix!" called Sister Anne, in a loud voice. It was the urgent opposite of her conspiratorial voice. "I bet we're fixing to have a gorgeous one—it's so dusty! You were saying last week, Cousin Felix, we already need a rain!"

Then to my amazement she came and rested her foot on a stack of mossy books by the bed—I was across from her there—and leaned her elbow on her lifted knee, and looked around the room with the face of a brand-new visitor. I thought of a prospector. I could look if she could. What must have been a Civil War musket stood like a forgotten broom in the corner. On the coal bucket sat an old bread tray, split like a melon.

There was even a dress form in here, rising among the trunks, its inappropriate bosom averted a little, as though the thing might still be able to revolve. If it were spanked, how the dust would fly up!

"Well, he's not going to even know *me* today," said Sister Anne, teasing me. "Well! I mustn't stay away too long at a time. Excuse me, Uncle Felix! I'll be right back," she said, taking down her tomboy foot. At the door she turned, to look at us sadly.

Kate and I looked at each other across the bed.

"Isn't this just—like—her!" said Kate with a long sigh.

As if on second thought she pulled open the door suddenly and looked off after her. From the other part of the house came the creakings of the human tiptoeing and passing going on in the breezeway. A flash of light traveled around the bend. Very close by, a child cried. Kate shut the door.

Back came Sister Anne—she really was back in a minute. She looked across at me. "Haven't you spoken? Speak! Tell him who you are, child! What did you come for?"

Instead—without knowing I was going to do it—I stepped forward and my hand moved out of my pocket with my handkerchief where the magnolia-fuscata flowers were knotted in the corner, and put it under Uncle Felix's heavy brown nose.

He opened his mouth. I drew the sweet handkerchief back. The old man said something, with dreadful difficulty.

"Hide," said Uncle Felix, and left his mouth open with his tongue out for everyone to see.

Sister Anne backed away from us all and kept backing, to the front of the paper-stuffed fireplace, as if she didn't even know the seasons. I almost expected her to lift her skirt a little behind her. She gave me a playful look instead.

"Hide," said Uncle Felix.

We kept looking at her. Sister Anne gave a golden, listening smile, as golden as a Cape Jessamine five days old.

"Hide," gasped the old man—and I made my first movement. "And I'll go in. Kill 'em all. I'm old enough I swear you Bob. Told you. Will for sure if you don't hold me, hold me."

Sister Anne winked at me.

"Surrounded...They're inside." On this word he again showed us his tongue, and rolled his eyes from one of us to the other, whoever we were.

Sister Anne produced a thermometer. With professional motions, which looked so much like showing off, and yet were so derogatory, she was shaking it down. "All right, Cousin Felix, that's enough for now! You pay attention to that sunset, and see what it's going to do!—Listen, that picture made twenty-six," she murmured. She was keeping some kind of tally in her head, as you do most exactly out of disbelief.

Uncle Felix held open his mouth and she popped the thermometer straight in, and he had to close it. It looked somehow wrong, dangerous—it was like daring to take the temperature of a bear.

"I don't know where he thinks he is," she said, nodding her head gently at him, Yes—yes.

Before I knew it, his hand raked my bare arm down. I felt as if I had been clawed, but when I bent toward him, the hand had fallen inert again on the bed, where it looked burnished with hundreds of country suns and today's on top of them all.

"Please, ma'am," said a treble voice at the door. A towheaded child looked in solemnly; his little red tie shone as his hair did, as with dewdrops. "Miss Sister Anne, the man says it's one more and then you."

"Listen at that. My free picture," said Sister Anne, drawing breath like a little girl going to recite, about to be martyrized.

For whom! I thought.

"Don't you think I need to freshen up a little bit?" she said with a comical expression. "My hair hasn't been combed since four o'clock this morning."

"You go right ahead," said Kate. "Right ahead."

Sister Anne bent to sight straight into Uncle Felix's face, and then took the thermometer out of his lips and sighted along it. She read off his temperature to herself and almost sweetly firmed her lips. That was *hers,* what he gave *her.*

Uncle Felix made a hoarse sound as she ran out again. Kate moved to the trunk, where on a stack of old books and plates was a water pitcher that did not look cold, and a spoon. She poured water into the spoon, and gave the old man some water on his tongue, which he offered her. But already his arm had begun to stir, to swing, and he put the same work-heavy, beast-heavy hand, all of a lump, against my side again and found my arm, which this time went loose in its socket, waiting. He groped and pulled at it, down to my hand. He pulled me all the way down. On my knees I found the pencil lying in the dust at my feet. He wanted it.

My Great-uncle Felix, without his right hand ever letting me go, received the pencil in his left. For a moment our arms crossed, but it was not awkward or strange, more as though we two were going to skate off, or dance off, out of here. Still holding me, but without stopping a moment, as if all the thinking had already been done, he knocked open the old hymnbook on top of the mossy stack at the bedside and began riding the pencil along over the flyleaf; though none of the Jerrolds that I ever heard of were left-handed, and certainly not he. I turned away my eyes.

There, lying on the barrel in front of me, looking vaguely like a piece of worn harness, was an object which I slowly recognized as once beloved to me. It was a stereopticon. It belonged in the parlor, on the lower shelf of the round table in the middle of the room, with the Bible on the top. It belonged to Sunday and to summertime.

My held hand pained me through the wish to use it and lift that old, beloved, once mysterious contraption to my eyes, and dissolve my sight, all our sights, in that. In that delaying, blinding pain, I remembered Uncle Felix. That is, I remembered the real Uncle Felix, and could hear his voice, respectful again, asking the blessing at the table. Then I heard the cataract of talk, which I knew he engendered; that was what Sunday at Mingo began with.

I remembered the house, the real house, always silvery, as now, but then cypressy and sweet, cool, reflecting, dustless. Sunday dinner was eaten from the table pulled to the very head of the breezeway, almost in the open door. The Sunday air poured in through it, and through the frail-ribbed fanlight and side lights, down on the island we made, our cloth and our food and our flowers and jelly and our selves, so lightly enclosed there—as though we ate in pure running water. So many people were gathered at Mingo that the Sunday table was pulled out to the limit, from a circle to the shape of our race track. It held my mother, my father and brother; Aunt Ethel; Uncle Harlan, who could be persuaded, if he did not eat to much, to take down the banjo later; my Jerrold grandmother, who always spoke of herself as "nothing but a country bride, darling," slicing the chicken while Uncle Felix cut the ham; Cousin Eva and Cousin Archie; and Kate, Kate everywhere, like me. And plenty more besides; it was eating against talking, all as if nobody would ever be persuaded to get up and leave the table: everybody, we thought, that we needed. And some were so pretty!

And when they were, the next thing, taking their naps all over the house, it was then I got my chance, and there would be, in lieu of any nap, pictures of the world to see.

I ran right through, with the stereopticon, straight for the front porch steps, and sitting there, stacked the slides between my bare knees in the spread of my starched skirt. The slide belonging on top was "The Ladies' View, Lakes of Killarney."

And at my side sat Uncle Felix.

That expectation—even alarm—that the awareness of happiness can bring! Of any happiness. It need not even be yours. It is like being able to prophesy, all of a sudden. Perhaps Uncle Felix loved the stereopticon most; he had it first. With his coat laid folded on the porch floor on the other side of him, sitting erect in his shirtsleeves for this, he would reach grandly for the instrument as I ran bringing it out. He saddled his full-size nose with the stereopticon and said, "All right, Skeeta." And then as he signaled ready for each slide, I handed it up to him.

Some places took him a long time. As he perspired there in his hard collar, looking, he gave off a smell like a cut watermelon. He handed each slide back without a word, and I was ready with the next. I would no more have spoken than I would have interrupted his blessing at the table.

Eventually they—all the rest of the Sunday children—were awake and wanting to be tossed about, and they hung over him, pulling on him, seeking his lap, his shoulders, pinning him down, riding on him. And he with his giant size and absorption went on looking his fill. It was as though, while he held the stereopticon to his eye, *we* did not see *him*. Gradually his ear went red. I thought all the blood had run up to his brain then, as it had run to mine.

It's strange to think that since then I've gone to live in one of those picture cities. If I asked him something about what was in there, he never told me more than a name, never saw fit. (I couldn't read then.) We passed each other those sand-pink cities and passionate fountains, the waterfall that rocks snuffed out like a light, islands in the sea, red Pyramids, sleeping towers, checkered pavements on which strollers had come out, with shadows that seemed to steal further each time, as if the strollers had moved, and where the statues had rainbow edges; volcanoes; the

Sphinx, and Constantinople; and again the Lakes, like starry fields—brought forward each time so close that it seemed to me the tracings from the beautiful face of a strange coin were being laid against my brain. Yet there were things too that I couldn't see, which could make Uncle Felix pucker his lips as for a kiss.

"Now! Dicey! I want *you* to tell me how I look!"

Sister Anne had opened the door, to a flash from the front. A low growl filled the room.

"You look mighty dressed up," said Kate for me.

Sister Anne had put on a hat—a hat from no telling where, what visit, what year, but it had been swashbuckling. It was a sort of pirate hat—black, of course.

"Thank you. Oh! Everything comes at once if it comes at all!" she said, looking piratically from one to the other of us. "So you can't turn around fast enough! You come on Mr. Dolollie's day! Now what will I do for Sunday!"

Under that, I heard an inching, delicate sound. Uncle Felix had pulled loose the leaf of the book he had labored over. Now he let me go, and took both swollen fists and over the lump of his body properly folded his page. He nudged it into my tingling hand.

"*He'll* keep you busy!" said Sister Anne nodding. "*That* table looks ready to go to market!" Her eyes were so bright, she was in such a state of excitement and pride and suspense that she seemed to lose for the moment all ties with us or the house or any remembrance of where anything was and what it was for. The next minute, with one blunder of her hatbrim against the door, she was gone.

I had slipped the torn page from the book, still folded, into my pocket, working it down through the starch-stuck dimity. Now I leaned down and kissed Uncle Felix's long unshaven, unbathed cheek. He didn't look at me—Kate stared, I felt it—but in a moment his eyes pinched shut.

Kate turned her back and looked out the window. The scent was burrowing into the roses, their heads hung. Out there was the pasture. The small, velvety cows had come up to the far fence and were standing there looking toward the house. They were little, low, black cows, soot-black, with their calves among them, in a green that seemed something to drink from more than something to eat.

Kate groaned under her breath, "I don't care, I've got to see her do it."

"She's doing it now," I said.

We stood on either side of the bed. Again Uncle Felix's head poked forward and held still, the western light full and late on him now.

"Never mind, Uncle Felix. Listen to me, I'll be back," Kate said. "It's nothing—it's all nothing—"

I felt that I had just showed off a good deal in some way. She bent down, hands on knees, but his face did not consult either of us again, although his eyes had opened. Tiptoeing modestly, we left him by himself. In his bleached gown he looked like the story-book picture of the Big Bear, the old white one with star children on his back and more star children following, in triangle dresses, starting down the Milky Way.

We saw Sister Anne at the table signing the book. We hid in the front bedroom before she saw us.

The overflow from outside was sitting in here. Thick around the room, on the rocking chair, on parlor chairs and the murmurous cane chairs from the dining room, our visitors were visiting. A few were standing or sitting at the windows to talk, and leaning against the mantel. The four-poster held, like a paddock, a collection of cleaned-up little children, mostly girls, some of them mutinous and tearful, one little girl patiently holding a fruit jar with something alive inside.

"Writing herself in, signing herself out all in one," Kate whispered, watching. "No! She mustn't forget that."

She gripped my wrist wickedly and we tiptoed out across the breezeway, and stood by the parlor curtain until Kate lifted it, and I saw her smile into the parlor to make watching all right; and perhaps I did the same.

Sister Anne was shaking out her skirt, and white crumbs scattered on the rug. She had managed a slice of that cake. The parlor in its plush was radiant in the spectacular glare of multiplied lights brought close around. The wallpaper of course was red, but now it had a cinnamon cast. Its design had gone into another one—it, too, faded and precise, ringed by rain and of a queerly intoxicating closeness, like an old trunk that had been opened still again for the children to find costumes. White flags and amaryllis in too big a vase, where they parted themselves in the middle and tried to fall out, were Sister Anne's idea of what completed the mantel shelf. The fireplace was banked with privet hedge, as for a country wedding. I could almost hear a wavery baritone voice singing "O Promise Me."

One with his camera and flash apparatus, the photographer stood with his back to us. He was baldheaded. We could see over him; he was short, and he leaned from side to side. He had long since discarded his coat, and his suspenders crossed tiredly on that bent back.

Sister Anne sat one way, then the other. A variety of expressions traveled over her face—pensive, eager, wounded, sad, and businesslike.

"I don't know why she can't make up her mind," I said all at once. "She's done nothing but practice all afternoon."

"Wait, wait, wait," said Kate. "Let her get to it."

What would show in the picture was none of Mingo at all, but the itinerant backdrop—the same old thing, a scene that never was, a black and white and gray blur of unrolled, yanked-down moonlight, weighted at the bottom with the cast-iron parlor rabbit doorstop, just behind Sister Anne's restless heel. The photographer raised up with arms extended, as if to hold and balance Sister Anne just exactly as she was now, with some special kind of semaphore. But Sister Anne was not letting him off that easily.

"Just a minute—I feel like I've lost something!" she cried, in a voice of excitement. "My handkerchief?"

I could feel Kate whispering to me, sideways along my cheek.

"Did poor Uncle Felix have to kill somebody when he was young?"

"I don't know." I shrugged, to my own surprise.

"Do you suppose she told him today there was a Yankee in the house? He might be thinking of Yankees." Kate slanted her whisper into my hair. It was more feeling, than hearing, what she said. "But he was almost too young for killing them....Of course he wasn't too young to be a drummer boy...." Her words signed away.

I shrugged again.

"Mama can tell us! I'll make her tell us. What did the note say, did it go on just warning us to hide?"

I shook my head. But she knew I must have looked at it.

"Tell you when we get out," I whispered back, stepping forward a little from her and moving the curtain better.

"Oh, wait!" Sister Anne exclaimed again.

I could never have cared, or minded, less how Sister Anne looked. I had thought of what was behind the photographer's backdrop. It was the portrait in the house, the one picture on the walls of Mingo, where pictures ordinarily would be considered frivolous. It hung just there on the wall that was before me, crowded between the windows, high up—the romantic figure of a young lady seated on a fallen tree under brooding skies: my Great-grandmother Jerrold, who had been Evelina Mackaill.

And I remembered—rather, more warmly, *knew*, like a secret of the family—that the head of this black-haired, black-eyed lady who always looked the right, mysterious age to be my sister, had been fitted to the ready-made portrait by the painter who had called at the door—he had taken the family off guard, I was sure of it, and spoken to their pride. The yellow skirt spread fanlike, straw hat held ribbon-in-hand, orange beads big as peach pits (to conceal the joining at the neck)—none of that, any more than the forest scene so unlike the Mississippi wilderness (that enormity she had been carried to as a bride, when the logs of this house were cut, her bounded world by drop by drop of sweat exposed, where she'd died in the end of yellow fever) or the melancholy clouds obscuring the sky behind the passive figure with the small, crossed feet—none of it, world or body, was really hers. *She* had eaten bear meat, seen Indians, she had married into the wilderness at Mingo, to what unknown feelings. Slaves had died in her arms. She had grown a rose for Aunt Ethel to send back by me. And still those eyes, opaque, all pupil, belonged to Evelina—I knew, because they saw out, as mine did; weren't warned, as mine weren't, and never shut before the end, as mine would not. I, her divided sister, knew who had felt the wildness of the world behind the ladies' view. We were homesick for somewhere that was the same place.

I returned the touch of Kate's hand. This time, I whispered, "What he wrote was, 'River—Daisy—Midnight—Please.' "

" 'Midnight'!" Kate cried first. Then, "River daisy? His mind has wandered, the poor old man."

"Daisy's a lady's name," I whispered impatiently, so impatiently that the idea of the meeting swelled right out of the moment, and I even saw Daisy.

Then Kate whispered, "You must mean Beck, Dicey, that was his wife, and he meant her to meet him in Heaven. Look again.—*Look* at Sister

Anne!"

Sister Anne had popped up from the organ bench. Whirling around, she flung up the lid—hymnbooks used to be stuffed inside—and pulled something out. To our amazement and delight, she rattled open a little fan, somebody's old one—it even sounded rusty. As she sat down again she drew that fan, black and covered over with a shower of forget-me-nots, languidly across her bosom. The photographer wasted not another moment. The flash ran wild through the house, singeing our very hair at the door, filling our lungs with gunpowder smoke as though there had been a massacre. I had a little fit of coughing.

"Now let her try forgiving herself for this," said Kate, and almost lazily folded her arms there.

"Did you see me?" cried Sister Anne, running out crookedly and catching onto both of us to stop herself. "Oh, I hope it's good! Just as the thing went off—I blinked!" She laughed, but I believed I saw tears start out of her eyes. "Look! Come meet Mr. Puryear. Come have your pictures taken! It's only a dollar down and you get them in the *mail!*"

And for a moment, I wanted to—wanted to have my picture taken, to be sent in the mail to someone—even against that absurd backdrop, having a vain, delicious wish to torment someone, then have something to laugh about together afterwards.

Kate drew on ladylike white cotton gloves, that I had not noticed her bringing. Whatever she had been going to say turned into, "Sister Anne? What have you been telling Uncle Felix?"

"What I *didn't* tell him," replied Sister Anne, "was that people were getting their pictures taken: I didn't want him to feel left out. It was just for one day. Mr. Alf J. Puryear is the photographer's name—there's some Puryears in Mississippi. I'll always remember his sad face."

"Thank you for letting us see Uncle Felix, in spite of the trouble we were," said Kate in her clear voice.

"You're welcome. And come back. But if I know the signs," said Sister Anne, and looked to me, the long-lost, for confirmation of herself the specialist, "we're losing him fast, ah me. Well! I'm used to it, I can stand it, that's what I'm for. But oh, I can't stand for you all to go! Stay—Stay!" And she turned into our faces that outrageous, yearning smile she had produced for the photographer.

I knew I hadn't helped Kate out yet about Sister Anne. And so I said,

"Aunt Ethel didn't come today! Do you know why? Because she just can't abide you!"

The bright lights inside were just then turned off. Kate and I turned and ran down the steps, just as a voice out of the porch shadow said, "It seems to me that things are moving in too great a rush." It sounded sexless and ageless both to me; it sounded deaf.

Somehow, Kate and I must have expected everybody to rush out after us. Sister Anne's picture, the free one, had been the last. But nobody seemed to be leaving. Children were the only ones flying loose. Maddened by the hour and the scene, they were running barefoot and almost silent, skimming around and around the house. The others sat and visited on, in those clouds of dust, all holding those little tickets or receipts I remembered wilting in their hands; some of the old men had them stuck in their winter hats. At last, maybe the Lady Baltimore cake would have to be passed.

"Sister Anne, greedy and all as she is, will cut that cake yet, if she can keep them there a little longer!" said Kate in answer to my thoughts.

"Yes," I said.

"She'll forget what you said. Oh the sweet evening air!"

I took so for granted once, and when had I left for ever, I wondered at that moment, the old soft airs of Mingo as I knew them—the interior airs that were always kitchenlike, of oil-lamps, wood ashes, and that golden scrapement off cake-papers—and outside, beyond the just-watered ferns lining the broad strong railing, the fragrances winding up through the luster of the fields and the dim, gold screen of trees and the river beyond, fragrances so rich I once could almost see them, untransparent and Oriental? In those days, fresh as I was from Sunday School in town, I could imagine the Magi riding through, laden.

At other times—perhaps later, during visits back from the North—that whole big congregated outside smell, like the ripple of an animal's shining skin, used suddenly to travel across and over to my figure standing on the porch, like a marvel of lightning, and by it I could see myself, a child on a visit to Mingo, hardly under any auspices that I knew of, by myself, but wild myself, at the mercy of that touch.

"It's a wonder she didn't let the Negroes file in at the back and have theirs taken too. If you didn't know it was Sister Anne, it would be past understanding," Kate said. "It would kill Mama—we must spare her this."

"Of course!" Sparing was our family trait.

We were going down the walk, measuredly, like lady callers who had left their cards; in single file. That was the one little strip of cement in miles and miles—narrow as a ladder.

"But listen, who was Daisy, have you thought? *Daisy,*" said Kate in front. She looked over her shoulder. "I don't believe it."

I smoothed out that brown page of the hymn book with the torn edge, that purple indelible writing across it where the print read "Round & Shaped Notes." Coming around, walking in the dampening uncut grass, I showed it to Kate. You could still make out the big bold D with the cap on.

" *Midnight!'* But they always go to bed at dark, out here."

I put the letter back inside my pocket. Kate said, "Daisy must have been smart. I don't understand that message at all."

"Oh, I do," I lied. I felt it was up to me. I told Kate, "It's a kind of shorthand." Yet it had seemed a very long letter—didn't it take Uncle Felix a long time to write it!

"Oh, I can't think even out here, but mustn't Daisy be dead?...Not Beck?" Kate ventured, then was wordless.

"Daisy was Daisy," I said. It was the "please" that had hurt me. It was I who put the old iron ring over the gate and fastened it. I saw the Cape Jessamines were all in bud, and for a moment, just at the thought, I seemed to reel from a world too fragrant, just as I suspected Aunt Ethel had reeled from one too loud.

"I expect by now Uncle Felix has got his names mixed up, and Daisy was a mistake," Kate said.

She could always make the kind of literal remark, like this, that could alienate me, even when we were children—much as I love her. I don't know why, yet, but some things are too important for a mistake even to be considered. I was sorry I had showed Kate the message, and said, "Look, how we've left him by himself."

We stood looking back, in our wonder, until out of the house came the photographer himself, all packed up—a small, hurrying man, blackcoated as his subjects were. He wore a pale straw summer hat, which was more than they had. It was to see him off, tell him good-bye, reassure him, that they had waited.

"Open it again! Look out, Dicey," said Kate, "get back."

He did not tarry. With paraphernalia to spare, he ran out between the big bushes ahead of us with a strange, rushing, fuse-like, Yankee sound—out through the evening and into his Ford, and was gone like that.

I felt the secret pang behind him—I know I did feel the cheat he had found and left in the house, the helpless, asking cheat. I felt it more and more, too strongly.

And then we were both excruciated by our terrible desire, and catching each other at the same moment with almost fierce hands, we did it, we laughed. We leaned against each other and on the weak, open gate, and gasped and choked into our handkerchiefs, and finally we cried. "Maybe she kissed him!" cried Kate at random. Each time we tried to stop ourselves, we sought each other's faces and started again. We laughed as though we were inspired.

"She forgot to take the pencil out of her hair!" gasped Kate.

"Oh no! What do you think Uncle Felix wrote with! He managed—it was the pencil out of Sister Anne's head!" That was almost too much for me. I held on to the gate.

I was aware somehow that birds kept singing passionately all around us just the same, and hurling themselves like bolts in front of our streaming eyes.

Kate tried to say something new—to stop us disgracing ourselves and each other, our visit, our impending tragedy, Aunt Ethel, everything. Not that anybody, anything in the world could hear us, reeled back in those bushes now, except ourselves.

"You know Aunt Beck—she never let us leave Mingo without picking us our nosegay on the way down this walk, every little thing she grew that smelled nice, pinks, four-o'clocks, verbena, heliotrope, bits of nicotiana—she grew all such little things, just for that, Di. And she wound their stems, round and round and round, with a black or white thread she would take from a needle in her collar, and set it all inside a rose-geranium leaf, and presented it to you at the gate—right here. That was Aunt Beck," said Kate's positive voice. "She wouldn't *let* you leave without it."

But it was no good. We had not laughed together that way since we were too little to know any better.

With tears streaming down my cheeks, I said, "I don't remember her."

"But she wouldn't *let* you forget. She *made* you remember her!"

Then we stopped.

I stood there and folded the note back up. There was the house, floating on the swimming dust of evening, its gathered, safe-shaped mass darkening. A dove in the woods called its five notes—two and three—at first unanswered. The last gleam of sunset, except for the threadbare curtain of wistaria, could be seen going on behind. The cows were lowing. The dust was in windings, the roads in their own shapes in the air, the exhalations of where people all had come from.

"They'll all be leaving now," said Kate. "It's first-dark, almost."

But the grouping on the porch still held, that last we looked back, posed there along the rail, quiet and obscure and never-known as passengers on a ship already embarked to sea. Their country faces were drawing in even more alike in the dusk, I thought. Their faces were like dark boxes of secrets and desires to me, but locked safely, like old-fashioned caskets for the safe conduct of jewels on a voyage.

Something moved. The little girl came out to the front, holding her glass jar, like a dark lantern, outwards. Kate and I turned, wound our arms around each other, and got down to the car. We heard the horses.

It was all one substance now, one breath and density of blue. Along the back where the pasture was, the little, low black cows came in, in a line toward the house, with their sober sides one following the other. Where each went looked like simply where nothing was. But across the quiet we heard Theodore talking to them.

Across the road was Uncle Theodore's cabin, where clumps of privet hedge in front were shaped into a set of porch furniture, god-size, table and chairs, and a snake was hung up in a tree.

We drew out of the line of vehicles, and turned back down the dark blue country road. We neither talked, confided, nor sang. Only once, in a practical voice, Kate spoke.

"I hate going out there without Mama. Mama's too nice to say it about Sister Anne, but I will. You know what it is: it's in there somewhere."

Our lips moved together. "She's common...."

All around, something went on and on. It was hard without thinking to tell whether it was a throbbing, a dance, a rattle, or a ringing—all louder as we neared the bridge. It was everything in the grass and trees. Presently Mingo church, where Uncle Felix had been turned down on "knick-knack," revolved slowly by, with its faint churchyard. Then all was April night. I thought of my sweetheart, riding, and wondered if he were writing to me.

EUDORA WELTY was born in 1909 in Jackson, Mississippi, where she still lives in the family home. Her books include The Wide Net, The Ponder Heart *and* The Optimist's Daughter, *for which she was awarded the 1972 Pulitzer Prize.*

Afterword

L I Z P A R K H U R S T &
R O D L O R E N Z E N

CHARLES ALLBRIGHT once wrote, in his column for the *Arkansas Gazette,* of a family Thanksgiving. "Call me crazy," his fictitious friend Reid observes, "but I believe families can love each other without making each other miserable."

Reid tells of glances exchanged and intercepted around the dinner table, glances that clearly indicate that everyone would rather be watching football; of broccoli casseroles tumped over in car trunks; of his mother upstairs, collapsed from "getting ready for all the good times." He devises a plan to leave an anonymous note on the family coffee table that reads: *They can't afford for us to be here.* He wonders how many will escape injury in the mass departure.

Reid's—and Allbright's—point is this: "We have to figure out how to love each other and spare each other at the same time."

Writers have been pondering that for a long time.

This collection brings together twelve stories that examine the family and the expectations we have of it in Southern life. In these stories, family is not merely incidental to plot or character or other aspects of fiction but is a tide that pushes and pulls its members along. These writers portray the family as—in the jargon of modern psychology—a single "emotional unit," where the members are bound one to another no matter where they roam.

In other words, our own emotional state is dependent on the moods and actions of other family members. In Alice Walker's "Everyday Use," for instance, a mother watches as one daughter wilts in the presence of her smarter, more sophisticated sister. In "Leaving," another mother fears she is contributing to her grown son's inertia by holding him ransom for the husband who abandoned her; she fears she is dependent upon his depression.

Southerners—Southern writers in particular—have been ahead of the psychologists for some time. We've always known what the doctors are only now documenting: that it is difficult to separate our own individual identity from that of our family.

People who achieve the most detachment from their families often seem to feel the most independent and willing to exist on their own terms. Not surprisingly, we find that writers fall into this category and that they are capable of writing about family relationships in ways that are uncompromising and sometimes painful. We find the innermost secrets of ourselves and our relatives and confront a real ambivalence about them—in part, we want to find a place in the family, and in part, we want to put the family in its place.

These conflicting needs—to belong to and withdraw from our families—are perfectly voiced by Evanelle, the narrator in Ruth Moose's "Happy Birthday, Billy Boy": "Seven days a week, twenty-four hours a day. How does he stand it? How do I? How do any of us stand each other? And somehow we'll go on putting up with each other until they put us off in a bed with sides and chairs with wheels to push like Billy Buttons in his stroller."

The concept of family has been an important and recurring theme in modern literature, often dealing with negative aspects such as the loss of family and an inability to maintain the family unit. Driving this concern, perhaps, has been a yearning simply to understand the family relationship and the reasons it has been accorded such a revered and historic place in Southern life.

The stories show that perhaps the idea of the nuclear family is not only dead but may have been as idealized and romanticized as a lot of other notions about the South. While modernization has made the South like other parts of the country, there is a lingering tendency by Southerners to see the South as a separate country that was conquered and later occupied, where the federal government and other intruders caused us to withdraw into a place where family and other familial institutions, such as the church, came first and often were the only sanctuaries available.

As Southerners continue to overcome a past full of racism and poverty, we know that the only way to understand it is through literature, and that the answer remains rooted in the past. Where psychology only attempts to describe human functioning, writers attempt to account for it. Writing about these aspects of Southern culture offers a way to look at how members of families are inextricably bound to one another both geographically and emotionally. If we overlook the source of our problems, it will be impossible to measure our gains. Where the first page has been ripped out of the family Bible, these writers can restore those names and their stories to the family tree.

The South long has been famous for its fictional treatment of the family in novels, but the stories here give us compressed and brilliant snapshots of how writers actually visualize their families. In this way, the family may be scrutinized, not scripted, so that its subtle workings are bared in fine detail. In these stories, we have found a number of ways to look at the South by native sons and daughters who remain, in one way or another, tethered by the umbilical cord of family and place.

One such way of seeing the South is through the notion of hospitality that is addressed by many of its writers. Turned outward to the guest, hospitality requires of the Southerner a deference, a determination not to offend; when these same attitudes are turned in to the family, the result is often a reticence, an internalizing, a "holding of the tongue," if not outright deceit or denial. *See everything, see nothing,* says the title character in Ellen Douglas's "I Just Love Carrie Lee." *Know everything, know nothing.* Nowhere is the downside of Southern hospitality summed up any more neatly.

In "Earl Goes to the Site and Stares Until He Sees," by Dennis Johnson, another woman chooses to hold her tongue. Having traveled to Washington, D.C., for at least the fourth time to fetch her husband, she realizes as the story ends that she will be doing it again, that there is nothing she can say to stop him. "I know that here, in this hollow space, if I dared to call out the truth to him," she observes, "my voice would carry up into the dome above us, and not be heard at all."

The reticence of the characters in Lee Smith's "Artists" has allowed a grandmother to create a fantasy world, one in which she pretends, among other things, that her husband has not been having an affair. The pretense only breaks down in the face of death—the death of her husband forces the mistress upon her in terms she can no longer deny. The realization breaks the grandmother but liberates her adolescent granddaughter from her own fantasy world.

Likewise, the death of his father forces Thomas Teague, the protagonist in Mary Hood's "A Man Among Men," to face a truth he has long been avoiding. In a painful exchange with his rebellious son, Dean ("Your granddaddy—" "Is dead and I'm not. I'm sure as hell not"), he realizes how his fear of Dean's death has set him at odds with him, and he is finally able to relinquish his anger and reconcile with his son.

Religion, another hallmark of Southern culture, is also addressed in these stories. In Nanci Kincaid's "Spittin' Image of a Baptist Boy," denominational differences divide a family, as happens so often in Southern life.

But in Larry Brown's "Old Frank and Jesus," religion presents Mr. P. with a much more complicated question. Mr. P. fears he has sinned by shooting his best friend, his dog Old Frank. Was he the dog's best friend or was he his god? In fundamental religious thought, gods have no way (because they have no reason) to seek redemption. Whether or not he considers himself eligible for it, Mr. P. has rejected the notion for redemption as the story opens, and he is thus contemplating suicide.

Fitting in is another concern families constantly express: will the new daughter-in-law fit in? Will her children? Even biological relatives sometimes feel out of step with each other. Family experts now say that the children who do not function well in families are those who, be they adopted or biological children, feel they don't belong.

In "A Man Among Men," Thomas is forced to confront the memory of his father, now delirious on his deathbed, telling him that it should have been Thomas, not his brother Earl, who was killed. "That was when Thomas knew," Hood writes, and what he knows is that he has been resented for years by his father for living.

In Eudora Welty's "Kin," Sister Anne, a distant relative, is kept at bay by her Jackson-based family. Because her ways are somewhat *declasse,* the family needs to make a point of not "claiming kin." Her stationery, her wardrobe, her every word—all of these are seized on, examined and judged as not worthy of the family name.

In Alice Walker's "Everyday Use," sister Dee, even though she is outnumbered, is able to make the rest of her family feel out of place. She has earned the awe of her sister and mother, but she has done so at the price of their affection. Her visit sets them both on edge, and they can only settle back into their own familiar relationship once she is gone.

But the stories here offer more than just the shortcomings of the family. Ultimately, there is acceptance, if not understanding. In "Earl Goes to the Site...," Earl's family has come to accept the sporadic trips to fetch him home from Washington as routine. In "A Man Among Men," Thomas finds the key to reconciling with his son when he visits a woman whose son has died of an overdose after committing a burglary. "Ray done bad?" she asks. "You don't love them for it, but you love them. There's good in between the bad times."

In "Leaving," the narrator comes to realize that accepting the terms our relatives impose on relationships may not fulfill our expectations but may be better than having no relationship at all. And in "Artists," Jennifer, after a period that she describes as a feeling of "not belonging," accepts the death of her grandmother and allows herself to grow up.

And Truman Capote—the old rascal who built a career out of not fitting in—pays tribute in his story to one treasured alliance in an otherwise imperfect family: "Other people inhabit the house, relatives; and though they have power over us, and frequently make us cry, we are not, on the whole, too much aware of them. We are each other's best friend."

With all these egos knocking about under one roof, how *do* families manage to love each other without making each other miserable? The authors of these stories offer a range of responses, from ultimate despair to rare moments of perfect unity. In a way, they provide the blueprint that Dennis Johnson's Earl seeks in the story included here.

In addressing such issues as independence, interdependence,

belonging and withdrawing, these stories ask us to confront the same painful aspects of our own family relationships, so that we might find in them—or in spite of them—the way to a homecoming where love and understanding abound.